A Phantom Enchantment

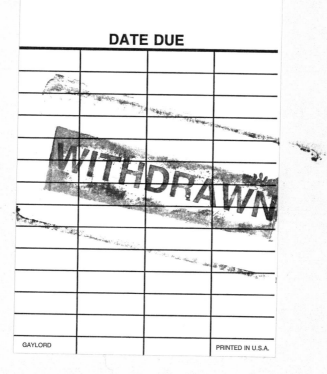

DATE DUE

Also by Eve Marie Mont

A Breath of Eyre
A Touch of Scarlet

A Phantom
Enchantment

Eve Marie Mont

KENSINGTON PUBLISHING CORP.
www.kensingtonbooks.com

K TEEN BOOKS are published by

Kensington Publishing Corp.
119 West 40th Street
New York, NY 10018

All Kensington titles, imprints, and distributed lines are available at special quantity discounts for bulk purchases for sales promotion, premiums, fund-raising, and educational or institutional use.

Special book excerpts or customized printings can also be created to fit specific needs. For details, write or phone the office of the Kensington Special Sales Manager: Kensington Publishing Corp., 119 West 40th Street, New York, NY 10018. Attn. Special Sales Department. Phone: 1-800-221-2647.

Kensington and the K Teen logo are Reg. U.S. Pat. & TM Off.

ISBN-13: 978-0-7582-6950-8
ISBN-10: 0-7582-6950-1
First Kensington Trade Paperback Printing: April 2014

eISBN-13: 978-1-61773-246-1
eISBN-10: 1-61773-246-X
First Kensington Electronic Edition: April 2014

10 9 8 7 6 5 4 3 2 1

Printed in the United States of America

To Phil and Pete, for being there . . .

ACKNOWLEDGMENTS

Coming to the end of a trilogy is bittersweet. I've been with these characters for four years now, and although their story never really ends, I have to let them go to make room for new characters and new adventures. But I'll never forget my journey with Emma, Gray, Michelle, Owen, and the rest of the gang. Nor will I forget those "real life" characters that helped me along every step of the way. An enormous and heartfelt thank-you goes out to:

Martin Biro, for his thoughtful and sensitive editing, and to the entire team at Kensington/K-Teen.

The Philly contingent of the Apocalypsies—Elisa Ludwig, Eugene Myers, Tiffany Schmidt, and Kate Walton—for being so much more than colleagues.

The Lower Moreland Commune, for supporting me through a difficult time and making the World Studies office a place I love to be.

Katya—poet, wise woman, and soul friend—you provide the best solace and cheerleading a girl could ask for.

Dave . . . for helping me with a new beginning.

Barb Kavanagh and Jay Thayakaran, for always being there to provide an ear, a ride to the mechanic's, or a glass of wine (or three) after a rough day.

Stephanie Breen, who taught me friendship can last thirty-six years and more.

Robin McNemar, who taught me I can still make new friends after forty.

Ashley Seiver, for her steadfast friendship and pilgrim soul.

Nola, for infusing my life with puppy energy.

My students, old and new, especially: Billie Jones, who came to visit me every day during hall duty and helped me brainstorm ideas for this book; and Nicole Distasio, who writes far beyond her years and will be a published author someday.

My parents, for reading early drafts of A Phantom Enchantment and cheering me and Emma to the finish line.

And all my family and friends who stepped in to support me in various ways; may I be able to repay the favor someday.

As one of my characters says, "Life is not a script to be followed; it's a novel to be written." Here's to filling many more pages with new adventures, friends, and joys.

If I am the phantom, it is because man's hatred has made me so. If I am to be saved it is because your love redeems me.

—Gaston Leroux, *The Phantom of the Opera*

A Phantom
Enchantment

CHAPTER 1

They say you're only fluent in a foreign language once you dream in it. The summer I turned eighteen, I dreamed in French. In fact, I did everything French that summer—ate baguettes for breakfast, drank French coffee, read French novels, watched French films. The only thing I didn't do French was kiss, but that's only because my boyfriend was a thousand miles away and there wasn't anyone else in the world I wanted to share my tongue with.

Two weeks ago, Gray had finished "A" School and was now in California, completing the final step in becoming a Coast Guard rescue swimmer: his EMT training. Unfortunately, by the time he finished and earned his leave, I'd be halfway across the world about to begin my senior year in Paris.

I don't know why the physical distance bothered me so much—something about an ocean separating us, I guess. Over land, one could hop in the car and drive almost anywhere. But once I crossed the Atlantic, it was no easy feat to uncross it, which somehow made our separation seem more permanent.

The headmistress of Lycée Saint-Antoine had booked me a red-eye flight that left Boston at eleven P.M. and arrived in Paris at eleven A.M. Despite the late hour, I arrived at Logan

Airport with a small entourage in tow: my dad, Barbara, Grandma Mackie, and my friends Michelle and Jess—now a couple. This fact made me feel a little less guilty about leaving Michelle, my roommate for the past two years, to fend for herself at Lockwood while I was off cavorting in Paris.

Jess announced, "If you come back with some phony French accent, we are not friends anymore."

"And you'd better not eat any horse meat," Michelle added.

Barbara, always one to remind me of the really important things in life, said, "And sweetie, don't wear your slouchy sweaters and jeans. You want to blend. Parisians wear black."

"Got it," I said with good humor. After all, they were only trying to help. "No accent, no horse meat, no scrubs."

"And what about some advice from your elders?" Grandma Mackie said.

"Of course, Grandma. What is it?" If there was anyone's advice I might actually listen to, it was Grandma's.

"French men," she said. "They're very charming, but in the end, all they care about is—"

"Grandma!" I said. "You don't have to worry about that."

"You didn't let me finish," she said. "All they care about is food." Michelle and Jess cracked up.

"Don't you think you're generalizing a little bit?" I said.

"Trust me, I know from experience," she said. "Learn to cook, and you can seduce any French man within a thirty-mile radius."

"Kilometer radius," I said. "Paris is metric. And why would I want to seduce any French men when I have Gray?"

"Emma," she said, "I love Gray as much as you do, but you are planning on having a little fun in Paris, aren't you?"

"If I must," I said, cracking a smile.

After checking my suitcases, we wandered to the escalator,

where I mentally prepared myself for the next moments. I hated good-byes. Jess and Michelle hugged me, Michelle wrapping her treasured red scarf around my neck, even though it was almost ninety degrees out.

"To remember me," she said.

"As if I could forget." Even so, I studied her face, trying to memorize the features I knew so well—the penetrating eyes, the copper skin, the stubborn mouth.

Then she handed me a tiny gift bag. "This is from Darlene, but she wants you to wait until you get to Paris to open it."

"That was so sweet," I said. "She didn't have to do that." Darlene was Michelle's aunt and caretaker and basically the closest thing I had to a fairy godmother. I clutched the bag to my chest, knowing it would take every ounce of willpower not to open it the minute I got to the terminal.

At the last minute, my dad insisted on accompanying me to Security. "We should get going," he said. "Otherwise, you won't make it to the gate the recommended two hours before flight time." My chest tightened in a wave of traveler's regret.

Barbara hugged me, then kissed me on both cheeks. "Remember, one kiss on either side," she said. "It's the European way."

My grandma clasped those same cheeks with her open palms, something she'd never done before in her life. "You squeeze as much fun out of Paris as you can," she said. "This trip is a gift." And then she kissed me on the nose, quite a loony thing for her to do. I wondered briefly if she wasn't getting a touch of dementia.

Before I could properly respond to her, my dad grabbed my carry-on in one hand and my arm with the other, leading me away toward the escalator. I watched the four of them wave from below, their figures shrinking as my dad and I sailed upward.

I wasn't sure why my father had insisted on coming with me to Security since he wasn't exactly imparting any last-minute wisdom. He and I had an interesting dynamic—either we strained to have the most mundane conversations or we bared our souls to each other in emotionally wrenching heart-to-hearts. Knowing the security line of an international airport was probably not the best place to have an emotional heart-to-heart, we stood woodenly beside each other, trying to think of things to say.

"Thanks for letting me go," I finally muttered. "Not every parent would have."

"I almost didn't, but you wore me down," he said, loosening up a little. "So make the most of it."

"I will."

"And write your grandma letters. She loves letters."

"And what about you?" I asked.

"I'll take what I can get," he said with a smirk.

My heart squeezed. This was what my dad had grown used to—taking what he could get from me. It was difficult to navigate our father-daughter relationship at this stage when all he wanted to do was cling and all I wanted to do was pull away.

"Be careful," he said, once we'd reached the front of the line. "Remember, you'll be in a foreign country. As much as I trust your judgment, I don't trust anyone else's. Use common sense."

"Of course," I said.

"We'll see you at Christmas."

I nodded, trying not to cry. I couldn't believe that my father, a man who hardly ever left Hull's Cove, let alone Massachusetts, let alone the country, was shelling out thousands of dollars to bring Barbara and my grandma to Paris for Christmas break.

"I can't wait," I said.

"It'll be here before you know it. I love you, sweetheart."

"I love you too," I said.

He hugged me a bit stiffly, and for a moment we both felt

self-conscious, but then I leaned into his hug and closed my eyes, comforted by my father's arms around me. When I sensed the people behind us growing impatient, I pulled away and smiled bravely, showed Security my passport and boarding pass, and wheeled my bag to the conveyer belt.

I waited until I'd gotten through the checkpoint, put my shoes back on, then turned just in time to see my dad walking away.

I should have turned around sooner. I should have waved good-bye. But there was nothing I could do about it now.

I was on my own.

CHAPTER 2

Well, not entirely on my own. Elise was at the gate, looking relaxed in a white cotton tunic with stylish jeans and knee-high boots, plus giant sunglasses and a plaid Trilby hat. Seasoned traveler and fashion icon.

If you'd have told me a year ago that I'd be spending my senior year in Paris with Elise Fairchild, I'd have said you were delusional. If you'd added that we would actually sorta-kinda be friends, I would have laughed in your face. Yet here we were.

"Hey," I said. "We made it."

Elise gazed at me through her immense sunglasses, no doubt sizing up my outfit. Then she propped the sunglasses on her head and said, "Emma, if I'm going to be seen with you in the most fashionable city in the world, we're going to need to work on your wardrobe."

"What's wrong with my wardrobe?" I asked, gesturing down at my *Doctor Who* T-shirt artfully accessorized with Michelle's red scarf, faded jeans, and Converse sneakers.

"Can you scream any louder that you're American?"

"To be fair, the T-shirt screams 'I'm British.' "

"And a nerd."

"Guilty as charged." I laughed. "Isn't the point that we're

going to be hurtling over the Atlantic for the next seven hours and might as well be comfortable?"

Elise rolled her eyes. I was a hopeless case. We chatted a little about our summers. I'd spent mine researching colleges and pining for Gray. Elise had spent hers taking advantage of the fact that her parents were divorcing, thus each was trying to get the upper hand by spoiling her rotten. As if Elise needed any more spoiling.

"They want to prove once and for all who I love more," Elise said.

"And?"

"My dad, of course. You've met my mom. Cruella de Vil has got nothing on her."

When boarding was announced, we got on the plane, and I gave Elise the window seat. Looking out plane windows always made me imagine engine explosions, fiery crashes, and watery graves. Better to get absorbed in a book and pretend I was on a train.

To calm myself down, I thought about Gray, scrolling through a mental record of our "greatest hits": our first kiss in his Jeep, dancing at the Snow Ball, me taking the prom to his house when he was on crutches and couldn't go, last summer when we'd been practically inseparable and had walked the beach together almost every night. This daydreaming must have done the trick, because eventually I fell asleep and when I woke, the flight attendants were already distributing coffee and breakfast croissants.

When we landed, Elise solicited a well-dressed gentleman to get her bag from the overhead storage bin while I wrestled my own to the floor. We disembarked and found a restroom, where I waited outside for Elise and texted my dad and Gray to let them know I'd arrived safely. Then we made our way to baggage claim and retrieved our checked luggage.

A hulking man stood a few yards away from us holding a sign that read: SAINT-ANTOINE.

"I guess that's our welcoming committee?" Elise said. "He looks like a vagrant."

"He does not," I said. "He looks like Jean Valjean."

Well, like the world-weary Jean Valjean, who's just carried Marius miles through the sewers. Even with the slight hunch in his shoulders, this man was well over six feet and looked like he'd once been powerful and vital until some misfortune or trauma had sucked the life out of him. His weathered face was shadowed in stubble, giving him an almost tragic air. But his gray eyes, the corners etched with lines, looked like they had once smiled for someone.

He introduced himself as Monsieur Crespeau and said he was "l'homme à tout faire" for the school, which I roughly translated into "jack of all trades." As if to prove this, he loaded our bags onto a cart and, without a word, began walking briskly toward the exit despite a noticeable limp. When we got outside, he tottered a little on a ramp, and I ran ahead to stop the cart from careening out of his grasp. He didn't smile or thank me; in fact, he looked irritated and re- sumed his task with even more single-mindedness, shoving our luggage roughly into the back of a van.

"Whoa, be careful!" Elise said. "That's precious cargo there."

I knew she was joking, but Monsieur Crespeau didn't seem to get her humor. I explained to him in French, "I apologize for my friend. She's a bit spoiled. She thinks she's the most precious cargo of all."

He just grimaced and got into the driver's seat without a word. Elise raised an eyebrow at our unlikely chauffeur, and we hopped into the back and buckled ourselves in, expecting a bumpy ride. But surprisingly, Monsieur Crespeau took great precautions to look behind him for traffic before pulling onto the road, proceeding to drive about twenty miles per hour the entire way to the school.

I was glad for the slow pace, as it gave me a chance to see the sights. What struck me first was how all cities look alike, to a certain extent. Somehow I'd been expecting Paris to beguile me from the moment the plane touched ground, but as we crawled along the highway behind a trash truck, passing railroad tracks and gas stations, I began to feel I'd been duped by Hollywood.

Even when we entered the city limits, the landscape looked like urban America with its MoneyGram and telecom shops, ethnic takeout places, characterless office buildings, and of course, the omnipresent McDonald's. It was a bit disheartening.

Until we went below an underpass somewhere around Gare du Nord. Then it was as if someone had waved a magic wand and transformed the city right before my eyes. Here was quintessential Paris—old, ornate, and sprawling. The ivory buildings were all decked with wrought-iron balconies, window boxes full of flowers, and mansard rooftops gilded by the sun. And each street corner was flanked by a church, a statue, or an obelisk—some grand monument to the city's history.

We came to a giant circle bustling with people, and Monsieur Crespeau took one of the narrow avenues that spiderwebbed from it. The road was tree-lined and framed by rows of buildings, houses, shops, and cafés. One building was so delicate and narrow I wondered how it didn't topple over. Another wedge-shaped building looked like a slice of wedding cake.

Elise told me we weren't far from Montmartre. In my mind I envisioned Sacré-Coeur's alabaster domes rising up against the blue sky, saw the painted ladies of Lapin Agile, squinted at the neon lights of Moulin Rouge.

We came to another circle with a statue of an armed woman

in the middle, and Monsieur Crespeau mumbled something, I think "Tout proche" or "Very near." I glanced up at a street sign and saw we were on Boulevard du Temple, a broad thoroughfare that separated the 3rd and 11th arrondissements. Along this road, we passed dozens of cafés, patisseries, boulangeries, charcuteries—all of them with brightly colored awnings and outdoor tables beckoning us to sit down and relax, stay a while. I'd never seen more eating establishments in one city block. My grandma was right—food did make the Parisian world go 'round.

I could see the July Column of the Bastille up ahead, so I knew we were almost there, and then we turned onto Rue Saint-Antoine. Monsieur Crespeau nodded at a building about three storefronts wide and five stories high, distinguished from its neighbors only by its arched blue doorway.

"Voici," he said.

He pulled into a tiny alleyway behind the school and parked the van, then told us he'd bring our luggage to our rooms so we could report to Mademoiselle Veilleux, the headmistress, who was awaiting our arrival. When I insisted we carry our own bags, he waved me off with his enormous hand.

Elise and I stood staring at a stone wall with a massive iron gate, but all we could see through its slats were narrow little trees. But when Crespeau opened the gate for us, we walked into an immense courtyard with green lawns, cobbled squares, and manicured walking paths. Who would have thought that hidden away in the middle of Paris was this dream of a campus?

Since school wasn't in session until next week, the courtyard was empty, so it seemed more like a church cloister than a schoolyard. We followed the main walkway across the quad and entered the administrative building, then walked down a long hallway, all gleaming floors and domed ceilings.

An arched doorway led to a spacious foyer with an even higher ceiling and a black-and-white-geometric-tiled floor.

A tiny woman came out of a hallway and began walking toward us, the click of her heels echoing off the walls. "Ah, bonjour," she said, her voice low and rich. "I am Mademoiselle Veilleux." She pronounced it *Vay-oo*. "Monsieur Crespeau just called to tell me you were here. Bienvenue, bienvenue!"

She kissed us both on each cheek and smiled warmly. Her black hair was pulled off her face in a bun, but instead of making her look prim and schoolmarmish, it made her preternaturally beautiful. Her porcelain skin seemed lit from within, and a rose-colored scarf only enhanced the effect. And as I'd come to expect from French women, she exuded style in a slim black skirt suit with impossibly high black heels.

"I am so glad you were able to come a few days early before the rest of the students arrive," she said in a charming French accent. "It will give you time to get acquainted with the building and its facilities and, of course, your schedules."

She handed us our course schedules, which pretty much had us occupied from eight in the morning until five in the evening every day. Our jaws must have dropped because she explained, "The French academic schedule may be a bit more rigorous than what you're used to. As you know, we had to schedule you at the Lycée Internationale for your Advanced Placement courses, so two days a week, you will take the Métro across town. But the school is right by La Tour Eiffel, and I think you'll enjoy doing some sightseeing after your classes. I'm sure right now you are very tired and would like to get situated in your rooms." She began walking us out the way we'd come. "Elise, your father took the liberty of having your rooms furnished and decorated. I hope you don't mind."

"Not at all," Elise said, flashing me a smug grin.

We crossed the courtyard to one of the dormitories, then took the stairwell five flights up. I was glad now that Monsieur Crespeau had been so insistent about carrying our bags up, although I wondered how he had managed with his limp.

When we reached the top floor, Mademoiselle Veilleux did not even seem winded. She led us down the hallway and hesitated at a door, then pulled out two sets of keys attached to velvet ribbons. "The large keys are for the school gate, which gets locked every night at six o'clock. The small keys are for your rooms, which share a bathroom. The room on the right is . . . well, it's a bit smaller, I suppose." She looked a bit flustered suddenly, like she'd momentarily forgotten her manners. Then she handed both keys to me. "It's just a trifle smaller, so perhaps you could flip a coin to decide. I'll leave you to your unpacking, but please don't hesitate to call me in the main office if you have any questions. Oh, and since the dining hall is not open yet, lunch is on me," she said. "Most proprietors in the neighborhood know who I am, so find a place you like and give them my card. I'll take care of the bill."

Awestruck, we thanked her and watched as she glided back down the hallway on those impossible heels.

Elise grinned. "Is this amazing or what?"

"Yeah, except for the nine-hour school day."

"I know. Are they trying to torture us because we're American?"

"Revenge for Disneyland Paris, no doubt," I said, dangling the keys from my fingers. "So, heads or tails?"

She cocked her head to the side and gave me her patented pout-smile. "I was hoping you'd take the smaller one, Emma. You don't need as much space as I do."

"Is that a jab about my height?"

"It's a jab about your luggage. You didn't pack nearly as much as I did."

I couldn't argue there. "Fine," I relented. "I'll take the smaller room."

It didn't matter. My room was bigger than the one I'd shared with Michelle at Lockwood by at least double, with a ten-foot ceiling to boot. The walls had been painted lavender with ivory trim, and Mr. Fairchild had bought us comforters to match. A plum-colored settee sat by a vanity table, and on the wall behind it was a full-length oval mirror with an ornately designed frame. My luggage sat neatly in front of a built-in closet, partially camouflaged by a purple organza drape. And the best part was a pair of immense French windows, opening onto a view of the rooftops of Rue Saint-Antoine. It was the most beautiful dorm room I had ever seen.

After a few minutes of inspecting and sighing happily, Elise and I met in the bathroom, which was equally impressive with a tub-and-shower combo, double sink, toilet and bidet, all of them fitted with gleaming brass fixtures.

"Oh, the long baths I will take here," she said. "With real French lavender."

"Mmm, that sounds nice."

"I would take one right now except I'm starving," she said.

"I know. All this luxury is exhausting," I said, trying for a joke that didn't take. "Where do you want to eat? Do you know of a good place?"

"I know of a thousand good places."

We ended up walking toward Place de la Bastille. Across the circle by the July Column was a large round building with a mirrored exterior. It was very modern and seemed out of place amid all the elegant historic monuments.

"What's that ugly building?" I asked.

"That's the Opera House."

My brow furrowed. I had seen pictures of the Opera House, had watched the movie version of *The Phantom of the Opera* twice. I knew that the Opera House was majestic and grand, with white columns and gold statues and a giant green dome, plus a grand foyer inside with that famous cascade of stairs. There was no way this was the Opera House.

Elise saw my confusion. "Paris has two opera houses. There's the Palais Garnier, the one you've seen in the movies. And there's this new one, Opéra Bastille. These days the old Opera House is mostly used for ballets, while the operas are usually performed here."

I remembered a pact Owen and I had made last spring to go to our first opera together. Owen was one of my best friends. At least he had been until I'd screwed things up by kissing him. He and our friend Flynn were in Europe for the summer doing some kind of backpacking pilgrimage/rock tour. Since Owen's family had money, he wasn't in any hurry to rush back to the States for college or a job. In fact, he and Flynn were coming to visit us in Paris in late September. I wasn't sure how long they might stay, but with Owen and Elise dating now, I imagined it might be a while. Awkwardness would surely ensue.

Elise and I turned toward the river onto Boulevard Henri IV, a street lined with produce stands, bookstores, flower stalls, and more eateries. Vespas and bicycles filled the stands on each corner, and Parisians on their lunch breaks crowded the outdoor cafés. Elise recommended a brasserie just a block from the river with ample outdoor seating and chalkboards advertising their specials.

I got shivers as the host seated us at a table with a view of the small park across the street. The interior looked like something from the set of *Amélie*—all dark wood and brass rails with art nouveau lamps and golden décor. It was thrilling to read a menu entirely in French and order in French.

Mademoiselle Veilleux had been right about her reputation at the local dining establishments. In fact, the chef came out from the kitchen to chat with us, reminding us repeatedly to tell Claire (Mlle. Veilleux's first name, apparently) that he missed her and sent his regards. He took our orders personally: a *croque-madame* and a glass of Beaujolais for me, salmon tartare and a glass of chardonnay for Elise.

A few moments later, the waiter brought our wine. Combined with our excitement about being in Paris and our jet-lag, the wine made us both a little giddy. When the food finally came, I was faint with hunger. My sandwich was rich and savory with layers of ham and melted Gruyère (is there anything better in the world than melted cheese?) and a Dijon-béchamel sauce and—in case I hadn't gotten enough cholesterol—a fried egg on top. A few vague concerns about fat and calories wafted through my brain, but I remembered that the French, despite their rich diet, were far healthier than Americans because they ate sensibly and walked a lot.

We would soon discover the rigors of walking through Paris for ourselves. After a leisurely lunch, we crossed the river and checked out La Rive Gauche, the Left Bank. Pausing halfway across the Pont de Sully, I nearly yelped when I saw Notre Dame in the distance. Elise, jaded from years of traveling to Paris, just laughed at me, but it was surreal to see this magnificent place I'd only read about or seen in movies suddenly here in front of my eyes, like Dorothy must have felt when she first spied Oz.

"It's kind of a long walk," Elise said, "but we can see it up close if you want. Actually, we should stop at Shakespeare and Company on the way. You are going to love this bookstore!"

We walked the Quai de la Tournelle and took a set of stairs down to the cobbled walkway that ran along the Seine. When I saw the ubiquitous riverboats, I had the cheesy tourist's desire to hop aboard, but I knew Elise wouldn't go for that. We continued walking on the shaded pedestrian path until we neared the bookshop. The neighborhood where we emerged was swimming with tourists, souvenir shops, and flashy restaurants. Shakespeare and Company was set back from the main street on a cobbled alley behind a median of trees.

Once inside we were joyfully bombarded by books of every color, genre, and size. I actually felt a little dizzy from the towering stacks and swirls of dust. A soot-speckled cat wandered by my ankles as we passed books piled shoulder-high, fine arts prints, ladders perched precariously against shelves, and quirky signs and postcards. This was clearly a place for people who loved the written word.

The smell of must and old books permeated the air, and I inhaled deeply, feeling a pang of disbelief and gratitude that I was here. I found a cozy nook off the main room and let my fingers graze along the spines of antique books. And then I spied a copy of *Le Fantôme de l'Opéra,* Gaston Leroux's Gothic masterpiece written in the original French.

Like almost every American, I had seen the Andrew Lloyd Webber musical, but I'd never read the book that inspired it. This copy was from 1965 and had a red cloth binding with a black-and-white illustration on the cover of a skeletal Phantom in a top hat clutching the fainting body of Christine Daaé. It was over-the-top and absolutely irresistible. I snatched the book from the shelf and handed over my ten euros at the front counter. Elise came up a few minutes later to pay for her selections, then we left with our spoils to go see Notre Dame.

Nothing could have prepared me for the splendor of this building. Yes, it was made of stone and glass like any other church, and I'd seen its image enough times on postcards to feel like I knew it. But the real deal made me breathless with wonder at its artistry. The west end impressed with its Gothic stone towers and rose-colored window gleaming under the sun, but it was the east end that floored me with its gravity-defying buttresses and that delicate spire, like a Christmas ornament made of spun sugar. I couldn't wait to come back and see it all lit up at night. But for now, Elise and I were the walking dead, so we deferred the tour of the interior for another day and started back toward school.

Everything was quiet as we entered our dormitory and climbed the five stories, listening to the creaking of our feet on the wooden stairs. Even though it was only a little after six o'clock, I was bone weary and ready to fall into that lovely lavender bed. After a deliciously cool shower, I wrapped myself in my fluffy robe and called my dad for a brief rundown of the day's events. When I called Gray afterward, his phone rang four times before the inevitable voice mail recording. I left him a message saying I missed him and wished he were here, not in a trite postcard way, but deeply and truly.

I went to stand by the window and flung open the panes to the Paris sky. The sun hadn't set yet, but it had dipped below the buildings, casting my little view in glowing silhouette. Rooftops gleamed ochre and patina green. Not a soul ventured through the alleyway, and except for the low rumble of traffic, it seemed for a moment as if I was entirely alone in the city.

My freshman year of high school, I'd had virtually no friends, and I'd struggled mightily over the past two years to solidify the friendships I had now. I was no stranger to loneliness. But tonight felt different. Standing at an open window in a virtually empty dormitory in a foreign city, it felt like loneliness was a presence in the room, sucking up half the air, making my heart thud against my rib cage. I closed the window and tried to slow my breathing.

Why didn't Gray call me back? Where was he tonight?

And then I remembered. In California, it was eleven in the morning. He was in the middle of his EMT training.

To distract myself, I unpacked my suitcases, slowly filling the closet with my wardrobe and setting my toiletries and personal items on the vanity. And that's when I found the gift bag from Darlene.

I riffled through the tissue paper and found a bottle of dried rose petals, a length of red yarn, and a compass. A tiny note was tied to the neck of the bottle that read: *Here are the instructions for the spell to reunite lovers. But remember, love casts its own spell.*

Darlene was a practitioner of voodoo and a believer in spells. I wasn't sure if I believed in them or not, but last year she'd given me one that seemed to have worked. I wasn't about to discount magic or superstition just yet.

I lay the bag on the table and looked at the mirror on the wall. I doubted this was one of Mr. Fairchild's purchases. It looked like a genuine antique, with scuffing along the frame and silver-black marbling along its surface. It not only looked old; it felt old, too, emanating some strange energy that only years of existence could yield. A shiver ran through me as I watched my reflection warp slightly in the aged glass.

For some reason, mirrors spooked me.

Last spring on Michelle's birthday, we had been playing a silly campfire game in which you spin around three times in a darkened room chanting "Bloody Mary" and then open your eyes in front of a mirror. Legend says you're supposed to see the face of your beloved in the mirror.

And I had. I'd opened my eyes to see Gray's ghostly image staring back at me. Of course, I had also screamed and we'd erupted into giggles and written it off as the power of suggestion. But there was something sinister about mirrors and their ability to reflect or distort reality.

Mirrors were also a powerful symbol of the self. Last year, I'd suffered from waking nightmares in which I'd occasionally wander away from campus, waking up hours later in the woods with no recollection of how I'd gotten there.

When these trips started getting dangerous, Darlene taught me a lucid dreaming technique that had ended my sleepwalking days forever. She told me, "When you get the sense that you're dreaming, create a mirror image of yourself and send the reflection into the dream so your real self stays put."

The first time I'd tried the technique, it had worked, and I'd been using it ever since to keep myself grounded in reality. But right now, I didn't want to imagine my reflection walking into whatever darkness lay on the other side of that glass.

Feeling fatigue overwhelm me, I crawled into bed, luxuriating in the satiny sheets, the plush pillow, the dense comforter. Even though it wasn't cold in the room, I wanted the security of thick blankets pulled tight around me.

As tired as I was, I decided to read a little before falling asleep. I grabbed my copy of *Le Fantôme de l'Opéra* from the nightstand and opened to the prologue. Reading a book in French took a lot more effort than reading in English, so I struggled to get through the first five pages.

Rumors about a phantom are flying through the dressing rooms of the Opera House. An unseen tyrant has been threatening the opera's managers into reserving a private box for him. And a scene changer has been found dead in a cellar, hanging from a beam. The police suspect suicide. But when they go to cut his body down, the rope has disappeared.

I shivered under the covers, imagining a body swinging from the rafters of a darkened theater. And then I heard a voice, faint and murmuring. It was so quiet I couldn't tell where it had come from or if the person was speaking French or English. Ordinarily, I would have assumed it was from a TV show, but our rooms didn't have television sets and no one else was in the building.

I held my breath and listened for a few seconds, hearing nothing but the distant sounds of traffic. I exhaled, but over my own breath I heard the whispering again, faint but haunting. It seemed to be coming from the hallway.

Maybe some students had arrived back at school a few days early. As jittery as I felt, I crept out of bed and padded to the door and stood there, heart racing, trying to drum up the courage to open it.

I sprang the latch and whisked open the door, looking left and right before going out to stand in the middle of the hallway, where I felt a current of cold air waft past.

No one was there.

Laughing at my superstitious nature, I went back inside. But the moment I'd shut the door, the voice resumed, still whispering but more loudly this time, like the person was in the room with me. It sounded as if it was coming from the mirror.

I'd gotten myself so worked up that I was afraid to look into the glass. But sometimes the only way to conquer a fear is to meet it head-on. I sat down at the vanity, my eyes glued to the cosmetics and toiletries there, feeling terror creep over my shoulders. Before I lost my nerve, I glanced briefly into the mirror. Some cold, menacing force made me recoil in fright, knocking over the settee as I did. The crash sent me dashing back to the bed, where I plunged myself under the covers, cowering with my head in my pillow, trying to erase what I'd just seen.

Because the reflection in the mirror had not been my own.

CHAPTER 3

The next morning, I took the purple organza panel from the closet and draped it over the mirror, trying to dispel the image I'd seen from my mind.

This was easy enough to do at first, because the next few days were more chaotic and busy than I'd imagined. The dorm quickly filled with the sounds of students returning for fall term. Unfamiliar French pop music echoed through the halls, and groups of stylish students congregated in little pods, chattering in incomprehensibly fast French. Elise had already made the rounds and introduced herself to the "cool kids," the ones who smoked fancy French cigarettes and dressed in effortlessly chic prep school garb. I found myself shy, feeling like an impostor among their tight-knit community. Perhaps when classes began I would make some friends and feel more at home.

The first week was brutal. When I woke each morning, I used the mirror in the bathroom to put on my makeup and check my outfit. This led to some tedious jockeying for time with Elise; however, we both managed to get out the door in time for a quick croissant and coffee at the cafeteria, followed by nearly ten hours of running ourselves ragged through a punishing schedule of coursework and homework.

By Friday, all I wanted was sleep. And Gray. Between his

EMT training, my rigorous schedule, and the six-hour time difference, we'd had a difficult time scheduling phone calls. But that evening I wanted so badly to hear his voice that I took a chance and called him, saying a silent prayer that he would answer.

Miraculously, he did.

"Gray! I can't believe you're actually on the line."

"I know," he said. "I just stepped out for lunch. You got lucky."

"I did, didn't I?" I said, smiling to myself. "How are you?"

Gray told me all about his training, which was grueling because they were basically fitting in a semester's worth of content into seven weeks. I told him about my courses and how I was adapting slowly to the crazy French schedule.

"Two days a week, Elise and I have to sit through these three-hour marathon AP classes at the international school. The professors are no joke, much more demanding than the teachers at home. But the city is beautiful, and I'm sort of excited all the time, wondering what I'm going to learn next. I really miss you. You would love it here!"

"I wish I could be there, walking by the Seine with you, holding you in my arms," he said. "I keep thinking back to your birthday last summer, that night we spent on the beach just before I left for Coast Guard training."

"You mean the night when we almost had sex?"

He laughed. "If you want to remember it like that," he said. "I like to think of it as the night I gave you my Scorpio dog tag."

"Aw." My heart swelled at the memory.

For my birthday, Gray had given me a dog tag with his horoscope sign on one side and a message etched into the other: *To Emma, the only antidote for my sting.* He wore an almost identical one with my Virgo angel, which he'd told me was his lucky charm. He wore it every time he had to travel somewhere, then took it off once he'd arrived safely.

"I also remember we were lying on our backs looking up at the sky," he said, "and I saw that shooting star and told you to make a wish. You never told me what you wished for."

"That's because it wouldn't come true," I said. But it already had come true. I had wished for Gray to come back to me, and he had. Eventually. "Of course you do remember that shortly after that romantic night, you callously decided to break up with me."

"Callously?" he said. "Don't say that. I thought it was what was best for you at the time. I didn't want to drag you into my drama."

"Oh, Gray, at this point, we're pretty much swimming in each other's drama," I said. "We're in so deep, there's no escaping each other now."

"I wouldn't want to escape," he said.

"Neither would I," I said. "I'm yours forever."

He made an adorable groaning sound. "I'm so glad you called," he said. "I feel so much better when I hear from you and don't have to worry whether you're okay. I know we can't talk as much as you'd like, but I think about you all the time. When I can't be with you, I daydream about our best moments together. It feels like I'm remembering a dream."

I laughed, thinking about how I had done the very same thing on the plane last week. "Well, it wasn't a dream," I said. "It was all real. And we're going to be together again very soon."

"Not soon enough," he said.

"Hey, maybe you'll get stationed in Cape Cod," I said. "Wouldn't that be amazing?"

He sighed a yes.

There was nothing I wanted more at that moment than to be reunited with Gray in Massachusetts at the end of this year, to be back in the comfort of my home with the man I would spend the rest of my life with.

Gray had to get off the phone—we'd talked through his

entire lunch break—so we reluctantly said good-bye. But the high from our conversation kept me buoyant for days.

It even helped me endure another arduous week of classes. Elise and I had opted to take a Gothic Architecture elective, which had us traipsing across bridges and through arrondissements to see countless cathedrals, cataloging every arch, buttress, vault, and spire. A tall student who looked like he'd forgotten to take the hanger out of his jacket often fell into step beside me on these jaunts, happy to have an "ignorant American" to impress. At first, I *was* impressed, and it was nice to have someone translating the professor's lecture for me. But after a while, his boasting began to grate.

One afternoon, we were crossing the bridge to Île de la Cité, one of the two remaining natural islands along the Seine and pretty much the heart of Paris. Coat Hanger Guy proceeded to tell me that all road distances in France were calculated from the 0 km point located in front of Notre Dame's towers.

"Really," I said, sighing, as this was about the hundredth gem of trivia he'd decided to impart to me today. "It's a wonder they don't have you teaching the class."

He didn't seem to pick up on my sarcasm. "True," he said. "Perhaps once I get my degree I will replace this *bouffon*."

I had to admit, Monsieur Laroche was a bit of a pompous windbag, and the young guy might have made a more entertaining teacher. At least he was easier to look at. He had longish sandy-blond hair, a rather prominent straight nose, intense blue eyes, and a crooked smile. He wasn't handsome in the conventional sense, but there was something about the way his features fit together that made him sort of fascinating to watch.

"I'm Jean-Claude," he said rather formally, as if he hadn't been talking my ear off for the last half hour.

"Emma," I said, involuntarily extending my hand.

He regarded my hand like an unappetizing hors d'oeuvre

and shook it reluctantly. I suddenly remembered my grandma's words. Was I meant to kiss him on the cheek?

Jean-Claude looked amused. "You are American," he said.

"Is it that obvious?"

"Well, yes, but Saint-Antoine is a small school. Anyone new stands out. Especially two beauties like you and . . . your friend."

I looked over at Elise, who was brownnosing the professor, no doubt asking him astute questions about apses and naves.

"So what do you think of our little school?" he said.

"I love it! Everything is so old and beautiful here. I couldn't believe it when we walked into our dorm room. Did the building used to be a hotel or something?"

"Actually, it used to be a prison," he said. "Well, not exactly. The building is nineteenth century, but the school was built on the grounds of the Bastille."

"No way."

"Oui. The neighborhood of Saint-Antoine was the center of the French Revolution. Legend has it that the ghosts of the Bastille still haunt the grounds."

I rolled my eyes, skeptical. But after my experience with the mirror, I wasn't so sure. Jean-Claude's eyes wandered back to Elise. "She has a boyfriend," I told him, cringing a little as I thought of Owen and Elise together as a couple. Some pairings just seemed unnatural.

Jean-Claude shrugged. "In Paris, we are not easily frightened by the existence of a . . . *boy*friend. He is not here now, eh?"

I had to give him props for his optimism. "No, but he's coming later this month."

"Quelle domage," he said. "Then we shall have to be . . . what do you Americans say? Friends with benefits." I burst out laughing. "You will introduce me?"

"Sure," I said.

Part of me was feeling generous of heart, and the other

part of me didn't mind the idea of seeing Elise cut this haughty Frenchman down to fry size.

We were approaching the Conciergerie, the medieval prison where Marie Antoinette had lost her head. I grabbed Jean-Claude's arm and led him to where Elise stood inspecting the tower.

"Elise," I said, "there's someone I'd like you to meet. This is Jean-Claude."

To my surprise, her perma-sneer turned into a winning smile. Jean-Claude smiled back, and in some sort of etiquette ballet, Elise edged her way toward him, and then they were air-kissing perfectly—once on the right cheek, once on the left.

Jean-Claude said, "Chez nous, c'est quatre" ("*Where I'm from, it's four kisses.*") and then he kissed her again. I tried to muffle a gagging noise.

Elise laughed charmingly and launched into her most lyrical and fluent French, and before I could say, "You're welcome," the two of them were flirting expertly while I stood beside them feeling like a total . . . *bouffon.*

After the prison, Monsieur Laroche led us to Sainte-Chapelle, our final destination for the day. Built in the thirteenth century to house the relics of King Louis IX, the chapel wasn't all that impressive from the outside—just a slender stone structure with a slate roof and wooden spires covered in delicate tracery. But the interior felt like something out of an illustrated fairy tale. The narrow chapel was surrounded by tall banks of stained-glass windows framed in gold, all of them capped by a vaulted ceiling painted to look like a night sky studded with stars. Standing in the middle and looking upward gave me the feeling of being a very tiny bird in an enormous gilded birdcage.

When our tour concluded, Laroche announced a quiz on architectural terms on Monday, and we headed back to campus. One of the most frustrating parts of the school schedule was the two-hour break for lunch. As much as I needed a rest, I would have rather grabbed a quick bite and finished my school day earlier, but a leisurely lunch was practically law in France.

Elise, Jean-Claude, and I headed to the cafeteria, which put Lockwood's dining hall to shame. Among the choices for lunch were green salad with duck paté, braised artichokes, Brie and apple slices, smoked salmon with asparagus and crème fraîche, roasted chicken with rosemary potatoes, Provençal vegetables, all served with sparkling water, and of course, the unparalleled baguettes that accompanied every meal. I could have happily survived on bread and Brie alone.

At the table, Jean-Claude introduced us to some of his friends. Since we were sitting, I didn't have to worry about the air-kissing quagmire, but I wondered what the protocol would be the next time I met them. His friends were nothing like the teens depicted on the front of our cheesy French textbooks. They seemed far older than American teens, more world-wise and sure of themselves.

They spoke French very quickly, interrupting one another and sometimes breaking into English for a few moments, then reverting back to French. For me, those moments of English were like air pockets, giving me split seconds to breathe before being thrust back into a tempest of French slang.

Eventually, I decided to sit back and take it all in, following their gestures and facial expressions since I couldn't follow their dialogue. There was Sylvie, who had the biggest brown eyes I'd ever seen, framed by dyed black hair with thick bangs. Yseult (pronounced Ee-sol) had exotic features and exuded sexual energy, especially when she was anywhere near Jean-Claude. Next to her was Louis with the spiky blond hair, suspenders, and high-water pants. And finally, there was adorable Georges with the crinkly eyes and honey-colored skin. His T-shirt immediately endeared me to him, as it reminded me of Owen. It featured a plate of sushi and the caption: *This is how I roll.*

After lunch, we went outside to sit in the courtyard. Immediately, they all lit up cigarettes. Jean-Claude offered me one, but I shook my head.

Yseult took a puff of hers and exhaled in a sultry way, like a movie star in a noir film. "So, which of the Americans has room five?" she asked, deigning to speak in English.

Since she hadn't directed the question to me, I didn't respond, even though room five was mine.

"That's Emma's room," Elise volunteered.

"Oh, so you're the lucky one," Yseult said.

"Lucky?"

She laughed. "That room hasn't been assigned to a student in years. But this class's enrollment was so high they had no other choice."

Louis narrowed his eyes and grinned a little deviously. "Rumor has it, room five was Mademoiselle Veilleux's when she was a student here almost twenty years ago. But some spirit in the room wanted her dead and set the room on fire. The school painted over everything, but it's still haunted."

"I don't think it was a ghost," Yseult said. "I think it was Monsieur Crespeau."

"More like Monsieur Creepo," Louis said.

"He went to this school?" I asked.

"Sort of," Georges said. "His parents were the caretakers, so he was allowed to take courses here. When his parents died, he took over for them a few years later."

"How did his parents die?" I asked.

"He killed them," Yseult said in a deadpan voice.

Louis broke into maniacal laughter.

"Don't listen to them," Jean-Claude said to me. "They are trying to scare the new girl with their stories."

"I know," I said, forcing a smile. But stories had to emerge from somewhere. And there was the unpleasant business of the mirror . . .

Later that afternoon, I sat in French literature class, listening to Madame Boulanger lecture about *Candide*. I tried not to think about Yseult's tale. Clearly, Elise and I were the American interlopers infringing on her territory, and Yseult was going to have a little fun at our expense. But I was no stranger to supernatural occurrences, and something about her story carried the ring of truth.

My final class of the day was Opera I. The teacher was originally from Kenya but had been adopted by a French family when he was six years old. His name was Lucas Odumbe, and he insisted we call him Luke. Unlike the other teachers, who were fairly strict and serious, Luke wore dreadlocks and layers of brightly colored shirts over faded jeans with high-top sneakers, and he never stopped moving as he lectured. He had that magnetism of people who truly love what they do. And he spoke French so differently from Madame Boulanger, slowly and deliberately, like he was making love to each word.

"My wife is jealous," he said in French. "She says opera is my mistress, and she is partly right. I sing my favorite arias in the shower, and when I finish sometimes I am weeping. Where else can you get catharsis like that? The first time my parents took me to the opera, I was nine years old. We saw *La Bohème*. Since then, I have seen it fourteen times. And each time it is different. And each time I am transported. Love, loss, magic, madness. It is all there on the stage. And it doesn't matter what language the opera is written in. A good opera needs no translation."

Those first weeks of class were all about storytelling, with Luke trying to get us as excited about opera as he was. He played us his favorite arias: "Dido's Lament" from *Dido and*

Aeneas, which Dido sings before throwing herself on her own funeral pyre; the final arias from *La Bohème* and *La Traviata*, in which both heroines succumb to tuberculosis; and finally, the Liebestod or "Love-Death" aria from Wagner's *Tristan und Isolde*, which ends with a suicide pact between lovers.

"Why do so many operas end in death, you might ask?" he said. "What could be more romantic than a love so immortal it transcends every obstacle, including death?"

He informed us that as members of this class, we were going to have the opportunity to participate in a Young Artists' libretto competition hosted by L'Opéra Bastille. We would work in teams, and our finished librettos would be due before the end of term. The top two librettos chosen by a panel of judges would advance to round two, in which the teams would develop their librettos into one-hour operas to be performed in L'Opéra Bastille's Studio space. The winner of round two would have their opera performed by a professional opera company next year!

Elise glanced at me, her eyes flickering with excitement. She thrived on any kind of competition. Maybe for once we would work together on something rather than being pitted against each other as rivals.

After class I walked back to the dorm, wishing I could talk to Gray but knowing he wouldn't be available. This weekend, he only had a short training session. He was supposed to call me Saturday around two o'clock his time, eight o'clock mine, so we could Skype. I couldn't wait to see his beautiful face on my screen.

My phone buzzed as I was about to enter the dorm, and I allowed myself to get excited thinking it might be a text from Gray. But it was from Michelle. I sat on the dorm steps and texted a long overdue message back to her. She'd been sending me a barrage of texts all week, making sure I was eating enough, that I was getting out and enjoying myself, that I wasn't homesick. Things had been so crazy I hadn't had time to respond with anything other than a quick yes or no.

I looked at my watch and figured it was ten o'clock in the morning in Massachusetts. Michelle would be sitting in third period right now. *Texting in class? Bad student!* I typed, then waited for her response.

Yep, she texted back. *Senior seminar. :- (*)*. I laughed at Michelle's *about-to-vomit* emoticon.

Poor you. I'm in Paris, I typed.

R u making the most of it? What r u doing this weekend?

Going to a club w/ 3 hot French guys. How bout u?

Staying in w/ 1 hot girl, Quentin Tarantino, and Orville Redenbacher.

A wave of nostalgia hit me. I wanted so badly to be somewhere familiar with people who knew me and accepted me even when I was a total dork and wanted to stay in and veg in my pajamas all weekend.

Tell Jess I love her, I texted.

I do every day. Miss you, Em.

Miss you, too.

I had told Michelle I wasn't homesick, but as I headed up to my room, my loneliness lingered there like a depressed roommate. I missed my family. My dad would be out on the boat right now, but maybe Grandma would be home. I dialed her number, but it rang and rang, making me even sadder.

I decided to write her a letter about my first week in Paris, then walked it to the post office, stopping on my way home to pick up a baguette and a hunk of cheese. I didn't feel like going to the cafeteria with Jean-Claude and his friends, being the outsider again. As nice as they might have been once I got to know them, they were still strangers to me. And I didn't have the energy to sit and be sociable with strangers for two hours. I needed to lie in bed, read a book, and get a good night's sleep.

As I walked back from the corner market, the streets were

teeming with people just off from work, outdoor café tables already filling with businessmen smoking and talking animatedly, the buzz of Friday night plans in the air. I felt like a spirit floating through other people's lives, able to observe but not participate. In a few months, I might feel like I actually belonged here. But for now, I felt apart.

When I got back to Saint-Antoine, Mademoiselle Veilleux was coming out of the bright blue main doors of the school. She was dressed in a body-skimming fuchsia wrap dress, and her dark hair, which I'd only seen pinned up, hung loose around her face in sexy waves.

"Bon soir," I said.

"Bon soir, Emma," she purred, descending the stairs gracefully in another pair of five-inch heels.

"Vous avez l'air très bien!" I said, marveling at how pretty she looked.

"Merci. I'm going out with a new beau. He owns a trendy brasserie on the Left Bank. Very handsome. Very young. And very rich. Wish me luck."

"Bon chance," I said as she darted into the crowds.

When I walked into the main lobby, Monsieur Crespeau was leaning against the far wall with a push broom in his hand. But he wasn't sweeping. He was standing there with an odd expression on his face.

"Bon soir!" I said, trying to quell the tremor of nervousness in my voice.

He muttered something unintelligible, then waved me off, disappearing behind a door. Despite his gruff demeanor, I couldn't see him as the psycho Yseult had made him out to be. There was a sadness in his eyes, something vulnerable that made a violent nature seem unlikely.

As I crossed the quad to the dorm, students were congregating in little clusters on the lawn, digesting their evening meal with cigarettes and coffee. Thankfully, I got back to my room unnoticed. The purple drape over the mirror was like a

garish neon sign announcing: SOMETHING SCARY UNDER-
NEATH! I half wondered whether the actual mirror would be
less distracting, but I couldn't stomach the thought of dodg-
ing my own reflection every time I passed it.

I changed into my pajamas and ate my baguettes with
Camembert and read a little more of *The Phantom of the
Opera* until my eyes were grainy and sore. I knew I should
stop reading and go to sleep, but as tired as I was, Yseult's rumors about my room still haunted me.

I snuck another glance at the covered mirror. It was only a
piece of glass, for God's sake. That first night when I'd heard
those whispers and seen the phantom reflection, I had been
severely jet-lagged, had drunk two glasses of wine with
lunch, and had walked three miles around the city before returning to an empty room. Most likely, what I'd experienced
had been the product of fatigue, dehydration, and my over-
active imagination.

I didn't want to give in to my fears. In fact, last year when
I was having those nightmares, the only thing that really
helped was acknowledging and confronting them. Once I
had realized they were just a product of my subconscious, the
nightmares had subsided and I'd regained control over my
life.

If I was going to survive living on my own in a foreign city,
I had to take control. I crept toward the mirror and stood in
front of it, issuing a challenge to some unseen foe. Before I
could reconsider, I tore the drape from the mirror so I was
staring at my own reflection. I didn't blink. And I didn't look
away.

My reflection was normal—no distortions, no other-
worldly voices, no ghosts. But the prickles of fear along my
neck lingered until I thought of a more permanent solution.
Why didn't I just take the mirror down?

Tentatively, I approached the mirror from the side and
grabbed it with both hands, pulling gently at first to try to

unhook it from the wall. But the mirror didn't budge. I tried again, tugging harder this time, but it remained fixed in place. If I ever succeeded in removing it, I'd probably take half of the wall with it. I drew back, out of breath from my exertions.

That's when I saw a flicker of light inside the mirror. I thought my eyes were playing tricks on me, but then the light began to recede slowly into the darkness until it disappeared completely.

I grabbed the drape and threw it back over the mirror, then jumped into bed. Every hair on my body stood on end. That light I'd seen had looked like a candle being carried down a darkened hallway and being snuffed out. But that was impossible.

Either I was going crazy . . . or Yseult's rumors were true. I wasn't sure which was worse.

CHAPTER 4

Saturday seemed interminable. I had a ton of homework to do, but I was finding it difficult to concentrate with a purple enshrouded mirror in the room. So I went to the library to study. Saint-Antoine's library was much smaller than the huge Gothic affair at Lockwood, but its intimacy suited me. It was on the second level of the administrative building so the windows overlooked Rue Saint-Antoine. I had to finish reading *Candide,* study for my Gothic Architecture quiz, write a three-page essay on the economic effects of the Black Death, analyze mythical allusions in Dante's *Inferno,* and write a proposal for the libretto contest for Opera class. I was pretty sure I wanted to do some kind of modern retelling of *The Phantom of the Opera,* but I wasn't sure how to adapt the story. Elise and I would have to get together and brainstorm some ideas.

After a few hours, I was so immersed in my work that I looked up and saw that the sun had passed over the school, casting Rue Saint-Antoine in shadow. I was starving. I gathered my books and took the stairs down to the cafeteria, but it turned out I was too late for lunch and too early for dinner.

On my way back to the dorm, I ran into Sylvie and Georges hanging out on the stairs. They both stood and air-kissed me, and I think I kissed them back without embarrassing myself.

"Are you going to Fool On Fair tonight?" Sylvie asked me. At least that's what I thought she said.

"Where?"

"The new nightclub. You must come!"

"Oui," Georges agreed. "Elise told us you are a . . . what did she say, Sylvie? A *homebody?*"

Sylvie laughed charmingly.

"I do stay in too much," I said. "The thing is, my boyfriend is calling tonight, and I haven't talked to him in a long time."

"Ah, *l'amour,*" Sylvie said. "Je comprends."

"We will . . . abduct you if you don't come," Georges said.

"Abduct me?" I said.

"Before your ghost does," Sylvie trilled. Georges flashed his beautiful white smile.

I forced a laugh, but my stomach clenched at the recollection of the moving flame in the mirror. I left them with a non-committal *maybe,* then raced up the stairs to my room.

A little before eight o'clock that night, I flipped open my laptop, checked that the camera and speaker were working, ran a brush through my hair, reapplied my makeup, and put on a white eyelet tank with a deep neck that showed the Scorpio necklace I wore for Gray. It almost felt like I was getting ready for a date.

I propped the laptop on a pillow in front of me and waited for Gray's incoming call. When the computer pinged, I clicked on the Skype icon and a big screen popped open.

"Hi," I said, feeling myself blush as Gray's face appeared on the monitor. My palms were sweating, and my insides fluttered with nerves.

"You're a sight for sore eyes," he said with a sigh. His deep voice made the hairs on my neck stand on end.

Although the camera quality wasn't great, I could see how tan he'd gotten over the summer and could make out a smattering of new freckles across the bridge of his nose. He looked older and a little tired but no less handsome.

"God, Emma, I've missed you," he said. "It's so hard to be away from you."

"I know," I said. "It's awful."

"Tell me everything," he said.

I told him all about my opera class and the libretto competition and about meeting Jean-Claude and making some real French friends.

"You look really happy," he said.

"Do I?"

"Yeah. You look like you're having a good time."

"I guess I am," I said. "I'm keeping busy. But I'm lonely without you."

"I know, me too," he said. "Is Elise keeping you company?"

"As much as that's possible," I said. Gray laughed. He and Elise had dated for six months during my sophomore year. We'd both witnessed her limitations in the friendship department. "How about you?" I asked. "You're almost finished. How does it feel?"

"Scary," he said. "But good. I got my first assignment. I'm going to be the rescue swimmer for the cutter *Dolphin* in Miami."

"Miami!" I said. "I'm so relieved. I was worried you were going to say Alaska."

"I know," he said, chuckling. "I'll only be three hours away. Well, once you're back in the States."

We talked for almost an hour, catching up and laughing. I didn't ever want to hang up. But we were interrupted by a knock at my door.

"Can you hold on a sec?" I balanced the laptop on the bed

and opened the door to see Jean-Claude, Georges, Sylvie, and Elise.

"Hey," Elise said, "we're leaving for the club soon and wanted to know if you were coming."

I looked back at my computer and thought about saying good-bye to Gray, having to put on dressy clothes, and maneuver through the fashionable crowds of some trendy nightclub.

"I'm still Skyping with Gray," I said.

"Well, how much longer do you think you'll be?"

"Maybe a half hour?"

"We can wait," Georges said.

"No, don't do that. I probably won't go."

"She probably won't," Elise confirmed.

"Come on," Jean-Claude said, a seductive lilt in his voice.

"The club's called Feu L'Enfer," Sylvie said, writing the name on a piece of paper. "It's in Le Marais. You can take a taxi."

"Yeah, text me if you decide to meet us," Elise said. "We'll look out for you."

"Okay, thanks," I said.

I watched them walk down the hallway in a haze of perfume and cologne, then hopped back up on the bed with my laptop.

"Who was that?" Gray asked.

"Just those friends I told you about."

"It sounded like they were going out for the night. Did you want to go with them?"

"Not really," I said. "They're going to a nightclub. You know I'm not into that scene."

"You should go," he said, his voice flat and unconvincing.

"I don't want to. I want to talk to you."

"But you're in Paris," he said. "You should be making new friends, not staying in to talk to your boyfriend. Besides, we can talk later."

"But I want you now," I said.

A groan escaped his lips. "I want you, too, Em. I hate this."

"Hate what?"

"That I'm not there with you. That I'm already feeling jealous. You're in Paris going to a club with a bunch of French guys, and I'm stuck here giving CPR to plastic dummies. I want to touch your face and smell your shampoo and kiss you. Really kiss you." The memory of Gray's kisses set my heart racing. I leaned into the screen and kissed the 2-D version of his lips. "It's not the same," he said.

"No," I agreed. "Not even close."

"Go out with your friends," he said with finality.

"But—"

"I mean it. I want you to have fun, Em. Even if it's not with me." But his jaw was rigid, like his conscience was fighting with his desires.

"You know, you don't have to be strong all the time," I said, joking.

"Emma, I'm not strong." His voice caught at the end. He pulled out his dog tags and flipped around the one with my Virgo angel. "This keeps me going. *You* keep me going."

A lump formed in my throat. I grasped at my neck for my own dog tag. "If you need me, I'm always here."

I could tell he was trying hard not to break down. "Me too. I love you, Em."

"I know."

He gave a sad laugh.

Gray and I had decided that we never wanted to say "I love you" as an automatic response. So we had adopted Han Solo's brilliant reply to Princess Leia right before he gets encased in carbonite in *The Empire Strikes Back*. It made certain that no matter how much we missed each other, the last thing we said to each other would make us both smile.

"Emma, I know this is hard, but—" He seemed about to

say something important, but the picture suddenly went wonky and the speaker lost sound. Then the screen went black. I tried to call him back, but the line just rang and rang. There was something wrong with our connection.

I knew I'd talk to him again soon but I felt inexplicably sad. I hated that I hadn't said good-bye, that we hadn't finished our conversation. It made me feel unsettled somehow.

As sorry for myself as I was feeling, I knew it was no good to stay in moping all night, so I decided to meet Elise at the club after all. Gray had given me his blessing, and if I stayed here by myself, I'd drive myself crazy staring at the mirror.

I took a quick shower and threw on a slim black dress, accessorized with Michelle's red scarf and my knee-high boots. When I came out of my room, the dorm was eerily quiet, emptied of students who'd fled in search of adventure or romance.

I texted Elise to let her know I was coming, then walked to the taxi stand on Place de la Bastille, waiting only a few minutes before one stopped for me. Paris was different at night, even more magical and fairy-tale surreal with its shimmering lights and golden reflections, all set against an epic blue sky. Flocks of people, young and old alike, thronged the narrow streets, making the city hum and throb to a jangling rhythm.

The taxi was turning onto Rue Beaubourg by the Pompidou Center when I got a text from Elise that said: *OMG, Emma, this place! It's owned by David Guetta! Dress to impress. Models and celebs everywhere. 30 min wait at the door and 20 euro cover, but so worth it!*

Inwardly I groaned. I hadn't even thought about a cover charge, let alone a long wait to get in. In fact, when we neared the club, the street was so crowded the driver had to drop me off a block away. The queue of young people waiting to get in snaked around four columns of velvet rope. The line was barely moving, but no one seemed to mind, as they'd started the party outside. The girls were dancing to the thumping bass line emanating from the club, and the guys were only too happy to watch.

For about two seconds, I considered getting in line. Then I looked down at my dress and my scuffed boots and knew I would feel hopelessly out of place. I looked up at the club's doors, immense faux-stone slabs painted with writhing figures that reminded me of Rodin's *Gates of Hell*. The club's name was emblazoned overhead in red Gothic lettering: *Feu L'Enfer*. Hellfire.

I remembered my dad's advice about using common sense. And right now, it made no sense to wait in line for almost an hour and spend thirty dollars just to stand around feeling lonely. I could do that for free in my room.

I texted Elise and told her I couldn't make it after all. I didn't tell her the reason, just that I wasn't feeling up to it. She'd give me grief about it later, but her lecture would be a lot easier to handle than this club.

The only problem was, I'd lost my taxi and had no idea how to find another one in this neighborhood. I put the school's address into my phone's GPS and followed the street away from the club, feeling the throb of dubstep slowly dissipate. Relieved, I turned onto Rue Rambuteau, a benign-looking street brimming with cafés and restaurants. I almost considered stopping in one for a drink, but I wanted to get back to school before it got too dark and deserted.

After walking a few blocks, I turned onto Rue Malher, hoping to find it well lit and occupied. But the roads were darker and narrower here, taking me through an old Jewish neighborhood of cobbled streets, bereft of people now. I shivered and quickened my pace.

Finally, I reached Rue Saint-Antoine and speed-walked the last few blocks to school. But once I turned onto the alley where the back gates were, a panic welled up inside me as I realized I wasn't alone. Someone had turned onto the alley, and I could see his shadow getting longer and closer behind me. I rummaged around in my purse for my keys but couldn't find them, and my hands were shaking. Helplessly, I knocked on the gate, hoping some students might be hanging out in the courtyard.

Okay, I told myself. *Calm down and walk the rest of the way down the alley until you come to a cross street.*

But then my fight-or-flight instinct suddenly fired, and I abandoned any pretense of remaining calm, lurching into a run down the alley. An intersection lay just fifty feet away, and my adrenaline drove me to the corner where I veered left and screamed as someone slammed into me from the opposite direction.

Actually, it was two people. One had gotten knocked to the ground by our impact, and the other stood over him, looking startled. There was a brief melee as I tried to rein in my momentum, and the guy still standing struggled to help the fallen guy, who was cursing loudly at me. In English.

I apologized for my clumsiness as the two of them brushed themselves off and moved under the light of a streetlamp. I nearly fainted with shock and relief.

"Owen?"

CHAPTER 5

Owen and Flynn were a little drunk. Well, Owen was a little drunk. Flynn was hammered.

"What are you guys doing here?" I asked.

"Our train got in a few hours ago, and we wanted to surprise you!" Owen said.

I looked at my watch. "A few hours ago?"

"Well," Owen explained, "we decided to get some food first."

"And some drinks, it would seem," I said, smiling. "I am so happy to see you guys, you have no idea."

Owen knit his brows in confusion, and I promised to explain later. Other than the furrowed brow, he looked exactly the same—sweet and comforting as a puppy dog. I threw my arms around him in an enormous, grateful hug. Then I hugged Flynn, who smelled of wine, smoke, and Froot Loops.

"What have you done to yourself?" I said, running my hand along Flynn's scalp. He had shorn all his gorgeous, raven-colored hair so he was nearly bald and a little scary-looking.

"What? You don't like it?" he said.

"It's . . . different," I said, taking a few moments to assess his new look. "So what was your plan then? To scale the walls of the school and break into my dorm room?"

"Actually," Owen said, "we were waiting at the gate for the last half hour, hoping someone would come along. But then Flynn had to . . ."

"Take a piss," Flynn said.

"Thank you," Owen said. "I was trying to be polite, but yes, we were looking for a place for Flynn to relieve himself with a little more dignity than this alley."

Flynn's face looked pained. "We didn't find it."

I laughed. "Okay. If I can find my keys, I can sneak you guys into my room. Wait till you see it; it's gorgeous!"

My keys had fallen to the very bottom of my purse, which I rarely carried. I'd have to find a better spot for them from now on, especially if I was going to make these late nights a habit. We tromped up the five flights of stairs, and Flynn was practically gasping by the time we reached my room. He quickly found his way to the bathroom.

"Wow, you weren't kidding," Owen said, checking out my new digs. "This room is amazing!"

"And check out the view." I walked him over to the window and pushed it open to reveal the night sky.

"Wow. This is ridiculous, Emma," he said. "I feel like I should shout something over the rooftops. Bonjour, Pa-ree!"

I peered down at the street and saw what seemed to be a red scarf, tied around the gate. I clutched my neck and realized my scarf was missing. It must have fallen off while I'd made my crazed dash down the alley.

"What's wrong?" Owen asked, seeing my worried look.

"Nothing. Just . . . when I was coming home tonight, I thought someone was following me." Then I explained about my scarf.

"Why were you on your own?" he asked. "Where's Elise?"

"Oh, you know Elise," I said, trying to sound casual. I didn't want Owen getting jealous. "That girl loves the nightlife."

"Who's she out with?" he said, his voice a little edgy.

"Just some friends," I said.

"Guys or girls?"

"Both."

He looked like he was about to say something but thought better of it. "I'm going to get your scarf," he said, abruptly leaving before I could stop him.

A moment later, Flynn came out of the bathroom, sighing. "I feel like a new man."

"Thrilled to hear it," I said. "The old you needed some work."

"Eff off," he said. "I'm drunk and unable to defend myself properly."

Flynn helped himself to my pillow and lay down on the bed with an arm thrown across his face. I sat on the settee by the vanity.

"So tell me about your tour," I said, trying to distract myself from the episode in the alleyway. "Are you guys going to be the next Death Cab for Cutie?"

He snorted from the bed. It turned out their European tour had been a bust. While they'd played a few gigs in London, the venues weren't big enough to attract crowds or agents. And Berlin was even worse. A few of their gigs fell through, and at one place, the owner kicked them out after Flynn almost came to blows with a bartender.

"He cut me off," Flynn said. "And I was barely drunk."

"The nerve!" I said, laughing. "Do you have anything lined up here in Paris?"

"Not yet," he said. "We might just lay low for a while. See what Zee Citee of Luvvv has to offer."

"You mean, be ugly Americans?"

"Bah," Flynn said, sitting up and holding his head like it was a ticking time bomb. "I happen to be a stunningly good-looking American." He smiled, then narrowed his eyes as they landed on something behind me. "What's with the purple sheet?"

"What?" I said, playing dumb.

"That purple curtain behind you. What's it hiding?"

I shook my head. "Nothing."

"Clearly, it's something," Flynn said.

"It's just an old mirror that creeps me out."

"Why?"

"Because I saw something in it."

Flynn raised an eyebrow. "What'd you see?"

"You're going to think I'm crazy."

"Too late."

I told him about the ghostly reflection and the moving candlelight.

Flynn's eyes lit up. "Oooh, a haunted mirror. Can I see it?" He popped up from the bed and ran toward the mirror, flinging off the drape with a dramatic flourish and examining it from all angles. "Yep, it's a creepy old mirror."

"So you agree it's creepy?" I said, thankful to have my fears validated.

The first thing he did was try to pry it off the wall, finding just as I had that it didn't budge. "That's weird," he said. "It's like someone bolted it to the wall. Maybe it's a two-way mirror, and there's some pervert who lives on the other side."

"Thanks a lot," I said. "You're really helping." I stood up and grabbed the drape from him, throwing it back over the mirror.

"I'm just kidding," he said. "You're really freaked out about this, aren't you?"

I felt foolish, close to tears for some reason. Owen came in a few seconds later holding my scarf and delivered it to me like he'd just found my lost kitten.

"Thanks," I said. "Did you see the guy who left it?"

"No, there was no one there. But he tied your scarf to the gates. That doesn't sound like something a serial killer would do. Why are you so spooked?"

"Because she has a ghost in her mirror," Flynn explained.

"Flynn!" I shouted.

"What? Owen should know about this. He can exorcise evil with one flash of those dimples."

"Dude!" Owen said, embarrassed.

But his dimples were so cute they should have been registered as weapons.

Feeling rather foolish, I debriefed Owen on the mirror's supernatural status. He came and sat next to me on the bench, tossing an arm over my shoulder. And then Elise came barging through the bathroom door and into my room.

"Emma, you'd better be on your deathbed or I'll—" Her mouth froze in place when she saw Owen. "Oh my God, you're here!" she yelled, throwing herself at him as if she hadn't just been grinding with Jean-Claude a half hour ago.

"Surprise!" Owen mumbled into her shoulder.

"You little shit! Why didn't you tell me you were coming?" she said, punching him in the chest.

"It's great to see you, too," he said, laughing.

Elise's face melted and she hugged him again, treating us to an unnervingly intimate kiss on his lips. Flynn glanced at me and rolled his eyes.

Once they had finished their smoochfest, Elise gave Flynn her requisite disdainful greeting. "Hey, Flynn," she said. "Nice haircut."

"Don't I get a kiss, too?" he asked.

"In your dreams."

"You don't have to pretend you're not thrilled to see me," he said.

"And so, the banter begins," I said, and Owen laughed.

We sat around for about an hour, catching up on our summers apart and making plans for the next few weeks in Paris. And then came the awkward moment when I looked over and saw Flynn asleep on my bed.

I was pretty sure Owen was going to spend the night with Elise, but I hadn't counted on sharing my bed with Flynn.

Owen glanced at me forlornly. "Are you okay with this? I'd be more than happy to wake him up and kick him to the floor."

"It's no big deal," I said. "He can crash here." I was a grown-up. I could share my bed with a male friend and not have it mean anything. Of course I could.

Owen and Elise left my room tangled in each other's arms, and I hoped that the walls were thick. I changed into my pajamas and then went to the bathroom to brush my teeth. When I came back in the room, I walked to the other side of the bed and gingerly crawled in, hoping not to wake Flynn. It was actually nice not to be alone in the room. I curled up about as far from Flynn's body as I could without falling off the bed.

I must have dozed off because, hours later, I nearly did fall off the bed when I woke to find Flynn's body curled against mine. I tried slipping out of bed without waking him, but his hand shot out and grabbed my arm before I could make my getaway.

"Emma?" he said groggily. "Where are you going?"

"I'm . . . going to take a shower," I said.

He struggled to make sense of where he was, sitting up against the headboard and rubbing his eyes. He looked so boyish and confused I couldn't help but laugh. "What happened?" he asked.

"You don't remember?" I said. "Flynn, it was incredible. A revelation."

His face looked panic-stricken. "Did we . . . ?" He was really buying it, and it was so absurd that I couldn't maintain the charade any longer.

"No, you idiot!" I said. "You passed out on my bed, and I had to sleep on the edge all night. You hogged the covers, too."

"Holy shit, Emma," he said. "Don't do that to me."

"Is it really so believable that I would fall into bed with you on your first night in Paris?"

"Well, yeah," he said. "I mean, look at this." He gestured down at his presumably hot bod. To be honest, it didn't hurt to look.

"You're too much," I said. "And now I really am going to take a shower."

"Really?" he said, running a hand along his scalp. "Want some company?"

"You're the most sex-crazed guy I know."

"No, I'm the only one who admits it," he said.

I rummaged through my closet to find him some necessities. "Here's a toothbrush, Casanova," I said, tossing it to him. "I'll be out of the bathroom in ten minutes."

He grinned, like he knew something I didn't.

It took the four of us a while to get ready sharing only one bathroom, and then we went and got coffee and breakfast at a café across from Opéra Bastille. I had two buttery croissants, fresh-squeezed orange juice, and the strongest coffee I'd ever tasted.

"I'm moving here," Flynn said as he inhaled a second croissant.

I tried to gauge the state of affairs between Elise and Owen, but they were being much more reserved this morning than they'd been last night.

"So is that *the* opera?" Owen asked, looking a little disappointed. I explained to him what Elise had told me about the two different opera houses.

"I suppose you two have already gone without me?" he said.

"Of course not," I said. "We made a pinky swear. We should go for your birthday."

"Yeah," Elise said. "We could double date."

"If you don't mind going with Mr. Clean over there," Owen said.

"Hey, lay off the bald jokes," Flynn said. "I'm a sensitive man."

Now that I'd had a chance to get used to it, I kind of liked Flynn's hair. It made his pale blue eyes look even more ethereally beautiful. He flashed me a smoldering look, and I cracked up.

"Speaking of opera," Elise said, "maybe you guys can help us with a school project we're working on."

"Aw, man, I'd forgotten about school projects," Flynn said.

Elise told them about the libretto contest and how the winning libretto would be developed into an opera to be performed at Opéra Bastille in the spring.

"We're going to write a modern retelling of *The Phantom of the Opera*," I said.

"I think Andrew Lloyd Webber beat you to it," Flynn said.

"No, I mean an updated version with a modern rock score. We're trying to think of a good premise."

"I don't know much about the story," Owen said. "Give me the basics."

I told him about the Phantom who haunts the Opera House and how his love for aspiring singer Christine Daaé makes him rig a performance that displaces the lead, Carlotta, so Christine can make her triumphant debut. "But what the Phantom doesn't know is that Christine's childhood sweetheart, Raoul, was in the audience, and he's in love with Christine, too."

"Ah, the ubiquitous love triangle," Flynn said.

"Exactly," I said. "But the Phantom isn't a phantom at all, just a man named Erik whose face is horribly disfigured. Since he's never been loved by a woman before, he feels he has to kidnap Christine and keep her trapped against her will until she falls in love with him and his music."

"Hmm," Owen said. "Maybe you could have your opera take place during a singing competition like *American Idol* or *The Voice*."

"Oh yeah," Elise said. "And maybe like on *The Voice,* the judges have their backs turned to the performers, so Erik's scars wouldn't matter."

"But when the judges turn around and see him, they recoil in terror," I said. "And then they cut him during the next round, which enrages him."

"But Christine makes it through," Flynn said. "And now Erik is determined to help her win so she'll fall in love with him. But another contestant falls in love with Christine, and Erik sets out to destroy him."

We started hashing out our ideas on paper, and Owen seemed really enthusiastic. "I don't know anything about opera," he said. "But I'm excited to help you guys with this."

"Yeah, we can pool our skills," I said. "I'll start writing the libretto. You and Flynn can work on the score."

"And what will I do?" Elise asked.

"You, my dear, will sing the part of Christine when we win the competition," I said.

This seemed to appease her for the moment.

But the opera project was the least of Elise's concerns over the next few weeks as a real love triangle emerged between

her, Owen, and Jean-Claude. Elise seemed to enjoy it, en-
couraging both of them when the other wasn't around and
making promises she had no intentions of keeping. All of this
made for some interesting screwball comedy scenarios that
might have been funny if Owen's feelings hadn't been at
stake.

Owen and Flynn were staying at a hostel a few blocks
from our dorm but frequently showed up unannounced. On
one of these occasions, Elise burst into my room with Jean-
Claude and asked me to let him hide out there until I heard
the toilet flush, at which point I was supposed to sneak him
out my door. The first time it happened, I acquiesced, but I
felt so guilty about it later that I finally confronted her in her
room.

"So what's going on with you and Jean-Claude?" I asked.

"We're just having some fun."

"What about Owen? I thought you liked him."

"I do," she said. "But what he doesn't know won't hurt
him. Besides we never said we were exclusive."

"Just because you never said it doesn't mean he can't be
hurt. He's my friend, too."

"Yeah, that's why you kissed Flynn last year even though
you knew Owen was in love with you?" she said, her voice
growing icy.

I felt like I'd been punched in the gut. "Whoa, this doesn't
need to get nasty. I knew that was a mistake and I was so
sorry for it. That's why I'm trying to prevent him from getting hurt again."

"I know, you're right," she said. "I'm sorry. It's just . . . my
parents' divorce is really getting to me. I think I've lost faith
in relationships. It seems easier to have a lot of meaningless
ones than to try to hold on to something real. Does that
make any sense?"

"I guess," I said.

"Can I tell you something?" she said. "I get freaked out when a guy starts getting all mushy and romantic. I think to myself, Can't we just have a good time and not start making big romantic proclamations to each other?"

I laughed, but inside I wondered if Owen had used the "L" word and scared her off. The thought of Owen telling Elise he loved her made me more jealous than I cared to admit.

"It sounds like you're afraid of getting serious," I said. "Because that's when hearts get broken."

Her briefly vulnerable attitude turned steely and remote again. "I'm not afraid of anything," she said. "I like boys, Emma. Cute ones. Do you know how many hot musicians go to Berklee?"

"Berkeley, California?"

"No, Berklee College of Music. It's in Boston."

"Is that where you're going next year?"

"If I get in. I applied early action, so I should know by the end of January. If I don't get in I'm going to kill myself."

"That's a little dramatic."

"No, Emma, you don't understand. I was meant to go there. That school is my soul mate." I couldn't help but laugh. Whatever commitment she lacked in her love life she certainly made up for in her college devotion. "What about you?" she asked. "Have you decided where you're going?"

"I'm leaning toward Amherst or Hampshire, but with Gray stationed in Miami, I applied to the university there. My dad doesn't know about it."

"Look at you, Miss Rebel," she said.

The truth was, I couldn't really see myself in Miami. But I wasn't sure I wanted to stay in Massachusetts, either.

In fact, it surprised me that Elise wanted to go to school in Boston so close to where we'd grown up. Because what I hadn't told her or my dad or Grandma or even Gray was that I'd applied to NYU, Johns Hopkins, and Emory, too. Not only did they all have stellar creative writing programs, they were all at least four hours away from Hull's Cove.

I'm not sure why this appealed to me so much. It was like coming to Paris had somehow made my home seem smaller, and I wasn't sure it would be big enough to hold me when I got back.

CHAPTER 6

With Elise juggling two boyfriends and me trying to hide it from Owen, he and I began working long hours on the libretto for our new *Phantom*. Even though we'd written an outline together, I was having a terrible case of writer's block and couldn't seem to get the songs down on paper.

Sitting at a café one afternoon, Owen asked me what was holding me back.

"I don't know," I said. "I'm afraid I might suck. I've never been comfortable sharing my writing with anyone. You know that. But this time, my words might be sung on a stage in front of a live audience. That terrifies me."

"Well, don't think about that right now," he said. "Just think of the story you want to tell. Imagine an audience of one, and write only to him or her."

It was good advice, because the minute I imagined myself telling the story to Gray, I could suddenly see how to incorporate elements of our relationship into the script.

"So what if I write a duet between Raoul and Christine as they're falling in love with each other, but Erik overhears it and gets really angry?" I said. "He decides he wants to destroy not only Raoul but the entire competition. So he plans to kidnap Christine during the finale and blow up the theater with everyone still inside."

"Oooh, that's good," Owen said. "Get writing."

So I did. Over the next few weeks, I wrote the duet between Raoul and Christine and a song called "The Phantom's Revenge." Now it was up to Flynn and Owen to set them to music. And I knew the perfect thing to inspire them: a trip to the opera for Owen's birthday.

The night was cool and crisp, and dry leaves scudded across the cobbled streets. Elise insisted we eat dinner at one of the swanky riverside cafés, and since she also insisted on paying, we didn't argue. We dined on a selection of bread and cheeses, garlicky escargot, asparagus in mousseline sauce, duck cassoulet, wild-mushroom-and-saffron ravioli, followed by lavender crème brûlée. I snuck a peek at our bill when it arrived and nearly gasped when I saw 150 euros.

On the way to the Opera House after dinner, we passed a guy selling padlocks at the Pont des Arts. Curious why anyone would sell padlocks here, we asked him what he was doing, and he explained that he was selling "love padlocks." A couple was supposed to write their names on the padlock and then lock it on to the bridge. Then they'd throw the key into the river as a symbol of their undying love. The only way to break the bond was to find the key at the bottom of the Seine and unlock the padlock.

"Let's do it," Elise said, grabbing Owen by the arm. I almost choked, as I'd been witness to Elise's double-timing with Jean-Claude on more occasions than I could count. I hardly thought their love was the undying kind.

While she was trying to talk Owen into it, I bought a double-hearted padlock. The guy had Sharpies available so I wrote Gray's name next to my own. The man helped me find a spot along the very crowded bridge and watched as I locked it in place, tossing the key into the Seine and feeling a rush of emotions—love, pride, fear, and dread.

"I suppose this means you and I won't be snogging after the opera?" Flynn said as I walked back to meet them.

"Not a chance," I said.

"I know that kiss we shared last year still haunts you. The memory is starting to fade, and you're beginning to wonder if it was as scorching as you remember."

I shook my head and laughed. Tonight Flynn looked like a handsome street urchin wearing the throwaways from some misbegotten marching band. He'd found this crazy tuxedo at a thrift shop, with toreador pants and a cropped jacket with silver embroidery and epaulettes. The weird thing was, he pulled it off.

Owen and Elise were still fighting over the padlocks, and I didn't want it to ruin the evening. Or Owen's birthday. "Guys, we should get to the theater," I said, my lame version of an intervention. "I want to take some pictures before the opera begins."

They reluctantly agreed, but despite the delicious meal we'd eaten, we all left with a sour taste in our mouths.

The Palais Garnier was even more magnificent than I had imagined. Its façade looked like an ornate Greek temple, topped with that famous green dome and a frieze flanked by two golden angels on either end.

But it was the interior that swept me away, taking me back to turn-of-the-century Paris. We walked past the buxom Greek goddesses holding the weight of this golden world on their heads and floated up the Grand Staircase in a daze, taking in the grandeur of our surroundings—the marble columns and arches, the ivory cherubs, the baroque intricacy of the ceiling, and the warm glow of a dozen candelabras.

Once on the second floor, we watched the parade of beautiful people below us strolling down corridors, kissing in alcoves, perching on gilded landings. I took a number of photos and texted them to Gray, Michelle and Jess, my dad, and Grandma.

The theater itself was immense, round, and sumptuous—like a decadent red velvet layer cake. The domed ceiling was awash with the vibrant colors of a Chagall painting, from which hung the famous chandelier, said to weigh six tons. No wonder Gaston Leroux had woven this into his Phantom story. Even with our modern knowledge of engineering, I still marveled at how it hung there, seemingly suspended in midair.

Finding our seats was an adventure, as we were on the third loge sandwiched tightly between dozens of seated guests. Elise squeezed into her seat first, followed by Owen, then me, then Flynn. Our seats were so close together I could smell Owen's and Flynn's colognes competing.

The opera was *Orphée et Eurydice,* a tragic myth about a man who descends into the depths of hell to retrieve the woman he loves. Of course it doesn't end well. Orpheus sings his emotional plea to the gods, begging them to bring Eurydice back to life. The gods agree given one condition: He must leave the underworld without looking back at Eurydice.

He agrees, and Eurydice is resurrected. But she doubts Orpheus's love and refuses to follow him unless he looks at her. Orpheus finally relents and turns to embrace her, but her body falls limp in his arms. A grief-stricken Orpheus sings his final lament: "What shall I do without Eurydice? Where shall I go without my love?"

At the height of this drama and passion, Flynn flopped onto my shoulder, sound asleep. "Are you for real?" I said, waking him up.

He startled, then laughed at himself. "Sorry. Too much wine."

As the curtains closed, the audience applauded, but there was an undercurrent of discontent. *How could the story end this way?* In general, people didn't like sad endings, even in France, a country that elevated the cruel ironies of life into an art form.

The four of us gathered our jackets and stumbled out of the Opera House onto Rue Scribe, the street made famous by

Gaston Leroux as the source of the hidden entrance to the Phantom's underground lair.

"So what did you think?" Elise asked, pulling out a cigarette.

"Flynn fell asleep," I said, bursting out laughing.

"Are you kidding?" Elise said.

"I told you opera wasn't my thing," Flynn said.

"Then how are you going to help us with our opera?" I said.

"Well, it's going to be a *rock* opera, right?"

Owen had been silent since we'd exited the theater, but now he said with an edge to his voice, "So you smoke now?"

"I only smoke when I'm in Paris," she said. "You know, *when in Rome . . .*"

"But we're not in Rome," Owen said. "If you were in Afghanistan, would you wear a burqa and let your father sell you off in marriage?"

"Of course not. You're being ridiculous."

Flynn shot me a look that said, *Uh oh, here we go.*

Knowing it was best not to get involved, I snuck a glance at my phone and saw that Michelle had texted me back.

So jealous! Miss you. Jess does, too.

My father had texted me as well: *Emma, please call home as soon as you can.*

That seemed a little urgent from him, but it had been five days since I'd last called home. Still, I felt uneasy as we walked back to school. What if something had happened to Grandma? She had been a little loopy these days.

While Flynn and Elise joked around and Owen sulked, I was in my own world of worry and angst.

"You guys want to get a drink?" Flynn asked. "The night is young."

"I need to call my dad," I said. "He just texted, and I'm a little worried. I think I'm going to call it a night."

"Aw, come on," Elise said. "You're no fun. What do you say, Owen?"

"I'll walk Emma back," he said. "You two go out and be French together."

"Owen, don't be like that," she said, sidling up next to him and flashing her most charming smile.

"I don't think Emma should walk home alone. It's late. And I'm not really in the mood to go out anyway."

"Fine." Elise pouted. "Flynn, you still up for a nightcap?"

"Have I ever said no to a drink?"

"Maybe we can call Jean-Claude and find out what he's doing."

Elise had pulled out the big guns and was pretty much dangling the threat of Jean-Claude right in Owen's face.

"All right, well, you kids have fun," I said, trying to keep things light. "I'll see you tomorrow morning?"

"Maybe," Elise said coyly.

Owen gritted his teeth, and I grabbed his arm and walked him away before tensions could flare any higher.

Poor Owen. It seemed he was always unlucky in love. Last year, Michelle had broken his heart when she revealed she was gay. Then I led him on by kissing him, and worse, by kissing Flynn a few months later. And now Elise was screwing him over, too. Why did it seem that nice guys truly did finish last?

We were walking past the Tuileries, all lit up like a fairy's garden. The Ferris wheel cast its giant reflection onto the fountain, and up ahead, the Louvre and Pei's pyramid lit up the sky like a fantastical mirage. The night seemed far too magical for the way we were both feeling.

"You okay?" I finally asked.

"I don't know, Emma. I can't figure Elise out. I mean, I knew the distance might be a problem this summer. But it's almost like she's trying to hurt me."

I took his arm again. "Look, I know it's no excuse, but her

parents are embroiled in this ugly divorce right now. She hardly ever mentions it, but I think she's having a more difficult time with it than she likes to let on."

"I know, but I'm tired of getting my hopes up only to be disappointed." I frowned and put my head on his shoulder as consolation. "And what about you?" he said. "Are you and Gray making it work despite the distance?"

"Yeah," I said. "Of course, I miss him. But I know it's only temporary. It sounds silly, but I think we're soul mates."

Owen scoffed. "You'd think if you were soul mates, the universe might make it a little easier for you to be together."

I tried not to look as hurt as I felt. "You think the idea of soul mates is stupid, don't you?"

"Not stupid. Just . . . optimistic."

"Well, you know me," I said. "Miss Sunshine and Roses."

That finally got a laugh out of him. "It's great talking to you again, Emma. I miss this."

"I know. Me too."

I shivered from the cold, or maybe from the sense of unease I'd had ever since getting my father's text. Owen noticed me bracing against the chill and suggested we take the Métro the rest of the way. I was grateful since I was anxious to talk to my dad. It was just around five thirty at home. Dinnertime. Barbara would be practicing some experimental dish in the kitchen, and Grandma would be sipping her first old-fashioned of the night. My dad might be stealing croutons from the salad bowl, and jazz would be blaring from the kitchen radio.

I was so enamored of my little scenario that I didn't realize we'd reached the Bastille Métro stop. Owen walked me to Saint-Antoine's back gate, which now filled me with dread. I paused with the key in my hand.

"Well, this is where I get off," I said.

"Want me to stay with you until you call your dad?" he said. "In case something's wrong?"

"Nah," I said. "You know me. I worry too much. It's probably nothing."

"As long as you're sure."

"I am. But aren't you forgetting something?" I said. He shrugged. "Last year, you may recall that I made a promise to sing a certain song to a certain someone on his birthday."

"No!" he said. "You remembered?"

"Yep."

"And after the karaoke debacle last year, you're still going to do it?"

"Yep."

"So let me get this straight. Emma Townsend . . . is going to serenade me in an alleyway in Paris. Don't you think I might get the wrong idea?"

"Don't worry. This will be anything but romantic. You ready?"

"Hit me."

I proceeded to sing Owen the most terrible rendition of "Happy Birthday" ever, using my unique Muppet stylings to make Owen laugh.

But then he got serious. "Emma, I know you like to joke around, but you have a much better voice than you give yourself credit for. Have you ever taken a singing lesson?"

I laughed. "Let's leave the singing to you, and I'll do what I'm good at. Writing."

"Or we could do both together," he said. "I've written a few songs in my day. I'd love to collaborate with you more on the opera. We make a great team."

"We do," I said, nodding and feeling about a thousand conflicting feelings, the strongest of which was guilt.

"I'm going to kiss you now," Owen said, and my face flushed to my earlobes. But he did the European air kiss on both cheeks, adding a joke: "You know, *when in Rome . . .*"

"Aw, Owen. You're the sweetest guy ever. And Elise knows this. She's just a little . . ."

"Confused. I know. I've been on this side of things before, and I have to say, it sucks."

This time, it was my turn to kiss Owen. On one cheek and very sincerely. "Happy Birthday, Owen."

"Thanks, Emma."

He waited until I was safely inside, then I ran to the dorm, feeling a slight unease at being on my own so late at night. Ignoring the feeling, I went up to my room, locked the door behind me, and crept onto my bed, pulling out my phone to dial my home number. My dad answered on the first ring.

"Emma, thank God," he said.

"Dad? What's wrong? Is everything okay? Is it Grandma?"

"No, Emma. It's not Grandma." Then, after a long pause, he said something that made my heart stop. "Honey, Gray is missing."

CHAPTER 7

Certain news comes with the complete inability to comprehend its significance. My father did his best to explain, but there was very little information to go on.

A few days ago, a hurricane had developed in the Caribbean and began barreling its way up the East Coast. A large schooner on a pleasure cruise tried to dodge the storm but ended up sailing right through the middle of it. When the ship began taking on water, the passengers were forced to abandon ship. Gray's unit had been sent by helicopter to rescue them, and Gray had been dropped into the ocean, where he managed to save most of the passengers and crew.

"But something went wrong," my dad said. "The winds were gale force, and the swells were too high. After the rescue, the helicopter had to ascend to avoid being taken down by the winds, and when it finally was able to descend, there was no sign of Gray."

"No sign of him? How is that possible?"

"We don't have all the details yet. But the Coast Guard is conducting an extensive search."

My tongue puckered in my mouth, and my skin felt like it was detaching from my body. "When did you find out?" I asked.

"Last night."

"And you didn't call me then?"

"Honey, I was hoping it would all turn out to be a misunderstanding."

"But it's not?" I said, starting to hyperventilate. "A misunderstanding?"

"Oh, sweetheart, it doesn't look like it." I felt the ground shifting beneath me. "Emma, I want you to be with someone right now," he said. "Are you with Elise? Don't stay by yourself."

"I'm not because I'm coming home," I said. "I'm getting the first flight out of here tomorrow morning."

"Sweetheart, that doesn't make any sense. Gray's parents are going to call the minute they know anything. I know it's hard to wait, but just hold out a little longer. Wait till tomorrow at least. We'll know more by then."

"How do you know?" I said.

"Just have faith, honey. I'll call you first thing."

We finally got off the phone, and I sat on the bed feeling like someone had beaten me with a club. Elise wasn't back yet, and I couldn't bring myself to call Owen. I only had enough energy to curl up on my bed. The tears hadn't come yet, and only a numbing sense of shock was keeping panic at bay.

All night, that fog of numbness and disbelief hovered around me, insulating me from the full impact of what had happened. I lay in a near-catatonic state, hoping I'd doze off and wake to find it had all been a bad dream. I must have drifted off eventually because I woke later and saw my cell phone still sitting on the bed, an awful reminder that this wasn't a nightmare. I scrolled through my call history to make sure my dad had really called, that our horrible conversation had actually taken place.

And then I remembered the last time I'd spoken with Gray, our connection had gotten cut off. Had that been some kind of sign, an omen that something terrible was going to happen and I was going to lose him?

Without thinking, I began dialing home.

"Hello," my dad mumbled, and I quickly remembered that it was the middle of the night.

"Sorry for calling so late. Have you heard anything?"

Of course, there had been no new news in the past five hours. I hadn't really expected any, but I had hoped. My dad talked to me for a few minutes to reassure me everything would be all right. It was a comfort to hear his voice, but when we got off the phone, I was alone again and Gray was still missing.

There are very few conditions that won't be at least temporarily improved by a hot shower, so I went into the bathroom and stood under a stream of hot water for ten minutes. But when I got out, I felt even more exhausted than before.

After getting dressed, I opened my laptop and did a search for news on the botched rescue. Dozens of articles popped up. I clicked on one from the *Miami Herald:*

COAST GUARDSMAN MISSING AFTER
HEROIC RESCUE OF "THE LADY ROSE"

The windjammer *The Lady Rose*, a 125-foot historic replica of an 18th-century clipper ship, set sail on a beautiful October day with eight passengers and a crew of six, hoping to enjoy a peaceful sail to the Bahamas. Despite hurricane warnings, Captain Ronald Walton continued with the journey, aiming to skirt the worst of the storm by sailing east, believing his passengers would be safer staying on the boat than attempting to outrace the storm.

"The rule of thumb is, a ship is safer at sea than at port," Walton said. "And the forecast models showed the storm hugging the coastline. But sometimes storms have minds of their own. I made a judgment call. It was the wrong one."

The captain only discovered his error as the ship sailed through the treacherous waters of the Bermuda Triangle about 500 miles off the Florida coastline. The hurricane took an unexpected turn east, and now it seemed as though the schooner was headed right into the eye of the storm. Late Thursday night, the ship began foundering as Walton made the decision to send the distress signal.

In the predawn hours, helicopter pilot Sheldon Boyers boarded a Jayhawk chopper with his co-pilot, flight mechanic, and rescue swimmer. When they arrived on the scene, Walton and his passengers had already been forced to abandon the sinking ship. Some had made it aboard a life raft, and others were at the mercy of the churning waters of the Atlantic.

"It was a nightmare scenario," Boyers said. "Swells were coming up as high as forty feet, and the winds made the chopper feel like a paper toy. Plus, we only had an hour to work before we'd run out of fuel. We had to act fast."

Boyers steadied the helicopter about 50 feet above sea level to prevent the propeller draft from overturning the lifeboat. Then they dropped rescue swimmer Gray Newman into the ocean. Newman rescued four passengers who were in the water before saving four who had sought refuge in the life raft.

One of them, Sandra Adelson, said of Newman's rescue, "He was so calm. He kept asking how we were doing and telling us not to worry, that we were all going to be fine."

After Newman delivered the passengers to safety, Boyers had a choice to make. Another chopper was scheduled to meet them at the scene within the next half hour. Boyers could try to pull out a few crewmembers and risk running out of fuel. Or he could leave the crew in the water with Newman and hope the second plane arrived quickly.

"It was the toughest decision I've ever had to make," Boyers said. "But if we ran out of fuel, we'd all die. The crew was in good hands with Newman, and another rescue swimmer was coming with the next chopper. I thought that gave them the best chance of survival."

After Boyers left, Newman began trying to secure the life raft in order to get the crew out of the increasingly dangerous waters. And then the unthinkable happened.

Captain Walton saw an enormous wall of water bearing down on them. "It was a monster wave, like something out of a movie," he said. "Somehow we missed the brunt of it, but it toppled right over the schooner and the life raft. The ocean caved and swelled, and we clung tightly to each other. I thought we were going to die."

Once the wave had passed, they heard an eerie sound. "It was my boat sinking," Walton said. "It sounded like a dying animal. I couldn't believe how fast it went down."

When the other pilot, Ronald Wexler, arrived at the scene, he couldn't believe what he saw. "It was chaos. The winds were shrieking and visibility was nil. *The Lady Rose* was gone. But men were still in the water, so we dropped our swimmer in and got to work. I had no idea Newman was missing until the captain and crew were safely in the chopper."

The second rescue swimmer, Todd Dolan, searched the area but was unable to find any sign of Newman or the life raft. "My heart sank," he said. "He must have gotten sucked down with the ship."

The Coast Guard continues its search for Newman in the hopes that he may have secured the life raft before the ship went down, but they are losing optimism. So far they've received no signal from his Emergency Position Indicating Radio Beacon.

Lt. Cmdr. Marcus Shilling of the U.S. Coast Guard's Miami base said, "In a storm like this, a life raft can drift more than fifty miles a day. And the currents will take it right into the Sargasso Sea. Without an EPIRB signal, it's going to be like looking for a needle in a haystack. Only in this case, it's a needle in a mass of seaweed."

He compared the sinking of *The Lady Rose* to the windjammer *Fantome,* a tall-masted ship that sank without a trace in 1998 during Hurricane Mitch. There were no survivors.

"This time," Shilling said, "due to the bravery of this rescue swimmer, we lost the ship but not the passengers."

Captain Walton concurred. "If I could give my life for that boy, I would. It was his first mission. He showed incredible bravery."

Despite the odds, flight mechanic Evan Wheeler said he isn't giving up hope for his friend. "I've never seen anyone work so quickly to save people's lives. If anyone could survive this, it's Gray."

I closed my laptop and shut my eyes. Was it really possible he was still alive? Or was this just wishful thinking?

I didn't know what to do or where to go. I couldn't face my friends. Telling them what had happened would be admitting it was real. That Gray was really gone.

But I couldn't stay here, cooped up in my room, either. I needed to get out.

I'd heard that Saint-Antoine had a chapel, but I'd had no reason to seek it out since I'd been in Paris. Right now I needed a haven where I could find some solace. After getting dressed, I made my way over to the main building. It was Sunday morning a little before eight A.M., and not a soul was on the quad.

The chapel was located on the second floor opposite the library. I half expected the door to be locked, but it opened into a tiny space—maybe fifteen by twenty feet at most. A small altar stood at the far end and two rows of four benches each provided enough sitting room for about thirty people.

I walked down the carpeted aisle and knelt down on the padded kneeler in front of the altar. A wooden cross hung on the back wall. I was relieved to see no dying Jesus suspended from it.

"Please, God," I said, feeling the kind of desperation that presses all the air out of your lungs. "Let Gray be all right. Let him be alive. Please, please, please."

I repeated that *please* over and over again, wishing there was something more I could do.

Mademoiselle Veilleux found me in the chapel an hour later and sat down next to me. "Your father just called," she said. "I'm so sorry, Emma." She put an arm around me, and that was it. I started crying—desperate, hiccupping sobs.

When I finally pulled myself together, Mademoiselle Veilleux said, "Don't lose hope, Emma. Here, this might help." She handed me a small card. It had the picture of a saint in brown robes holding the Baby Jesus in one arm and a white lily in the other.

"What's this?" I asked.

"It's a prayer card," she said. "Turn it over."

The other side of the card read: *Saint Antoine est invoqué pour retrouver les objets ou personnes perdus.*

It was only then that I realized Saint Antoine, the school's namesake, was actually St. Anthony.

The patron saint of missing things.

I remembered a verse I must have learned as a child: *Dear Saint Anthony, please come around. Something's lost that must be found.*

I recited it to myself all the way back to my room, where I fell into a mercifully dreamless sleep. And when I woke in the morning, I relived the nightmare all over again by telling my friends what had happened.

Over the next few days, they did everything in their power to comfort me. Owen rubbed my back and made me tea. Elise sat in my room with me after classes, not talking, just making me feel less alone. Flynn just wanted to fix things, asking over and over, "What can I do?"

But there was nothing to be done.

My father called every night to make sure I was okay, and every night I startled at the sound of my ring tone, my heart clenching with fear that this would be the call that would seal Gray's fate forever.

*   *   *

The days idled by, and I went robotically to my classes, then came back to my room, feeling grief descend on me like a lead blanket. Despair turned to disbelief to numbness to anger and then back again to despair. I felt lost. Broken. Grief took me by degrees, as I vacillated between hope and despair, sometimes within the same day.

After two weeks, the Coast Guard gave up their search, listing Gray as "missing in action," which usually meant *dead*. Gray's little sister, Anna, seemed to be the only one who hadn't given up hope. She began texting me numerous times a day.

Mom and Dad are so sad. They think he's dead even though they won't say. But I know he's alive. I just know it.

I wanted to have Anna's faith. I'd gone through the same false belief at her age when I'd lost my mom. Because when someone goes missing like that, there's no body. No closure. You think to yourself, *She can't really be gone.* Or *He's only presumed dead; where's the proof? There's got to be some other explanation. People don't just disappear.*

Only sometimes, they did.

Darlene's spell bag sat on the vanity. I knew with sudden clarity what I needed to do. I took my favorite photo of Gray out of its picture frame and dropped it in my knapsack along with the ingredients for the spell, then ran all the way to the bridge where I'd locked the padlock. I rolled up the photo of Gray, placed it inside the bottle of rose petals, and sealed it with a cork, tying the length of red yarn to its neck.

I pulled out the compass and stood so I was facing north, repeating the words Darlene had written: "Fate links you to me." I turned east and repeated the incantation, then south, then west, finally returning north. Holding the bottle in my hand, I said the final prayer of reunion: "Like the tides that recede and come back to shore, we belong to each other forevermore."

The river had turned ochre from the lowering sun, and the wind off the water had the chill of winter in it. I kissed the bottle once and tossed it in, feeling a tiny stab of hope strike somewhere deep inside me.

CHAPTER 8

Now there were two relics of our undying love in the River Seine—the message in a bottle and the key to the padlock. It wasn't until I got back to the dorm that I considered the unforeseen consequences of the spell. Because if Gray was really dead, then the spell meant I would need to die in order for us to be reunited.

Could I give up my life, like Orpheus had done, to be with the one I loved?

At the opera, that notion had seemed romantic. But now it made my stomach churn. I ran up the five flights of stairs and unlocked the door to my room, feeling a sick chill run through me. I didn't know why at first, but then I saw that the purple drape had been returned to its rightful place in front of the closet, leaving the mirror exposed on the wall. It seemed to stare accusingly at me.

My first instinct was to back away and leave. But as I glanced around, I noticed that the rug was freshly vacuumed and all of my belongings had been tidied up. It was probably only Monsieur Crespeau, come to do his weekly cleaning. There was no way he could have known about my dread of the mirror.

Then again, what difference did the mirror make now that

Gray was gone? I had confronted my deepest fear already. Nothing could scare me now.

Night fell quickly, and tiny squalls whistled along the rooftops. Later that evening, I sat down at the vanity and lit a candle. If something truly resided in that mirror, I wanted to meet it face-to-face right now while I felt fearless.

I stared into the mirror without blinking, watching my reflection flicker in the candlelight. The wind outside seemed to knock against the windowpanes. I imagined tendrils of air creeping through the seams, finding passage into my room.

As I gazed at the mirror, my face began to soften and blur, and after a few minutes, it was as if I was no longer looking at myself but at some other girl. The reflected candlelight began to flicker erratically before it blew out entirely, plunging me into complete darkness.

"Emma?" a voice whispered. Only this time, the voice didn't frighten me. Because I knew whose it was. I had almost expected it.

Just as it had the other night, a small flame appeared in the mirror and began receding into the darkness as if someone was carrying it away. My eyes followed it, mesmerized, until I felt myself falling into that trancelike state I'd experienced last year. This was a critical time for me—that moment between wakefulness and sleep when I could get lost in my dream world and stray into danger.

I wanted to follow the light, but in order to do so safely, I'd have to split myself into two like Darlene had taught me. Here in my room was a little girl, terrified of the wind and mourning the loss of her beloved, but there on the other side was the reflection of a girl who looked like me but was wise and fearless, as if she knew something I didn't.

I felt a psychic tug pulling me forward, so I narrowed my eyes and imagined sending my reflection down that long dark corridor. And suddenly I was that bold girl standing on the other side of the mirror, ready to follow the light wherever it led.

As soon as I passed through, a strange sense of peace overcame me, as if I'd stepped into a warm bath. Suddenly, I didn't care whether I was dreaming or not. I only wanted to cling to that drowsy feeling of well-being. I followed the dot of light until I saw a shadow stretch around a corner and disappear. I kept moving even as the floor seemed to slope downward and the hallways zigged and zagged until I had no idea where I was. Only my feet seemed to know where we were going.

And then I heard the sound of water—not just a lake like the one in the Phantom's lair—but the churning, resonant whoosh of the ocean.

When I turned a final corner, a black door stood at the end of the hallway, emblazoned with carvings of flames. And just on the other side, the sound of waves. The intersection of fire and water.

Feeling like Alice gone down the rabbit hole, I opened the door and stood paralyzed as I took in the sight before me. It was a beach at nighttime with rose-colored dunes and sea grass that smelled of spices and wild roses. Beyond the dunes was an expanse of metallic sand, flickering in some unearthly light, while a stormy sea tossed its waves upon a silver shoreline. It looked like the beach at the corner of my street at home, only enchanted by some mystical force.

I caught a glimpse of something black being jostled out on the waves. A boat? Just as I was about to investigate, something lifted me off my feet and carried me toward the water at frightening speed, like the night itself had abducted me. Moments later, I was lying on the bottom of a skiff, being buffeted by sea spray and the ocean's rough chop. Someone was on the boat with me, and he was rowing us through the maelstrom.

I must have lost consciousness because when I woke, the sea had calmed, and the night sky had changed from a soft pinkish-gray to a deep midnight blue. A pair of arms lifted me out of the boat and carried me to shore, depositing me onto a beach of black sand. There was no light here, no dynamic sound of the sea, just a flat landscape of darkness broken only by a formation of black rocks, slick and shiny as onyx and somber as tombstones. This beach smelled not of brine and sea spice but of volcanic ash and death.

The man stood camouflaged by one of the large stones.

"Where am I?" I asked, my voice sounding strange to my ears.

"You're safe," the man said, and my eyes welled with tears because it was Gray's voice.

"Gray! But how—" I began to say, standing up and advancing toward him.

He retreated behind the rock so I couldn't see him. "Don't come near me," he said.

"Why?"

"I don't want you to see what I've become."

"What do you mean?"

"I'm different," he said. "I can't explain it, but I'm . . . not real anymore. Like a ghost."

I tried to look at him again, but he shied away. "It's okay," I said. "It's just like before, how we met in our dreams. But just because they're dreams doesn't mean they're not real on some deeper level."

"You've always believed in us, haven't you?" he said. "Even when things have been difficult."

"Of course," I said. "Haven't you?"

"I don't know anymore." My face must have fallen because he finally stepped forward, moving out of the shadow of the rocks to approach me.

His hair was long and blonder, grizzled at the ends, and his face was gaunt and scarred, the skin brown and puckered from too much wind and sun. And he was thin, painfully thin. I tried to hug him, but he was all angles and bones. His ribs poked through the material of his shirt, and his arms had no strength to embrace me.

He rested his head on my shoulder, and I could feel his hot breath on my neck. My limbs fell slack, as if I were suddenly under the influence of some narcotic drug.

"It's like I'm wasting away," he said. "Disappearing."

I grabbed his hand and pulled his knuckles to my lips. "Can you feel this?" I said. "You're not disappearing."

As soon as I kissed his hand, he drew away, like he was ashamed he'd let me touch him. "It's not good for you to be here," he said. "You shouldn't waste your time with me."

"I'd give up much more for you," I said. "Gray, I love you."

"I know," he whispered, and I laughed. He managed a sad smile. I knew then that there was hope. "The light is changing," he said, turning to face the sky, which was beginning to lighten. "You have to go or you'll be stuck here like me."

"What do you mean?"

"There are rules here," he said. "Don't ask me how I know, but I don't want this fate for you. You have so much life ahead of you."

"Gray, I don't want a life that doesn't include you," I said, reaching out to grab on to him. He pulled away again.

"You must leave. Or I won't have the strength to let you go. Please don't make this any harder than it is."

"But how will I find you again?"

"The same way you did this time. Listen for my voice, and come to me."

I was torn between ignoring his advice and trying to find a way to get back home. If I had somehow sent my spirit out to Gray as I'd done in the past, it meant my body was still in my room in Paris. All I had to do was send my mirror image back through that black sea and through the doorway, but that meant leaving Gray here on this beach, perhaps never to see him again. It nearly killed me to say good-bye.

"Close your eyes," I said.

"Why?"

"Just close them. I want to try something."

He closed his eyes, and I moved slowly toward him, reaching up on tiptoe to kiss him gently on the lips. He didn't pull away. In fact, his lips grew warmer as we kissed and my touch seemed to breathe some life into him. When I pulled away, there was color in his cheeks.

"Keep that memory until I see you again," I said.

A tiny smile formed on his lips, and before I could change my mind, I turned away from him and ran into the ocean. The water was frigid and made me numb with cold. Trudging out waist-deep felt like wading through molasses. But eventually the water grew deeper and warmer, more buoyant. I had the sensation of waves swelling beneath me, carrying me for miles until they delivered me onto that more familiar shore.

I ran up the beach and toward the black door that hovered like a mirage beyond the dunes and opened it, feeling a rush of hot air, like the backdraft of some immense fire. My body was swept up in the whirl, rushing madly forward until it collided with something both hard and soft. The impact felt precise and right, like a lock clicking into place.

When I opened my eyes, I was sitting in front of the mirror, my reflection staring back at me in wide-eyed surprise as if she, too, had just witnessed a miracle.

CHAPTER 9

My reunion with Gray made me feel alive again, full of adrenaline and excitement and the pleasure of a delicious secret I couldn't share with anyone. But when I sat down at the mirror in the cold light of day, it looked so ordinary. I began wondering if the visions had just been my mind's desperate attempt to deny the obvious. That Gray was dead.

Even Gray's parents had come to this conclusion, but Anna had convinced them to delay the memorial service. Her faith that he was still alive, or perhaps their own desire to avoid such finality, led them to postpone the service until after the holidays.

But I believed he would be found by then. I knew I sounded as naïve as Anna, but I didn't care.

In the days that followed, I was flooded with creative energy. I suddenly had the urge to write songs for Gray, and my hand couldn't move quickly enough to capture all the ideas flowing through my brain. Before I knew it, I had half the pages of my notebook filled. One of the songs captured how I felt sitting at the mirror, longing for a man who might never return.

Come to me again.
I'll let you pull me under.

Let me hear your voice—
A whisper like thunder.

You may be a ghost;
An ethereal infatuation.
But what I want most
Is pure imagination.

I beg you to take me
To your shores of black sand.
If I'm asleep, don't wake me.
Take me by the hand.

I'll be your guardian angel
If you'll be my tragic muse.
Between this world and yours,
I have no will to choose.

Take me in your arms,
Don't let me answer no.
And when I say I love you,
Tell me that you know.

I put the pen down, tears streaming down my face. The emotions that had poured from my heart scared me because they were full of such surrender and passion.

Each night I stared into the mirror, waiting for that voice to echo through the room or for that pinpoint of light to appear, but each night, nothing happened. I began missing classes as the lure of the mirror took hold and I found myself unable to leave its side.

The following Friday, I had cut a morning class and was sitting at the mirror when I heard a knock at the door. At first, I pretended I wasn't in, but then I heard the latch unlocking. I almost screamed when a hulking body appeared in the doorway until I saw it was only Monsieur Crespeau come to do his weekly cleaning.

"God, you scared me!" I said.

"Je suis désolé," he said. "I thought everyone was in class."

"Oh, right," I said. "I'm not feeling well."

"Pardon," he said, turning to leave.

"No, wait. It's okay," I said. "You won't bother me."

He eyed me suspiciously, then took his bucket into the bathroom and closed the door behind him. I sighed and stood up from the vanity, wandering over to my bed. I could hear Crespeau moving efficiently through the bathroom, moving all of Elise's toiletries and then placing them back just so. It felt a little strange sitting and eavesdropping while some old guy cleaned, so I grabbed my copy of *Phantom* and began reading.

Eventually, Crespeau came out of the bathroom. "Would you like me to clean your room now?" he asked.

"No, that's okay," I said. "I'll do it later."

On his way out, he bent down to pick up my red scarf that was on the floor. He wrapped it over a doorknob and said, "This is a good scarf. Cashmere. You keep dropping it on the ground."

The truth dawned on me. "That was you," I said, recalling the man who had followed me down the alley and tied my scarf to the gate.

"Oui," he said.

I sighed in relief. "I'm Emma."

"Monsieur Crespeau," he said.

"I know who you are. Can I ask you something?" I said. "A few weeks ago when you cleaned my room, you took the drape off the mirror and put it back on my closet."

He knitted his brow, trying to remember. "Was that wrong?"

"No, no. I was just . . . well, I was a little scared of the mirror."

"And yet I found you sitting at it this morning."

I laughed. "Well, I'm not scared anymore."

"I've always loved that mirror," he said with a sigh. "I used to imagine it was an antique from the time of the Revolution. Perhaps it was a witness to magnificent and terrible things." His English was excellent, and once he got talking, he was not nearly as creepy as everyone thought.

"Is the mirror really an antique?" I said. "Do you know where it came from?"

"No. I only know it's been here as long as I have."

"And how long is that?" I asked.

"Oh, I guess since I was about your age," he said. "Twenty years or so." I quickly calculated in my head. Crespeau was a lot younger than he looked. "That mirror even survived . . ." he began to say. "Well, it has endured much."

"Was this your room?" I asked, wondering how he knew about the mirror's history.

"No." He paused, like he was considering whether to tell me something or not. "This was Mademoiselle Veilleux's room."

"Oh," I said. So Louis had been telling the truth, at least about Mademoiselle Veilleux attending Saint-Antoine. And if Crespeau knew about the mirror, he must have had reason to enter her room. Very intriguing.

"So what got you over your fear of the mirror?" he asked.

"It's silly, really," I said. "I lost someone important to me. And . . . sometimes I think I can see him in the mirror."

He looked down at the copy of *Phantom* lying on the bed beside me.

"So now you wait for him like Christine waits for the Phantom?" he said. "Or maybe like the Lady of Shalott, observing life through the mirror instead of participating. You know what happens to her, don't you?"

"I know," I said. "As soon as she turns around and looks at the real world, a curse befalls her and she dies."

He considered that, then unveiled a wise and cynical smile. "I do not think it is the curse that kills her," he said. "I think it is all the years spent staring into that mirror and not living. Think how willingly she gets onto the boat that takes her to Camelot and how she sings during its journey. I believe she turns around because she is ready to die."

"That's an interesting way to look at it," I said.

"I understand this woman," he said. "I have known loss, and in my grief I have hidden from the world, too."

"Can I ask what happened?"

He hardened his jaw. "My parents were killed many years ago."

"I'm so sorry," I said. "How did they die?"

"A car crash," he said. "I was in the backseat and survived."

So that explained the hunched back. And the pervasive shroud of melancholy that surrounded him always. Then he blurted out, "It was my fault."

"Oh, no, I'm sure it was—"

"My parents were driving me to the train station because I wanted to make a grand romantic gesture to the girl I loved. I was rushing my father, telling him to drive faster."

"You can't blame yourself," I said. "It was an accident."

"Nevertheless, they are gone and they will never come back." He shook his head like he was dispelling demons from it. "I'll return tomorrow to vacuum," he said suddenly, as if he'd shared too much, then gave me a formal nod.

"Wait," I said, not wanting him to leave. But I didn't know what to say. I decided on the truth. "The person I lost?" I said. "It was my boyfriend. He's dead."

It was the first time I'd uttered those words out loud.

Monsieur Crespeau came over to me and put a large hand on my shoulder. "I am very sorry, Emma." And then he quietly let himself out of the room.

Writing was the only thing that kept me sane over the next few days. Owen and I worked on revising the poems I'd written, and we polished the outline so I could turn it in to Lucas on Monday. We tentatively titled our opera *Voice of an Angel*.

Even though it was a little premature, Owen was excited to begin scoring my poems just in case we advanced to round two. So he, Flynn, and I decided to take a working lunch in Chinatown in Belleville, the once sordid neighborhood where members of the Paris Commune had bathed the streets in their own blood, and much later, a destitute Edith Piaf had sung her ballads to drunken soldiers at the cabarets. In recent years, the area had transformed into a multicultural mecca with ethnic restaurants, shops, and a lively music scene. The atmosphere was busy and colorful and, most important, distracting. The streets overflowed with outdoor market stands, colorful paper lanterns, neon signs, and graffitied walls.

We ate at a tiny hole-in-the-wall that boasted excellent dim sum. Even though the outside of the restaurant was nondescript, once inside, we sat on red silk chairs and ate off white tablecloths, enjoying delicate ginger dumplings, pork-stuffed bao, prawn raviolis—all served with tangy dipping sauces and very hot, strong black tea. I hadn't realized how hungry I was until the waitress came around with a trolley of desserts. We sampled the egg tarts, mango pudding, and an almond sponge cake served with jasmine tea.

After lunch, Owen and I strolled through the shops while Flynn went to the nearby North African neighborhood, where he'd been told he could score some hashish.

"You seem a little better today," Owen said as we navigated the Saturday afternoon crowds.

"I feel a little better," I said. "But maybe that's the dim sum talking. How are *you* doing?"

"You know me, Emma. Another girl breaks my heart. I'm used to it."

"Oh, Owen, I'm sorry," I said.

He exhaled deeply and put on a brave face. "She told me straight up that she wanted to see other people. She said she didn't want to be in the world's most romantic city and be tied down."

"Geez, that's cold," I said.

"Depends how you look at it. At least she didn't string me along." An unwelcome dose of guilt jolted through me. "But I can't imagine what you're going through," he said.

"It's like my mother all over again," I said. "Except this time I'm not eight. I understand that gone means gone."

He put an arm around me, and I nestled into his embrace. "Wanna go into this gift shop for some retail therapy?" he said. "I'll buy you something. Big spender, here."

"Sure," I said, smiling.

The shop was long and narrow with four aisles stocked with all manner of food, trinkets, and kitsch. There were herbal teas and elegantly wrapped candies, exotic incense and rare oils, colorful dragon kites and big-eyed kewpie dolls, silk flowers and lush brocade slippers—a world of visual and olfactory stimulation.

After we'd found our way around the entire store, we were still empty-handed.

"I have to get you something," Owen said. "A souvenir."

I spied a little box of green-and-gold grasshopper charms, studded with fake diamonds. The sign on the box was covered with Chinese symbols.

Owen asked the clerk what the sign said. She translated: "May your good fortune be as plentiful as grasshoppers."

"I like that," Owen said. "A good-luck grasshopper. I'm buying you one. You need some good luck."

"Aw, thanks, Owen," I said. "What should I get you?"

"I don't know," he said, grinning boyishly.

"Wait here. I saw something you might like."

I jogged back to one of the aisles and found what I was looking for, a steel harmonica with some Chinese characters etched onto the surface. I had no idea what they said, and it cost a little more than I'd wanted to spend, but Owen was worth it.

When I got outside, Owen was beaming, dimples and everything.

"Here, let me pin on your charm," he said. "Maybe some of its luck will rub off on me." He fastened the pin to my coat lapel, and I stared down at the smiling green face.

"My own Jiminy Cricket," I said.

"It's a grasshopper, not a cricket," he said, laughing.

"What's the difference?"

"Crickets are brown and ugly; grasshoppers are bright green and cute. Like you."

"I'm bright green?"

"Shut up, smartass," he said. "Now where's mine?" He held out his hands and wriggled his fingers.

"Okay, okay, Mr. Impatience." I pulled the harmonica from the bag and placed it solemnly in his hands, like I was presenting a gift to royalty.

"A harmonica!" he said, taking the instrument and holding it up to his mouth. "I've always wanted one of these."

"Do you know how to play it?"

"A little," he said. He blew into it while swiping from side to side, creating a joyful glissando of sound. "Thanks, Emma. It's perfect."

And then we heard a snide voice from behind. "How come every time I come upon you two, I feel like I've interrupted a scene from a romantic comedy?" It was Flynn, looking very pleased with himself, holding a suspiciously unmarked brown paper bag.

"We were just exchanging souvenirs," I said.

"And you didn't get one for me? I'm hurt. Truly. But I'll forgive everything if you help make one of my dreams come true," he said. "One of my life goals is to smoke pot in front of Jim Morrison's grave at Père Lachaise."

"I think you need to set your sights a little higher," I said.

"Come on," Flynn pleaded. "It's a small wish. Besides, it's on our ugly tourist destination list."

"But it's Saturday," Owen said. "It's going to be so crowded."

"Yeah," Flynn said. "I hear people are dying to get in there."

Owen shook his head at me. "He did not just say that."

The cemetery wasn't a far walk from Belleville, and it was rather crowded, with several tour groups assembled at the entrance. But once we got inside the main gate, the place was so vast and sprawling it didn't feel that congested. We walked down an alleyway of trees that cast eerie shadows onto the pale headstones. Brittle fall leaves huddled along the path, and everything looked a bit ghoulish in the late afternoon light.

As we strolled, we stopped by the graves of some of the more famous people buried there: Oscar Wilde, Edith Piaf, Molière, Victor Hugo. Hugo's tomb boasted an enormous statue, but the other graves were more modest. Surprisingly it was the graves of people I'd never heard of that were the most macabre.

The creepiest had to be the stone crypt with a statue of a dead man lying on his back holding his own head in his hands. Another sarcophagus was festooned with stone roses and skulls and frightening winged creatures. One depicted a dead man trying to break out of his own grave.

Many of the tombs were accompanied by hooded or robed figures lingering graveside. A particularly eerie one showed a woman weeping outside the gates of a mausoleum, where her loved one surely rested. If there was one dominant motif, it seemed to be resistance against death, despite how inevitable we all knew death to be. The natural world seemed to know just what kind of place this was, sending its gnarled roots and thorny tendrils onto the grave sites, the bodies inside becoming one with nature.

The strangest thing was that people were camped out alongside the graves, smoking cigarettes and drinking wine and eating Brie, as if all of this were a perfectly lovely setting for a picnic.

When we finally got to Jim Morrison's grave, it was a simple stone block with a small area beneath it, recessed for flowers or other gifts.

"Here we are," Flynn said.

"Kind of anticlimactic," Owen said. "I was expecting a giant statue with girls fawning all over it."

"There are lots of flowers here," I said. "And apparently, a pair of pink panties."

"No way!" Flynn said, moving to get a closer look. "Musicians have the best job in the world."

"Until they choke on their own vomit," I said. "So how are you going to . . . achieve your lifelong dream with all these people around? Did you see that cop earlier?"

"From what I've heard, the cops don't care so much about pot," Flynn said. "And anyway, I'm going to roll the hashish in papers, so it'll look like a regular cigarette."

He took his bag behind one of the larger mausoleums to roll his joints, and Owen and I sat down on a little stone bench nearby. The wind howled softly through the treetops, almost like Jim Morrison himself were whistling from the other side.

"So I wrote a few more songs for the rock opera," I said, "and I wanted to get your opinion."

I took the handwritten sheets from my bag, ironed out the creases, and passed them to Owen, feeling that stab of vulnerability I always got when I shared my writing with anyone.

Owen began reading, and about halfway through, he began nodding his head and making little humming noises.

"Are those grunts of disapproval?" I said.

"No, I'm getting a melody in my head. These are really good. You got a pen?"

He quickly sketched some bar lines and jotted musical notes along them, his fingers working so fast he looked like a mad scientist. Then he got out the harmonica and played me a few measures.

"What do you think?" he said. "Of course, you've got to imagine it with sweeping guitar chords and a piano building to a crescendo."

In fact, I was already imagining it like that, and the result was haunting and melancholy and absolutely perfect—part Andrew Lloyd Webber, part Rachmaninoff, part The Cure. "How did you do that in five minutes?" I said. "That's exactly what I was hoping for. You're a genius!"

"See? It happened again," Flynn said, sitting down to join us with a grin on his lips. "Only this time, it's not a romantic comedy. More an epic love story."

"Please," Owen said, blushing. I might have been blushing, too. "I'm setting Emma's poems to music. Are you still in?"

"Me?" he said. "In like Flynn." He passed a joint to Owen, who took a puff and nodded approvingly. Then Owen handed Flynn my lyrics, and I watched Flynn's canny blue eyes scan the page.

"Aren't they good?" Owen asked.

"Yeah, Emma, they are. Really good."

"And she wrote them all in, like, two weeks," Owen said. "How did you do that with everything else that's been going on?"

"I was inspired, I guess," I said, feeling myself deflate as I recalled my dream reunion with Gray on the beach and the fact that I hadn't been able to duplicate it since. "Can I tell you guys something?"

"Sure," Owen said, and Flynn nodded.

Reverently, as if Gray might be listening, I told them about my trip through the mirror and what I thought it meant. "What if Gray is still alive and that's why I was able to talk to him in my dream?" I asked.

Owen gave me a pitying look. "Emma," he said, "I know that's a tempting fantasy, but it's just that."

"How do you know?" I said. "It's happened to us before, this connection even when we're far apart. Besides, wouldn't I know in my heart if he were dead? Wouldn't I have gotten some premonition that night at the opera? Instead, all I feel is hope. He's so close, I can feel it."

I was standing now. And kind of yelling.

Owen looked concerned. "Emma, it's great that you're writing lyrics and starting to feel hopeful again. I just don't want you setting yourself up for disappointment."

"Why is everyone so certain he's dead?" I said. "Isn't it possible that I'm right?"

Owen and Flynn fell silent. They didn't know what to say to their heartbroken friend who had clearly lost her marbles. Suddenly, I couldn't wait to get out of that cemetery. All that death and longing—it hit too close to home. I wanted to get back to my room, back to my mirror to see if I was right or, maybe, if I was crazy like everyone thought.

"Okay, this is awkward," I said after a too-long silence. "I'm out of here." I picked up my bag and turned to leave.

Owen stood and grabbed my arm. "Don't go, Emma."

"Yeah," Flynn said, coming over to me and holding out the joint. "Sit down with us and have a smoke. It'll help you relax."

"I don't need to relax and I don't want your stupid joint," I yelled. "You guys escape your way, and I'll escape mine."

And then I fled, running through the maze of paths, surrounded by the ghosts of scores of dead people.

The thing was, I didn't really want to be alone. But I also didn't want to be told I was insane for believing Gray was alive.

Two years ago when I got struck by lightning and fell into a coma, I had slipped into a fantasy world where I was given the chance to communicate with my mother, who had been dead for eight years.

Maybe that was what had happened the other night. Maybe Gray was dead after all, and I had only been communicating with his ghost.

No matter how much it would hurt to know the truth, I had to find out.

CHAPTER 10

As soon as I got back to my room, I shut the curtains, making the space as dark as possible. I lit candles and sat at the mirror as I'd done before, trying to re-create the conditions that had allowed me to travel into that dark world, a world in which Gray still lived and breathed.

I listened intently for my whispered name to echo from the glass and peered into the mirror searching for that flickering candlelight, trying to put myself into that trancelike state again. But the mirror wouldn't let me in.

What is missing? I thought.

And then I remembered. It wasn't just Gray I was searching for in the mirror. It was that other girl—the one who looked like me but had no fear. Last time I'd stared at my reflection until my face had grown distorted, softened, and melded into hers. It was that mirror image that had allowed me to travel into the dreamscape while my body remained here.

I stared into the mirror again, letting my eyes blur slightly until the image in the mirror no longer looked like my own reflection but like a separate being who happened to resemble me. But when I frowned, my mirror image seemed to smile.

And then I felt myself splitting into two, my spirit flinging itself into the mirror and attaching itself to that other body, who was slowly making her way down the corridor. This time, I didn't need Gray to call me. I could go to him on my own.

When I arrived at the black door, it was half open, like it was waiting for me. I knew exactly what to do. I ran through the portal and onto the beach, jetting straight to the water and diving in with a certainty and fearlessness I hadn't felt in a long time.

Once more, the water cooled and condensed, like it was stuck in some limbo state between liquid and solid. Almost ice.

Despite the numbness setting into my arms and legs, I plowed through the water until I made my way to the black sand beach. My body dried instantly although the chill in my bones remained. I walked up to the rock formation to look for Gray and was surprised to see him huddled against one of the stones, building a sand castle.

"Gray," I said.

When he looked up, the manic intensity in his eyes terrified me. "Emma!" he said, struggling to stand. He had to grasp on to one of the stones to steady himself, and that's when I noticed he'd grown even thinner and more skeletal-looking. He began limping toward me.

"What happened to you?" I asked.

He gripped my shoulders to balance himself or to hug me, I'm not sure which, and nearly toppled me with his embrace. I held him up and studied his face, brown as a walnut and nearly as wrinkled, like he was shriveling up, or as he had feared, wasting away.

"I'm so weak, but seeing you makes me stronger," he said. "Don't leave me again."

"You asked me to leave," I said. "And then you never called. I was waiting every night. I didn't know how to get back to you."

"But you found a way," he said. "You came back."

"I promised I would." He leaned away from me, collapsing against the stone and crumpling to the ground. I joined him down on the sand. "What are you doing?" I asked.

"Making a sand castle," he said, his voice sounding a little unhinged. It was the most pathetic sand castle I'd ever seen, mounds of sand piled in a haphazard way around a flimsy foundation. In the flat middle section he had carved our initials. "I know it must look awful," he said. "I can't see very well."

"Why? What's wrong?" I said, reaching out to touch his face.

He clasped my hand to his cheek and held it there, looking so pitiful I didn't know whether to hold him or pull away. "I don't know. It's like the whole world's gone fuzzy," he said. "But I can see you. You're so beautiful, Emma."

His hand was pressing against mine so forcefully that I felt claustrophobic and a little afraid. "You look so tired, Gray."

"I am," he said. "I've been drifting in and out of sleep, and when I woke and called for you, my voice wasn't strong enough. It felt like you were so very far away."

"I wasn't. I've been sitting by the mirror every night."

"But now that you're finally here, you feel more distant than ever."

"What do you mean?" I asked. But I knew what he meant. I felt uneasy looking at him, like he really was dead, and this phantom before me was the last figment of whatever essence remained.

He reached out for me, and I bristled as his clammy hand came around my neck. "What are you doing?" I asked, feeling his fingers tighten around my throat.

"I'm looking for your dog tag," he said. "I want to make sure you're still wearing it."

"Of course I am."

"But there's something else," he said, his voice growing hard as flint. His finger dropped from my neck to the grasshopper pin Owen had bought for me. "What's that?"

"Just a good-luck charm," I said without thinking.

"This has always been my good-luck charm," he said, pulling out the Virgo angel he wore around his neck. "It's all I need because it reminds me of you. But you need something more than me, I think."

"I don't need more than you, Gray," I said.

"Who is it from?" he said.

I couldn't lie to him. "Owen." He jerked away and stood, his jaw clenching in anger. I rose and grabbed his arm. "Gray, don't be like that."

"Like what?" he said, flinching violently away. "Jealous that another man claims your heart when you swore it to me? What did you expect?"

"It's not like that, Gray."

"I know exactly what it's like. Why do you think it was so hard for you to hear my voice? Because you were listening to someone else. Someone who sings your own words back to you."

"How do you know that?" I asked, feeling an unwelcome terror snake through me.

"Emma, you can't hide things from me. We can't hide from each other. You see me in my world, and I see you in yours. You wanted to know what I've become. Well, this is what I am now. Jealous and bitter and half-dead." As he spoke, the ocean began churning behind us, so violently that it flung black spray onto our bodies. "Separation has brought out the worst in me, and only you can make it stop. But you're disgusted by me now."

"No, I'm not!" I said, but my voice faltered.

"Yes, you are. And how can I blame you? Look at me. I'm disgusting. I warned you that I was changing. You just didn't know how much. You didn't know what a monster I'd become."

"You're not a monster," I said. "You're my Gray. And I still love you."

"Do you?" It was the first time he hadn't answered, *I know*. "You write songs about us and sing them with him."

"Gray—"

"You'll be my guardian angel if I'll be your tragic muse," he said, mocking my words. "You lied, Emma. You took our story and gave it to him."

"I only lent him the words so he could set them to music," I said. I felt desperate to appease him. "So that everyone could know how much I love you."

The ocean began hurling itself farther up the beach, the tide coming in all at once so Gray's sand castle was in danger of being obliterated. "You're still lying," he said. "Your love used to be pure and true. Unbroken. But now you've split your heart in two." He reached for the grasshopper pin, plucked it off, and threw it to the ground. I gasped and reached down to retrieve it before the tide could take it out to sea. "I knew it!" he said, smashing his foot down on the sand castle over and over.

"Stop it, Gray. You're scaring me!"

My voice made him stop his frenzied destruction, but he lost his balance and fell to the ground on the ruined sand castle, sobbing piteously. Slowly, the oceans calmed and retreated. The sky lightened like it had the last time, and I knew I would have to leave soon. I knelt down beside him.

"Gray, I'm sorry for what you've been through. I do love you. Why are you pushing me away?"

"I'm pushing you away before you leave on your own," he said. "I don't want to imprison you here. But I can't bear to lose you again."

"You won't lose me, Gray," I said. "Not if you stay strong. But if you start giving in to the anger and the bitterness, I'll be left with no choice but to leave and never come back. If you can be patient with me, I promise I'll return."

"I know," he said, reaching for my hand. I held his firmly

and felt his bony fingers, so fragile and weak. "You won't give up on me?"

"I won't give up on you, Gray. I promise."

"And you'll never take my necklace off?"

"Never."

"And you won't wear Owen's pin?"

"Gray, I—" But I saw the ire flaming in his eyes. "No. I won't wear it."

With palpable relief, he drew me to him and buried his head in my shoulder. Once again, I felt his hot breath on my neck, only this time it felt oppressive and sickly. I couldn't wait to leave. With what little strength he had, he squeezed my shoulders—not so much in a hug as a restraining hold. Considering how weak he'd become, his grip was surprisingly tight.

"Gray, I can't breathe," I said. But he continued to crush me against the stone until I was thrashing about, trying to break free from his clutches.

"Don't struggle so much. You're like a caged bird," he said. And that's exactly how I felt.

In a burst of fear, I threw his arms off me and ran down the beach toward the shore, diving into the icy water and swimming through that ocean of black tar, using every ounce of my strength to keep moving until the sea changed, until my strokes met no resistance, until I was able to stand and walk freely out of the water and onto dry land.

But when I reached the door on the dunes, it was locked. I banged on it as if anyone on the other side might be able to hear me. Had I waited too long? Had I breached some curfew that would keep me trapped here forever?

My double had found her way back before, and the reunion had felt natural and inevitable, like coming home. But maybe Gray was right. Maybe I had split my heart in two, and the part of me that wanted to stay with Gray was trapping me here. I felt torn, scared by what I had seen with Gray but guilty about leaving him. His biggest fear was that I would run away, and that's exactly what I had done.

I tried prying the door open, but it wouldn't budge. It was only then that I saw the keyhole in the door. When I peered into it, I saw the long corridor that led back to my room. All I had to do was unlock it.

I scoured my pockets for something to pick the lock, finding Owen's grasshopper pin. Bending down, I stuck the pin inside, struggling to find the right motion to release the latch. Sweat poured off my forehead from the heat coming behind the door, that intense backdraft that would propel me back to my body if I ever got past the threshold. Above the tumult, I heard a voice faintly calling my name from the other side. I jostled the pin back and forth until I heard a pop, and then the door swung open, and a whoosh of heat carried me through the corridor like a bullet through the barrel of a gun.

The next thing I remember was falling off my chair and opening my eyes to see Elise's face peering down at me.

CHAPTER 11

Apparently, I had been in some kind of trance, and Elise had grabbed hold of my shoulders and shaken me, so forcefully that she'd knocked over the chair I was sitting in. She also seemed to have knocked some sense back into my muddled brain.

"What happened?" she asked.

I tried to explain about my trip into the mirror and the appearance of Gray and how frightened I'd been in his presence. "He wasn't Gray anymore," I said. "And he wouldn't let me leave. I couldn't get away. It was like he wanted to trap me there with him."

"I've never seen anything like it," Elise said. "Your eyes were open, but you couldn't see me or hear me."

"How did you know to come in my room?" I asked.

"I heard some struggling and a kind of strangled cry. But when I knocked, you didn't answer. I could see candlelight flickering under the door, and I got worried so I let myself in."

Thank God she had. What if she hadn't heard me? Would I still be stuck in the mirror? Would my body have fallen into some kind of eternal slumber, waiting for its other half to return?

Elise insisted on staying with me the rest of the night to make sure I was okay. When she finally left, I slept fitfully, replaying my trip through the mirror over and over again in my head. If Gray was really dead, then it was his ghost that wanted to lure me permanently into his world of illusion and death. I couldn't let that happen again.

It was only after this epiphany that I really began to mourn him, to accept that he was truly gone from my life. The grief I felt over that next week was almost unbearable. The worst part was that I wanted to remember Gray as he had been in life, the heroic Coast Guardian and my faithful boyfriend for so many months. But the most potent memories now were of that frightening specter from my dreams.

Despite my best efforts to move on, Gray haunted my steps. And not just figuratively. On my way to and from classes, I felt his presence at my side, felt his eyes on me while I waited in line at the patisserie or picked up my mail at the administration building. I covered up the mirror again, but on some nights, that purple shroud seemed to glow from within, as if Gray's spirit lingered in its depths, just waiting for the moment to break through to the other side.

Thanksgiving came and went, and I felt a wave of homesickness that nearly incapacitated me. I began spending more and more time with Elise. With things so rocky between her and Owen, she had begun helping Jean-Claude write his libretto, a retelling of *Cyrano de Bergerac* set at a punk rock club in Manhattan circa 1973. In his version, Cyrano is a gifted singer-songwriter and club owner with a very large nose. Even though he should be the lead singer of his band, he decides to hire the vocally mediocre but physically stunning Christian to pose as their front man. But when Cyrano writes a song dedicated to the lovely Roxanne and Christian "performs" it, Roxanne falls in love with Christian instead of him.

"If Jean-Claude advances to the second round, I'm going to sing the part of Roxanne," Elise said. "Jean-Claude will play Cyrano, and Georges will play Christian."

It was perfect casting. And all team loyalties aside, I had to say the concept was really strong. I wondered if my Phantom even had a shot.

The following Friday, Luke came into our opera class beaming. I knew what was coming and steeled myself for disappointment.

"I have very exciting news," he said. "This morning I received word that not one but two of our student groups have qualified to advance to the second round of L'Opéra Bastille's libretto contest. Those students will have the opportunity to perform a student-produced version of their operas in L'Opéra Bastille's smaller Studio space for an audience of two hundred guests. Judges from the opera company will choose the best of the two, and that opera will be produced by professional members of the opera company in next year's fall season!"

Gasps and excited murmuring filled the room as we waited to hear the results. "The first winner advancing to round two is . . . Jean-Claude Bourret."

Everyone clapped, and Jean-Claude and Georges hooted and hollered.

"And the second winner to advance," Luke said, "is our American guest, Emma Townsend!"

The class applauded again, and I felt a surge of adrenaline and excitement that made my entire body buzz with energy. Luke eventually calmed the class down. "Congratulations to the winners. There is much work ahead. I'm sure Jean-Claude and Emma will be calling on some of you to help with the next steps of the process: writing the score, casting and directing, costumes, makeup. It is all very exciting!"

Elise shot me an enthusiastic smile, and then my euphoric feeling turned to sudden dread when I realized what this meant: I was going to have to pull together a one-hour opera for a live audience. I knew I couldn't do it alone. And I needed Owen and Flynn, the very friends I'd alienated a few weeks ago.

That afternoon, I walked to Owen's hostel with my completed libretto in hand, marked in red with all of Luke's notes and suggestions. I knocked on the door to his room, but Flynn answered instead.

"Emma!" he said. "Love of my life! Where have you been hiding?" At least Flynn was no longer angry with me.

"I've been taking that class again on how not to be a raving lunatic," I said by way of an apology.

"And how's that going for you?" He flashed me a cocky grin.

"I'll let you know after they release me," I said. "Where's your better half?"

"I assume you're referring to Owen, who at this moment is drowning his sorrows at his favorite Gallic watering hole."

"Name, please?"

"I'll do better than that. I'll take you there."

I can't tell you what a relief it was to chat with Flynn, who despite all outward shows of misogyny and hedonism, was really a big old softie. His hair had come back in, lush and black, and he had grown a scruffy beard for the winter.

Sometimes I wished I could be like Elise, sampling cute men as one might sample *macarons*. But I just wasn't built that way. I longed for a deeper connection. I wanted the real thing.

We arrived at a splendidly debauched-looking bar, appropriately called Café Rabelais. Once we walked inside, it might as well have been midnight for the lack of windows and the tea lights lined up along the bar. I didn't think of Owen as the type to idle away hours at a bar, drinking liquor and listening to Edith Piaf songs, but there he sat, head cradled in his palm as he drunkenly watched the candlelight flicker in the mirror.

"There's our cowboy now," Flynn said, "in need of a feisty wench to get those spurs back in action." He winked at me and goosed my side, and I slapped him accordingly.

"Might the feisty wench have a few minutes alone with the cowboy?" I asked.

"Sure. I see a damsel in distress who needs tending," he said, leaving my side and approaching a woman at the bar.

I took a seat on the stool beside Owen. "Howdy, partner," I said, continuing Flynn's joke even though Owen had no idea what I was talking about.

"Oh, hey," he said, looking surprised to see me.

We sat in silence for a few seconds until the bartender came to take my order. I shook my head and asked for water. Owen needed a sober sidekick more than a drinking buddy.

"So I wanted to give you something," I said.

"Is it my heart on a platter? Oh no, Elise already gave me that."

I laughed a little and put a hand on his shoulder. "I wanted to give you the finished libretto for the Phantom opera. I was hoping you could help me finish the score, seeing as I advanced to the second round."

It took a few seconds for that to sink in. "Really?" he said, his eyes lighting up.

"Really."

"Oh, Emma, that's fantastic!" He got up from his stool, teetering a little drunkenly, and hugged me with such force I thought he'd knock us both over.

"Will you help me?" I asked.

"Of course," he said. "Why wouldn't I?"

"Because I haven't been very nice to you lately," I said. "I wanted to apologize for being a jerk at the cemetery. I'm sorry I yelled at you."

"It's okay," he said.

"No, it's not. I acted like an idiot."

"You were hurting," he said.

"And I still am. I probably will be for a long time, but it wasn't fair for me to take it out on you. You were only trying to help me face the truth. That's what friends do."

"Friends," he repeated. "Always just friends."

I knew exactly what he meant. Owen was the guy you would marry someday, not the guy you made out with passionately at the back of a nightclub. I'm sure his future state of marital bliss didn't make it any easier to accept girls rejecting him now.

"So, I've been thinking," I said, trying to distract him from his wallowing.

"Never a good idea."

"Ha. Seriously, it's so cold in Paris right now, and you've been depressed, and we've got tons of work to get this score ready. What if we went away?"

"You mean, the two of us?"

"No, I meant you, me, and Flynn. A sort of writers' retreat." I couldn't help but catch his look of disappointment. "What if we took the train to . . . I don't know, Provence maybe. Arles! We'll get inspired by van Gogh and write songs on the verge of beauty and madness."

"When?"

"What about next weekend?" I said. "We can take the bullet train, tour the town, have some dinner, split a hotel room, and stay up late writing."

Owen seemed to be wrapping his head around my proposal. "Let's do it," he said, and I beamed. Owen was always up for an adventure. We laid some money on the bar and hopped off our stools to tell Flynn about our travel plans. When we neared the front of the bar, I saw that the woman Flynn had gone to hit on was Mademoiselle Veilleux.

"Emma!" she said. "I see you discovered my favorite café."

"I guess I did," I said, surprised because this sordid little place didn't seem to suit her more elegant persona. I introduced her to Owen, who extended his hand to shake hers. She gripped his hand and pulled him in to kiss her cheek and said, "Enchanté." Owen looked a bit stunned.

"I'm sorry we spoiled your secret hideout," I said. "I'm sure you don't like running into students off-hours."

"Oh, I don't mind," she said. "In fact, your friend here has been excellent company while I wait for my date, who is becoming more unforgivably late by the second."

"Is this the guy . . . ?" I was going to ask if it was the man she had gone out with before, the owner of the Left Bank brasserie.

"Oh no," she said, finishing my thought. "Philippe, *c'est l'enfante terrible*. Terrifically talented, but his ego took up the entire room."

"Ah," I said.

"Flynn has been regaling me with stories about your modern version of *The Phantom of the Opera*. I had no idea you were interested in opera, Emma."

"Well, I wasn't until this year. I'm taking Luke's opera class, and I just found out today that my libretto passed on to round two of Opéra Bastille's competition. We're going to be producing a version of it this spring in their Studio space."

"Emma, why didn't you tell me?" Flynn said.

"I don't know," I said. But I did know. I wanted to tell Owen first.

"Congratulations, Emma," Mademoiselle Veilleux said. "I am envious of you. You will have so much fun planning this production. Did I ever tell you about my opera days?" I shook my head. "I played Carmen, Ophelia, Manon, Mimi." Her face grew flushed from either the wine or the memories.

"Did you ever sing at Palais Garnier?" I asked.

"Oh no, I was not that good," she said. "Believe it or not, we performed on a barge."

"A barge?"

"*Oui*. It was called La Péniche Opéra, and we sailed down the river and performed in various locations on the Seine. We were quite *les bohèmes* ourselves, dressing up each night in garish costumes and performing under neon lights, then drinking till dawn at the cafés or roaming restlessly through the parks. We were a veritable mob. But oh, it was fun."

I couldn't reconcile this image of her as a bohemian opera singer with the sophisticated woman sitting here in a floral scarf and silk dress.

"That sounds so cool," Flynn said.

"It was. Although it began as a way to spite my parents when I didn't get into La Conservatoire. They could not forgive me for that, and so I made them regret ever giving me singing lessons in the first place." She smiled faintly, and then she looked directly at me. "Never pursue something to fulfill the wishes of another. It will only lead to unhappiness." I didn't know how to respond to that, so I just nodded as she got down from her stool and flung her bag over her shoulder. "It seems as though I have been stood up," she said. "Alas, it was not meant to be."

"But the man of your dreams is right here," Flynn said, winking.

She gave him a kiss on both cheeks. "You are adorable and *trés dangereux.*"

He clutched his heart as she left the café. As soon as she was gone, he asked us, "Do you think it would be inappropriate if I asked Claire out on a date?"

"Claire?" I said. "You two are on a first-name basis?"

"I've got mad skills with the ladies," he said, and Owen and I cracked up.

We told him about our idea to go to Arles next weekend, and Flynn was on board with the plan. Shortly afterward, we left the café, tightening our coats against the winter chill. I was listening to Flynn wax poetic about the need to incorporate some eighties post-punk style into our opera when I caught sight of a man walking opposite us, bundled in an overcoat and wearing a Cossack hat. A scarf partially obscured his face, but I spotted the familiar crow's feet by the eyes and the salt-and-pepper scruff on his chin.

It was Monsieur Crespeau, and I was pretty sure he saw me, too. But as he passed us, he pretended I was a stranger.

We continued on our way, Flynn rattling off some musical inspirations he wanted to include in our songs: The Cure, Echo & the Bunnymen, Joy Division.

"I think that style would go well with your lyrics," Flynn said. "What do you think, Emma?"

"Huh?" I was still mulling over Crespeau's snub.

"Post-punk? Eighties sound?"

"Sure," I said. "Sounds great."

"These are your lyrics, Emma," Owen said. "You should care what we do with them."

"I know. And I do care. But I don't know music like you guys do."

"Why do you do that?" Owen asked.

"Do what?"

"Sell yourself short like that. I saw you crying during the opera. You appreciated it more than any of us. Just because you haven't studied music formally doesn't mean you don't know what's good. You know what moves you, right? That's all we're asking for. We want your opinion. We want to know what you want." And then Owen said the one thing I'd been dreading, the thing that terrified me most. "In fact, now that Elise has gone over to the dark side, you're going to be our new Christine."

CHAPTER 12

I don't know where my fear of singing came from. I wasn't tone-deaf. I could sing on key, at least in the shower. But ever since I could remember, I froze up at the thought of singing in public, even at friends' birthday parties.

My mom used to have a beautiful voice and sang often. Genetically speaking, I was 50 percent predisposed to carry a tune. But there was something about singing that laid all my insecurities bare. As soon as I heard my own voice, it triggered all my inhibitions and I became a stuttering, incoherent mess.

So despite the beauty of the scenery out the train window as we made our way to Arles that next weekend, I was in turmoil about just how badly I was going to screw this all up. By the time we arrived at the station, the sun had burned off the clouds, and the sky was a color I could only describe as Provençal blue. Walking into Arles was like traveling back in time. The city was ancient, compact, and crowded with buildings, like someone had shrunk Rome down to 10 percent of its size. The buildings were a sooty white color with red tile roofs, and the narrow terraced streets would have been a nightmare for anyone in heels. Luckily, I was wearing my Converses.

Since we were only staying the night, we splurged on a

hotel close to the sights instead of staying at a hostel. Our hotel room looked like it had been decorated by Dr. Seuss—turquoise walls and bright yellow curtains, whimsical furniture with curvy lines, polka-dotted wallpaper in the bathroom, and giant round headboards with a red-and-white swirl design.

We stashed our luggage in the closet, washed up, then grabbed a map of town from the hotel lobby before heading out to the famous Amphitheatre, which looked like a miniature Coliseum. Owen and Flynn were like little boys running through the arched tiers and hiding behind columns while I took photos of the arena and the gorgeous views of the Rhone. Supposedly our hotel had a rooftop deck with stunning views, and I was looking forward to scoping it out later.

When we went down to the performance area, Flynn, dressed all in black, pretended to be a matador to my reluctant bull. "Come on, Emma, charge me!" he kept saying.

Owen laughed. "I hope that's not code."

"Sexual innuendo from Flynn?" I said. "Surely not."

After the Amphitheatre, we walked to the town square, which had an obelisk in the center surrounded by some civic-looking buildings and a church. We ducked into the church of St. Trophime and strolled through its Cloisters, which were practically empty, making the experience feel solemn and meditative. I took some great pictures of the sun coming through the columned arches and the weathered statues of saints who seemed to be surveying the grounds.

"Where's the van Gogh café?" I asked.

"You want to go to that tourist trap?" Flynn said.

"I know you're a complete iconoclast, but one of the main reasons I wanted to come here is because I love van Gogh. I want to see the yellow café."

"Oh, all right," Flynn groaned.

We checked our map and made our way to the café, pass-

ing by a tiny restaurant tucked in an alley. A chef stood outside the entrance cooking a pan of paella that must have been
three feet wide.

"Please tell me we can come back and eat that for lunch,"
Flynn said.

"Fine by me," I said.

We finally came to the famous yellow café, which except
for the daytime sky beyond, looked just like van Gogh's *Café
Terrace at Night.*

"Let's go in," I said. "Just for a drink."

Flynn grudgingly agreed, but the inside was not nearly as
impressive. There were a few phony van Goghs on the walls,
and the service was a bit surly.

"See?" Flynn said. "Tourist trap."

Eventually, the waiter managed to brings us our *citron
pressés,* drinks made from the juice of an entire lemon with
just a dash of sugar. They were just a little less sour than our
server.

By the time we got our check, we were starving. We found
our way back to the little restaurant we'd passed before. The
paella man was no longer outside, but a host promptly met
us at the entrance and took us into a dining area that made us
feel like we were guests in someone's home. The kitchen beyond was open, so the homey scents of roast meats and
seafood wafted our way.

Flynn and I both ordered the paella, and Owen got a
chicken dish infused with thyme and rosemary. We shared a
carafe of Grenache that tasted faintly of blackberries and
lavender. After dessert, we began discussing the opera over
the last of our wine.

"So we should assign roles so we can try out the different
parts to see if the songs are working," Owen said.

Flynn said, "I don't know what you guys think, but I'd be
perfect as the Phantom."

"Agreed," Owen and I said at the same time.

"Should I be offended that it was so easy to come to a consensus on that one?" Flynn asked.

"No," Owen said. "I just think I'd make a better Raoul."

"Which leaves me as Christine," I said. "Are you sure you and Elise can't make up so she can play the part?"

"Definitely not," Owen said. "Besides, we have an idea to get you over your fear."

We paid the bill, and the two of them led me through the narrow streets of Arles until we came to the ruins of an ancient Roman theater. The semicircular seating area was largely intact, but not much was left of the stage except for two columns that stood in eerie silence now, watching over nothing. We were the only spectators.

I stood there, marveling at this architectural wonder. "This is so freaking cool."

"Yeah, especially since it's been here since 14 B.C.," Owen said, reading from the map caption. "It used to seat ten thousand people."

"Wow," I said, trying to imagine the seats filled to capacity.

"They still use it for concerts," Owen said. "Sigur Rós played here just a few months ago."

"Can you imagine performing here?" I said.

"Actually, we can," Flynn said. "And that's exactly what we're going to do."

"What do you mean?" I said, feeling my stomach drop.

Owen grinned. "We're going to start your singing lessons right here, so the ghosts of ancient Romans can spur you on."

"Guys, I don't think this is such a great idea," I said. "It's getting late, and—"

"Emma, it's three o'clock," Flynn said. "We have a couple hours before we lose daylight, but we only have a few months to get you in singing shape, so we've got no time to spare."

"Can I just say that I hate you?" I said.

"Look," Flynn said. "Think of this as singing boot camp."

"Yeah," said Owen. "The acoustics here are great, and despite Flynn's snide comment, I know you can sing after—"

"The event that shall not be named," I said.

"I know you don't believe me, but you've got potential."

"Fine," I said. "But you're both a bunch of bullies."

"You know you love us," Flynn said as they dragged me to the center of the performance area.

"Most of your issues come from your fear of being judged," Owen said. "And we promise not to judge. What an audience really wants is to be told a great story. So think of singing as one way to tell a story, and your voice is the instrument to tell that story. Emotions and authenticity are far more important than perfection. Remember, Christine wasn't a perfect singer, either. She needed lessons, too."

"Yeah, just consider us your angels of music," Flynn said dramatically. I couldn't help but crack a smile.

"Eventually, we're going to work on vocal techniques, breathing exercises, and all that," Owen said, "but for right now, all we want is to get you over the fear of your own voice. So we're going to play a little singing game."

We sat in a circle at the center of the "stage" and passed around Owen's iPod, which was set to shuffle. When a random song came up, the person holding the iPod would hum the tune until one of the others guessed it. You got bonus points if somebody guessed correctly in fewer than ten seconds.

Humming instead of singing made the game a lot less intimidating, and after a few rounds I wasn't feeling as nervous anymore. I was just laughing and having a good time.

"Okay, now we're going to step it up a little," Owen said. "This time, you have to sing the words. If you don't know them, you can look up the lyrics on your phone. But you have to try and imitate the singer's style. We'll start with classic rock."

I groaned, but the reality was that it was much easier to sing if I was pretending to be someone else. I could let loose with a Robert Plant scream or the raspy growl of Janis Joplin. We quickly graduated to more recent songs—punk, pop, and hip-hop. And I found that, despite everything, I was having fun.

Later that night, exhausted from our vocal exertions, we found a little pizzeria and shared a few slices as we strolled by the river, which looked exactly like van Gogh's *Starry Night Over the Rhone* except the stars weren't quite as sparkly as they were in van Gogh's vision.

When we got back to the hotel, there was a little verbal scuffling over the sleeping arrangements. The room had two double beds, so the consensus was that I would share my bed with one of the guys.

"Emma and I have already slept together," Flynn said, "and I thought it went quite well, didn't you?"

"Fine by me," Owen said, but his voice was a little gruff.

"Yeah," Flynn said to Owen, "in case you get back together with the Ice Queen, I don't want you to do anything that might blemish your reputation as the perfect gentleman. I, on the other hand, have no reputation to speak of."

"And what about my reputation?" I said, feeling mildly insulted that I wasn't being consulted on the matter.

"Spotless as always," Flynn said. "This will be a charitable gesture on your part, allowing a bum like me to crash in your bed. Some would say you're downright saintly."

He stripped down to his boxers and T-shirt, and Owen went into the bathroom. I waited until he came out, then went in to brush my teeth and change into my pajamas. Flynn was already cozied up in the center of the bed, and I had to forcibly move him over to make room.

"Good night, Owen," I said, reaching over to turn off the bedside lamp.

"Good night," he said softly.

I scooted over to the far side of the bed and tried to sleep. It should have been easy. We had traipsed all over Arles that day. I was exhausted. But I couldn't stop thinking about Gray. Getting away from Paris with Owen and Flynn had been a great distraction, but tomorrow the illusion would end, and I'd be back at school facing my demons. Well, one demon in particular.

As I lay there painfully awake, I remembered that I'd never gone up to explore the rooftop balcony. I wondered if it would be accessible at night. I tiptoed out of bed and threw on my jacket over my pajamas, creeping out of the room and taking the elevator to the top floor. A door led outside to the roof, and I strolled to the balcony railing and peered out over the river, calm and smooth as glass.

After a few minutes, I heard the door open behind me and wheeled around.

"Owen, you scared me!"

"Sorry. Couldn't sleep, either."

He came to join me by the edge, and our arms were nearly touching as we leaned against the railing.

"What kept you up?" he said.

"I can't stop thinking about Gray," I said. "Today was probably the first time I stopped thinking about him every second. And I have you to thank for it. I had so much fun today. I felt almost . . ."

"Happy?" he said.

"Yeah."

He grinned at me. "I want you to be happy, Emma," he said. "And believe me, you will be happy again."

I shook my head. "Sometimes I wonder." The night's silence grew around us as we stared off into the distance. "Why couldn't you sleep?" I asked.

"Honestly?"

"Yeah."

"Because you were in the bed right beside mine."

"Ah," I said, feeling a little confused and a little self-conscious in my pajamas. "Were you mad that Flynn got to sleep with me?" I said, going for a joke.

"I was mad that I wanted to," he said. He ventured a shy glance at me. "Emma, as much as I try, my feelings for you don't go away. I know it's not fair to put this on you with everything else you're going through. But it's so hard to just be your friend when I want to be so much more."

I was flustered by this late-night confession. "What about Elise?" I said. "You guys just broke up."

"Emma, I never loved Elise. We had fun for a while, and I know everybody thinks I was devastated by the breakup, but the truth is, I'm going crazy because I can't seem to find a way to get over you."

I could feel my throat growing tight and my underarms beginning to sweat. Just a few hours ago, we'd been humming and singing songs like total dorks, and now he was here on the roof with me making romantic proclamations.

Only unlike Elise, I didn't mind romantic proclamations. I wasn't afraid of commitment and true love. The problem was, I was still in love with Gray.

I thought back to what Crespeau had said about me being like the Lady of Shalott, watching shadows through a mirror instead of living my life. For once, I wanted something real, *someone* real who was standing right in front of me, not an illusion in a mirror.

Owen turned to me and let his finger drop to the grasshopper pin on my coat. "Has it brought you any luck?" he asked softly.

I bit my lip, feeling nervous and shy. My head felt swimmy. "Not yet."

He smiled a little. "Sometimes you've got to make your own luck." Then he leaned down toward me, his lips barely grazing mine. The brush of his lips made my cheeks flush. I felt so lightheaded my eyelids seemed to flutter.

He kept his face close but didn't kiss me. He wanted me to be the one to initiate. He wanted me to want more.

And I did. At that moment, I wanted a lot more. But I felt this dark presence looming over us, watching us. And I couldn't bring myself to kiss him. It wasn't the right time. I had to put things to rest with Gray before I could move on with somebody new. I owed that to his memory.

As difficult as it was not to press my body into Owen's and kiss him hard on the mouth, I drew away. "Owen—"

"Stop," he said. "I know what you're going to say. You don't think of me that way. You just want to be—"

"No!" I said. "Owen, believe me, I want to. So much. It's just . . . complicated. With Gray."

"I'm sorry."

"You've got nothing to apologize for," I said. "I want to be fair to you. And right now, I'm afraid there would still be . . . Gray's ghost between us."

"I know," he said. "I can feel that you're not entirely here with me. Part of you is somewhere else."

I frowned because I knew he was right. "Owen, I want you to know that as much as I value your friendship, I could see you and me together someday. As . . . something more."

"Really?"

I nodded, smiling. "Really."

We resisted the urge to continue where we'd left off and headed back to the room. Owen pouted as I crawled into bed beside Flynn. I rolled my eyes, reassuring him that nothing would ever happen between me and Flynn again. He flashed me a boyish grin that could very well have kept me smiling for days.

If we hadn't had to go back to Paris the next morning.

Because when I got back to my room at school and sat down to unpack my things, I realized that at some point in all that traipsing around Arles, I had lost Gray's scorpion necklace.

CHAPTER 13

The first thought that ran through my head was, *Gray is going to kill me*. I knew that was ludicrous because Gray was dead. But I feared him anyway.

Over the next few days, I spent more and more time out of my room, finding any excuse to study at the library or in a café or sometimes at Owen and Flynn's hostel. Midterm exams were coming, and even though my transcripts had already been sent to colleges, I wanted to do well here to prove to my father that this year abroad hadn't been a waste of time and money.

But as I walked to and from classes, I couldn't shake the feeling that someone was following me, that Gray's spirit had found its way out of the mirror and was haunting my steps. It felt like no matter how much I tried to move on with my life, some force of love or obsession between us would never let me go.

Paris in December was the perfect antidote to my fears. Trees along the Champs-Élysées were bedecked with lights, and the city council had set up an ice-skating rink on the square in front of the Hôtel de Ville. No matter where you walked, you'd stumble upon holiday markets selling decorations and gifts and the irresistible winter treat, *chocolat chaud*.

With the Christmas break in sight, everybody turned their attention to the Bal Masqué, the annual masquerade ball held at Saint-Antoine each December. This year's theme was Fin de Siècle, celebrating the decadent lifestyle in Paris during the turn of the nineteenth century. In between classes, students gossiped about whom to ask and what to wear.

Jean-Claude told Elise about a fantastic flea market where you could buy old costumes from opera and theater companies. We decided to try our luck there a few weeks before the ball, taking the Métro to a colorful but poor district on the outskirts of Paris, a neighborhood where the old rag-and-bone men used to hawk their scavenged wares.

The flea market was enormous and teeming with people. We didn't know where to begin, so we wandered past the various stalls, taking in the sights of antique furniture, vintage clothing, costume jewelry, rare collectables, along with a fair amount of garden-variety junk. If you were looking for something eccentric or strange, chances were you could find it here.

Interspersed among the vendors were people selling fragrant but greasy-smelling street food, and the occasional opportunist, hoping to con a tourist into parting with his money in exchange for having his portrait sketched or his fortune told.

"If you see something you like," Elise said, "don't look too excited. They'll peg you for an American and take you for everything you've got. Haggle. They always come down if you bargain with them."

We finally found the vendor that Jean-Claude had told us about. Elise scooped up a few dresses in a matter of minutes, while I stood overwhelmed at the colors and over-the-top drama of the costumes. I was particularly drawn to a red velvet dress with a lace crinoline and gold embellishments, imagining it paired with a gold domino mask.

Of course, there were no dressing rooms. I held the gown up to my body and tried to imagine whether it would fit. A plump woman with a ruddy face approached me and said, "Ça vous plâit?"

Okay, Emma, lie. Don't look too excited. "I love it!" I heard myself say. So much for playing hard to get.

"Elle est très belle sur vous," she said.

She was using flattery now, but I wouldn't be seduced. "Combien?" I asked, placing it back on the rack like I was losing interest.

But she picked it back up and held it against me. "Pour vous? Cent euros."

One hundred Euros. I quickly calculated it to about a hundred and thirty dollars. For a used opera dress that I would wear once. "Non," I said. "Trop pour moi. Je suis un étudiant." I was trying the sympathy card, playing the destitute student.

She frowned, considering. "D'accord. Quatre-vingts."

Should I keep haggling? I wondered. "Oui," I finally said.

"Bon. Elle sera beau regard sur vous!"

She took the dress and walked it to her cash register. Elise was standing there waiting, holding a long black dress. After I paid for mine, Elise and the woman negotiated like pros until Elise smiled and handed over fifty euros.

As we walked back into the market, I marveled at Elise's tactical skills. "How did you get her down from a hundred to fifty?" I said.

"Confidence," she said. "She knew I wasn't going to back down, and she wanted to make the sale. The buyer has the upper hand. I can always take my business elsewhere. It's the same thing with guys, Emma. When you look like we do, you can take your pick. Never settle for the first offer. Wait for the one you want." She gave me a sly look.

"And have you figured out who you want?" I asked.

"I'm still weighing my options," she said.

The Métro dropped us off back in town, and we walked the few blocks to Saint-Antoine.

"Can I see your dress?" I asked Elise once we got inside the warmth of our rooms.

"Of course," she said, pulling it out of the shopping bag and draping it over her body. It was narrow, black, and beaded, with a plunging back. It looked like something out of an Aubrey Beardsley painting.

"That is gorgeous," I said. "It doesn't even look like a costume. You could wear that anywhere."

"I know," she said. "Let's see yours." I drew mine out of the bag and modeled it over my clothes. "It's very . . . sweet," she said.

"You say that like it's a bad thing."

"No, it's not bad at all. It's very you."

"Somehow that still sounds like an insult."

"Emma," she said, pulling my arm and drawing me aside like she was about to unveil one of the mysteries of the universe. "I know you were probably saving yourself for Gray. And I totally get that. It's incredibly romantic. I just want to remind you that you're human. And you'll never be this young and hot again. There are some really cute guys at this school. Georges is freakin' adorable! He always asks why you don't come out with us more."

"He does?"

"All I'm saying is you should wear something sexy, and try to get lucky."

"I like this dress!" I said.

"I know. And it's not a bad dress. It just looks like something I would have worn when I was . . . five."

"Great."

"Never fear," she said. "All it needs is the right pair of shoes and jewelry." She shuffled me into her room and stood me in front of her dresser. "You need to accessorize," she said. "Or as Tim Gunn would say, 'Use the accessory wall very thoughtfully.' Hey, maybe I could cut a slit up the side of that thing."

"You are not coming near this dress with scissors!"

"Fair enough. Then we'll need higher heels. And maybe fishnet stockings."

More crucial to my enjoyment than any accessories I might wear was who I was going to go with. Elise hadn't actually ruled out Owen as her date, but after all her carrying on with Jean-Claude, I didn't think Owen would consent to that. So the question remained: How did I feel about Owen? While I had always relegated him to the dreaded friend zone, had that only been because of Gray? And was I going to keep closing myself off to the possibility of new love out of guilt and grief?

Owen had made it pretty clear in Arles that he didn't want to get hurt again. Asking him to the dance seemed weighted with expectation. In the end, I took the coward's route. I asked Owen and Flynn to come as my guests. "We can go as friends," I said, echoing the same words Owen had said during our sophomore year when he'd asked both Michelle and me to the Snow Ball. That dance hadn't ended well for any of us. I tried to ignore the sinking feeling I had that this dance, too, would end in disaster.

I couldn't wait for my parents and Grandma to come visit. My father had just e-mailed me, asking what I wanted for Christmas. Christmas had never been the same without my mother. I had such vivid memories of decorating the tree with her and singing carols in the neighborhood and venturing to the beach for the first snowfall. She used to take our whole family to visit the beautiful crèche at the local chapel, and even though we only went to church twice a year, my mom sang the hymns louder than anyone else there. Since she had died, Christmas was only a painful reminder of what could have been had my mother lived.

Suddenly, with every fiber of my being, I was glad I wasn't going home for Christmas. When I'd first arrived in Paris, I'd felt homesick and scared and lonely. But something had changed over the past few weeks. Maybe it was my blossoming friendship with Elise or working on the opera with Owen and Flynn or the fact that I'd finally stopped having nightmares.

But mostly, I think I was relieved not to have to face Gray's family. Ever since my mom died, we'd taken efforts to make sure our two families remained close, celebrating each other's milestones and getting together for every holiday. If I went home, I couldn't avoid them, but seeing them without Gray might undo me.

The term came to an anticlimactic close one Thursday afternoon after the last midterm exam had been given. As far as I could tell, I'd aced most of them, with the slight possible exception of AP European History. It was rumored that the exam was harder than the actual AP test.

By the weekend, the entire student body was ready to blow off some serious steam. On the evening of the dance, Elise and I had the bathroom doors open so we could come freely into each other's rooms for hair and makeup advice. Elise wanted to stand in front of the full-length mirror in my room, and I wanted to avoid the damn thing altogether. I didn't want to think about Gray tonight.

"So what do you think?" I asked Elise, showing her a flash of the fishnet stockings she'd lent me.

"They look fantastic," she said. "Very French bordello."

"That's exactly the look I was going for," I said, and she laughed. "You look amazing, Elise. Very Morticia Addams."

"Morticia Addams wishes she had this dress," Elise said, twirling around in front of the mirror, watching the black gossamer fabric swirl around her. "I'd better get back to my room. Jean-Claude's going to be here soon, and I don't want him hanging around my door when Owen arrives."

"No, we wouldn't want that," I said.

Elise didn't catch my sarcasm. She went back to her room, and I tried to finish my hair. I was attempting to use a curling iron to give myself big, romantic curls, but mostly I succeeded in burning the nape of my neck. Around eight o'clock, someone knocked on my door.

I opened it to see two of my favorite people, both looking incredibly handsome in their own ways. Owen had loosely interpreted the fin de siècle theme, sporting an outfit inspired by Sherlock Holmes—a wool serge suit with a vest and double-breasted jacket and a tweed flat cap. All that was missing were the pipe and magnifying glass. Flynn went more melodramatic, wearing a fuchsia-lined trench coat over a purple-and-black leopard-print suit, sort of Bram Stoker meets David Bowie.

"You look delectable," he said, taking my hand and kissing my knuckles, adding a little tongue just to be Flynn.

"Thank you very much. Now I have to wash my hands," I said in mock anger.

"What you should say is, *Thank you very much. I'll never wash this hand again,*" he teased.

I smirked and pulled my hand away, giving them each their tickets. Then Flynn popped into the bathroom, leaving Owen and me to stand together awkwardly, no doubt wondering how this evening would play out.

"So . . ." I said.

"So . . . you look so pretty, Emma."

"Thanks," I said shyly. "Elise thought the dress was too sweet."

"I happen to like sweet," he said.

I was blushing as Flynn came out of the bathroom, rolling his eyes. "Oh, would you two get it over with?"

"Get what over with?" Owen asked.

Flynn sighed, exasperated. "We all know why I'm here tonight," he said. "I'm your freakin' chaperone so you two have another excuse to drag out this . . . whatever it is you have. But you don't need a chaperone. You need a coach, someone to shove you out on the field in the middle of a big play and see what you're made of. I'm out of here."

"What are you talking about?" I said.

"I'm off to find *Claire*—I love saying her name—and to leave you two to figure it out. I'll see you kids later. Go, Team Owen!"

And with that, he exited the room with a flourish of his coat, leaving the two of us alone. Again. To my surprise, Owen didn't look awkward anymore. In fact, he held his arm out to me and said, "Shall we?"

I linked my arm in his, and we walked toward the door. But as we did, I got the strangest sensation of someone at my back. I glanced behind me once before leaving the room and could have sworn I heard someone faintly calling my name.

The ball was being held in the main lobby of the administrative building, which had been transformed to look like a Gothic ballroom. The cavernous space was dimly lit by old gas floor lanterns. Tables had been set with white tablecloths, red napkins, and dramatic candelabras; and the walls had been swathed with purple velvet fabric that reminded me of the mirror in my room. A string quartet played elegant classical music, and most of the guests were strolling here and there, checking out one another's costumes rather than dancing. Across the room by the stairwell was an enormous Christmas tree trimmed with white lace, gold ornaments, and a cranberry-and-silk garland, topped with a magnificent gold angel.

The best part was the long table by the entrance, covered in masks of every shape and size. Owen and I sorted through them, each of us searching for the perfect mask that would define our personas for the evening.

After scavenging for a few minutes, Owen settled on a simple black mask that had a Zorro vibe. I found one that looked like it had been fashioned from tiny gold wires that made delicate scrolling patterns around my eyes and forehead. We donned our masks and took a stroll throughout the ballroom, looking for people we knew.

As expected, Flynn was against the wall chatting up Mademoiselle Veilleux, wearing a black mask with silver rivets along the edges. Elise and Jean-Claude were doing a rather formal waltz to the classical music. Jean-Claude had opted for a clichéd white half-mask like the Phantom's, and Elise's mask was adorned with appliquéd roses. In their black streamlined costumes, they looked statuesque and stunning.

"Are you okay?" I asked, watching Owen's face as he took in the sight of them.

"Yeah," Owen said, shrugging.

"Just for the record, Jean-Claude doesn't hold a candle to you. Can I tell you what I thought the first time I saw him?"

"What?"

"That he'd forgotten to take the coat hanger out of his jacket."

Owen laughed. "I always knew something was wrong with him. His posture's too good."

"Yeah. Never trust a guy with impeccable posture," I said. "He's hiding something."

Owen smiled and grabbed my hand, leading us to the refreshments table, where we sampled some punch—sparkling wine mixed with cranberry juice—and tried each and every one of the hors d'oeuvres: roasted apricots with Brie, mushroom-and-Camembert tartlets, bacon-wrapped figs in a port wine reduction sauce.

By the time we finished eating, the music had shifted from staid classical pieces to more moody, romantic sonatas. I looked over at the string quartet and saw that someone had joined them on the baby grand piano. The dance floor filled up as the swoony music permeated the room. Most couples swayed in conservative little box steps, but a few of the more skilled dancers made dramatic arcs across the tiled floor.

I turned to Owen, feeling emboldened by the music, the atmosphere, the sparkling wine. "Would you like to dance?"

Owen gave a rueful smile. "Emma, haven't we danced this dance one too many times?"

I knew what he was saying. "I think tonight's different," I said. "Something new is in the air."

He wet his lips a little, looking boyish and nervous. "I'd be honored."

On our first dance we were shy, holding each other a little woodenly as we tried our best to do the foxtrot. We stepped on each other's toes, laughing at ourselves as Flynn and Mademoiselle Veilleux sailed by.

"I think she's leading him," Owen said.

"Wouldn't surprise me in the least."

"They actually look pretty cute together."

"As opposed to us, the blind leading the blind." I immediately felt sorry I'd said it because Owen looked a little hurt.

I wanted to lose myself in the moment, but that same mantle of dread I'd felt in Arles hovered over me now. As absurd as it was, I felt as if Gray still stalked us, like a pair of disembodied eyes was watching over us from behind the velvet drapes. When the song ended, I asked if we could take a break. Grateful for the reprieve, we walked off the dance floor and toward the band to find out who the piano virtuoso was. All I could see was a broad back straining in its tuxedo jacket and some dark hair peeking out beneath a top hat. The pianist had begun a lovely Chopin nocturne, and I marveled at how one man could create such rich sound, his hands dancing across keys and his body lunging left and right as he channeled his energy into the instrument.

Owen and I walked the perimeter of the dance floor, talking now and then, but mostly watching people, everyone playing a role tonight, hoping for some magical transformation that would bring passion and romance into their lives. Mademoiselle Veilleux had switched partners and was now dancing with a man closer to her own age, although still younger than she. He was dark-skinned and movie star handsome with finely sculpted features, sensuous lips, and dark eyes covered by a silver mask. I wondered if this was the elusive Philippe from the Left Bank.

"She's got a busy dance card tonight," Owen said.

"Yeah, she has a lot of admirers."

"Well, she is beautiful." I must have given him a funny look because he added, "For an older woman."

I laughed. "She's also got that French thing."

"What French thing?"

"You know, that magnetism older French women have . . . that *je ne sais quoi*."

"I think the word you're looking for is confidence."

"But it's more than that," I said. "It's confidence and sex appeal and a certain . . . indifference, like she doesn't care if you like her or not."

Elise showed up beside us, coyly holding a long black glove that she had taken off. She smiled and took Owen's arm. "Emma, I'm going to borrow Owen for a dance, if you don't mind."

I stared at her in disbelief, trying not to bite a hole through my tongue.

And before I could speak, Owen was walking out onto the dance floor with Elise. Elise, who had cheated on him and had come to the ball with Jean-Claude! She hadn't even given Owen the option of saying no.

I realized that even though she wasn't French, Elise had it, too—confidence, sex appeal, indifference. And right now, I wanted to kick her right in her *je ne sais quoi*.

I was standing by the Christmas tree watching Elise hijack my date when I got a text message from my dad. All it said was: *We'll be there for Xmas. I love you.*

I was beaming. Suddenly, it didn't matter that Owen was dancing with Elise. Or it didn't matter quite as much. I scanned the room looking for Flynn, Sophie, Georges—anyone to talk to—but it seemed everybody but me was on the dance floor. And then the music stopped, and the piano player rose from his bench.

The quartet continued with their next song—"Air on the G String," which always made me laugh as a title—and the pianist turned around and began walking toward me. I was struck dumb when I realized who it was. No young maestro hired from the Paris Philharmonic, but our very own Monsieur Crespeau. He wore a tux and tails and a decorative black mask embroidered in red thread, but it was still unmistakably Crespeau. He walked over to the refreshment table and grabbed a bottle of water, took a large swig, then returned in my direction toward the piano, stopping when he saw me.

"All alone?" he said, tipping his hat a charming way.

"For the moment," I said.

"Quelle tragédie," he said. "Une belle fille comme vous?"

"My date is dancing with someone else."

"Ah," he said. "The Lady of Shalott stands on the sidelines again. We are alike in that way. We both sit out when we should dance." He peered into the crowds and spotted Mademoiselle dancing with her Romeo, and his face grew wistful, his eyes narrow as if he was conjuring distant memories that pained him.

And then I knew. I couldn't believe I hadn't seen it before. Monsieur Crespeau was in love with Mademoiselle Veilleux.

Perhaps she'd even been the young woman he had followed to the train station in order to profess his love all those years ago.

"I'm not choosing to sit out," I said, anxious for him to know I wasn't a wallflower. "What else is there to do when the person you came with is dancing with someone else?"

"You must dance with someone else as well," he said, holding out his arm.

"Moi?"

"Bien sûr."

I took his hand, and he led me to the middle of the dance floor, so we were right next to Mademoiselle Veilleux and her young beau. And then the song changed, and the music switched tempo.

"They are playing a tango," Monsieur Crespeau said. "Do you know how?"

"Are you kidding?"

"Just follow my lead," he said, shocking me.

Once we began dancing, you would never have known this guy had a limp, much less a hunched back. It was almost as if the costume, the music, the dance with a much younger woman—all had combined to transform him, making him forget who he was and what his limitations were.

He led me artfully across the dance floor, and though I tried my best to match his steps, he was so fast and skilled that sometimes I found myself holding on for dear life. But I have to say, it was intoxicating to lose control like that, to be swept quite literally off my feet.

At one point I noticed people staring, watching us dance, and instead of freezing me up like it might have, it energized me, so I found myself picking up my pace and keeping up with his moves. Mademoiselle Veilleux and her partner had stopped dancing to watch, and so had Elise and Owen and Flynn and Sylvie and Yseult and Jean-Claude.

When the song ended, the crowd applauded, and Crespeau took a tiny bow before walking unceremoniously off the dance floor, his limp subtly reasserting itself.

"Whoa," Owen said. "I had no idea!"

"I know. He's amazing, isn't he?"

"I meant you," he said.

I laughed. "I didn't do anything but follow," I said.

"That's not true. I was watching you. You anticipated his moves, imitated his steps."

"He's a great lead."

"It takes two to tango," he said, cracking me up.

Crespeau took his rightful seat at the piano, and the quartet began playing a passionate rendition of Beethoven's "Moonlight Sonata." Jean-Claude was dancing with Yseult, and Georges with Sylvie. Elise was standing behind Owen, waiting for him to turn around and rejoin her on the dance floor.

I was about to bow out and let the two of them dance when I realized Owen was right. I was a good dancer. And I was even a decent singer. Although I had little experience in both, I had good musical instincts. That was exactly what I was lacking in the romance department—instinct. That ability to read people and know what they wanted before they knew it, to anticipate what they were going to do before they did. I was watching Owen now, alert to any signs of what he wanted. And he wasn't looking at Elise. He was staring straight at me.

I didn't ask him to dance, just slid my body into his, no hesitation, no fears. My left arm fell around his shoulder as he placed his hand on my waist, gripping it firmly. Our hands entwined, and we slowly began moving to the music, our bodies so close I could smell his cologne, feel his breath on my neck.

I closed my eyes and rested my head on his shoulder, letting the emotion and energy of the song surge through me, imagining myself giving up control with Owen like I had during the tango. Not losing control in a submissive way but in a way that showed him I trusted him with all my heart, in a way that showed him how much his friendship meant to me and how much I truly loved him.

Loved him as a friend. But not only that. Loved him in ways that made me temporarily forget my sorrows so I was fully present, drinking in this moment, feeling a little dizzy in his arms.

I pulled away slightly so I could see his face, and a thought entered my head that nearly knocked me over. *I could look at that face for the rest of my life and never grow tired of it.* Every dimple and curve and line was familiar and honest and true. Yes, Owen Mabry's face was maybe my favorite face in the entire world.

Owen seemed to have some sense of what I was thinking and swallowed nervously. I watched his Adam's apple lurch as he summoned the courage to kiss me. He didn't have to. It was my turn to lead.

I leaned in, wrapping both arms around his neck, and imagined kissing Owen—no little peck but a full-throttle kiss. It didn't matter that there were dozens of people around us or that the sonata had ended. Owen would pull away briefly and take off his mask, then carefully remove mine, and we would grasp each other's hands and run out of the ball and into the rain, seeking shelter in my room, where I might let Owen remove more than just my mask.

I was about to do it, just lean in and kiss Owen on the mouth, when Elise strolled up beside us, her cheeks pink and her eyes fierce. "What do you think you're doing?" she said.

She was looking at me. "Um, taking your advice and getting lucky," I said.

Elise scoffed. "I can't believe you."

"Why? You're with Jean-Claude."

"No, I'm not. We broke up," she said.

"Since when?"

"Since tonight."

"You dumped him? I thought you really liked him."

"He dumped me, Emma."

Flynn must have caught the scent of girl drama because he suddenly appeared beside us and interjected, "Who dumped you?" I could tell he was drunk because his words slurred a little.

"Stay out of it, Flynn," Elise said.

"What's going on, man?" Flynn asked Owen.

Owen looked pained watching all of this unfold. "Jean-Claude and Elise broke up," he said. "I don't know why."

"Because he knew I still had feelings for you," Elise said, turning her full attention to Owen. Owen stood silent, his face betraying nothing. "He even cut me from the musical, the bastard. Gave Yseult the role I've been rehearsing for months."

"I'm sorry," Owen said.

"What an asshole!" Flynn said, puffing up his chest a bit. My sinking feeling from earlier in the night began to return. "Dude," he said, going up to Jean-Claude, who was still dancing with Yseult. "Did you really ditch Elise at the masquerade ball? That's a dick move."

Jean-Claude sneered. "Articulate, and he can hold his liquor," he said. "A worthy combination."

"You better *ferme* your *bouche* before I shut it for you," Flynn said.

But Jean-Claude, who towered over Flynn, just quipped, "I am trembling in your formidable presence."

We were teetering on the brink of a very deep shithole, and I racked my brain for anything to defuse the tension. "Everyone just calm down," I said, pulling out the "temporary détente" card they always used in the movies. "Look, both of our teams made it through to round two. Which is incredible. So why don't we call a truce and save all these feelings of aggression and competition for the showdown in April?

Come on, we don't need to cause a scene after Mademoiselle spent so much time planning such a beautiful event."

Jean-Claude seemed to soften a bit, but Flynn still looked like he needed to pummel someone. "Can you get him out of here?" I asked Owen.

"I can try," he said. He put an arm around Flynn, who shrugged off his best friend in anger.

"I'm sorry it had to be this way," Jean-Claude said to Elise. "But like you said, you weren't looking for anything serious."

And then Elise told him to eff off.

Jean-Claude and Yseult sauntered away, looking smug, and Elise turned back toward me. "Why, Emma? Why are you doing this to me again?"

"What are you talking about?"

"You know what I'm talking about! You stole Gray our sophomore year, and now you move in on Owen before we had even officially broken up."

"Elise, listen to yourself. You just said that Jean-Claude broke up with you. How could he break up with you if you were still with Owen?"

"Owen and I agreed to see other people," she said. "We didn't break up."

"Well, maybe he wants to see me."

"You don't do that to a friend."

"I'm sorry, Elise," I said, sick to my stomach over the whole thing. But as I watched Elise wiping away crocodile tears, I realized what was really going on. "No, you know what? I'm not sorry. You can't stand not being the center of attention, not having every guy fall madly in love with you. But you're the one that pushed Owen away. And then Jean-Claude dumps you, and you suddenly want him back? That's not fair to Owen. Or me."

We both looked up and saw Owen walking toward us. His

face expressed all the grace and generosity of a saint. And then a strange moaning sound came from the ceiling. Everybody looked up, and someone screamed as the Christmas tree began teetering, looking like it might topple to the ground.

"The tree!" someone shouted. "It's coming down!"

Everything seemed to lurch into slow motion as dancers scattered from the dance floor and hundreds of glass ornaments pelted the tiles, their impacts sounding like torrential rainfall. The stampede toward the back exit created a logjam, keeping us trapped near the tree. I looked up to the top of the stairwell where the gold angel had hovered just seconds before. But now I saw a demon standing there. A demon that looked an awful lot like Gray.

The last thing I remembered was reaching out my hand toward Owen as if I could somehow pull him to safety, and then we heard the creaking grow louder and louder until the final explosive thud as the tree came crashing to the ground.

CHAPTER 14

Five of us in total were rushed to the emergency room. Although from the look of things, the entire student body of Saint-Antoine was at the hospital, wanting to get in on the gossip and spectacle. My wounds were superficial—lacerations on my face and arms, mostly from glass shards on the floor. Flynn's were about the same as mine. Another couple had received severe contusions from falling branches.

But Owen had borne the brunt of the fall. The tree had pinned him to the ground, and Monsieur Crespeau had been forced to cut branches away with a chainsaw so the medics could pull out Owen's body. They'd rushed him to the hospital since he was losing so much blood, and although his condition sounded grim, a nurse came to my room to tell me his injuries were not life threatening.

When all was said and done, Owen had suffered a fractured rib, a broken nose, and multiple cuts and lacerations. Somehow, Elise had made it through the ordeal unscathed.

When I was finally given the green light to leave my bed, I asked the nurse if I could visit Owen and found him laid up in his bed with Flynn and Nurse Elise at his side. He looked so vulnerable lying there in his hospital gown, connected to IVs and an oxygen mask.

"He's heavily sedated," Elise told me, placing a proprietary hand on his arm. "But he's going to be okay."

"Thank God," I said.

"How are *you* doing?" Flynn asked.

"I'm okay. They want to keep me overnight for observation, but mostly I'm just scary-looking."

Flynn smirked. "You can say that again. That's gonna leave a scar," he said, tracing one of the cuts on my face.

"You're no beauty yourself," I said.

"Chicks dig scars," he said. Damned if that wasn't true.

"How long do you think they'll keep him here?" I asked Elise. I don't know why I was deferring to her, but she did have a pretty convincing Florence Nightingale routine going.

"A few days, probably," she said. "The doctor said something about blunt trauma."

"That doesn't sound good," I said. "I can't believe the tree fell on him. How do you think that happened?"

"Just a freak accident, I guess," Flynn said.

But I wasn't so sure. I thought about the ghostly image of Gray I'd seen at the top of the stairwell. Probably just a hallucination brought on by my terror. Still, I'd been having these feelings for weeks now, some sixth sense that someone was following me, watching me, and that this presence bore me ill will.

We stayed in the room for about an hour until the nurse told us we had to leave. Somehow Elise convinced her that she was Owen's girlfriend and was allowed to stay. But Flynn and I went back to our respective hospital rooms. I barely slept at all. Finally, I drifted off sometime around four A.M. but was awoken just a few hours later by a stream of hospital attendants coming in and out of my room. All I wanted to do was check on Owen, but it seemed to take hours for them to get my discharge papers ready and release me. Flynn succeeded in getting discharged before I did, so he came and waited for me and we went together to visit Owen.

Owen had been moved in the middle of the night to a room in the IC unit, but the one thing that hadn't changed was Elise's presence. There she sat, still by his side as if she'd been his ever-present girlfriend for all these months. I really didn't care anymore. I was too happy to see Owen sitting up and smiling, making some hilarious face when he tried the protein smoothie Elise was trying to make him drink.

"I swear this has spinach in it," he said.

"It does," said Elise. "And bananas, blueberries, avocado, sweet potato, soy milk, and psyllium husk."

"Sillum what?" Owen asked.

"Husk. Tons of fiber. It's from this great juice bar I found on Rue Quincampoix." Then she pulled out a cardboard carrier with two clear plastic cups filled with mint-green liquid. "Look, I got you guys bubble tea."

She handed Flynn and me our teas, complete with blue tapioca balls at the bottom.

Flynn said, "Oh, we didn't warrant the protein smoothies because our injuries weren't severe enough?"

"Be grateful, dude," Owen said, grimacing as he tried to stomach another swig.

"Why are you being so nice to us?" I asked.

"Well," Elise said, "because I want to apologize. I know I've been a bitch over these past few months, and I've disappointed you all by defecting to the dark side, but I'm willing to work extra hard to make it up to you. Here's what I propose. You have to put together an opera in less than four months, complete with songs, singers, costumes, and sets. Now I'm not saying you should just give me the lead after everything I've done, but you know I can sing. And you know the part of Christine would look incredible on my transcript if I get into Berklee. But this isn't about me. This is about putting on the best opera we can. And you guys need me."

Flynn was nodding traitorously, and I gave him an evil look. "What?" he said. "She's right."

I sighed, feeling irritable and tired and desperate for my own bed. "Look, you guys do what you want to do. I'm going to my room to try and get a little sleep. I'll be back later tonight. Owen, text me if you need anything. I love you."

I said those last three words with the casual air of one saying "God bless you" after a sneeze. Still, it meant a lot for me to utter those words to him.

"Wait, I'll come with you," Elise said. "I've got to grab some things from the hostel for Owen."

"I can do that, man," Flynn said.

"No," Elise said. "I'm happy to do it. Remember, this is payback time."

"Thanks, Elise," said Owen. And the sincere look in his eyes made me want to cry.

I really didn't feel like walking back to school with Elise. I wanted to be on my own. But Elise insisted on accompanying me, so I had no choice but to talk to her, even though I was still fuming over what she had done last night.

"Didn't Owen look so adorable all helpless like that?" she said.

"I prefer when he's able to walk around and move his head, but that's just me."

"You're still angry," she said. "About last night."

"Yeah, I'm angry."

"I know," she said. "It wasn't fair, what I said to you. And it wasn't just because Jean-Claude ditched me. It's just . . . well, I still have feelings for Owen, Emma. And when I saw the two of you dancing, I went a little crazy."

"Yeah, you did," I said, quickening my pace. It was really cold, and Paris didn't seem quite so magical as it had last night.

"I know. I'm sorry. But I figured out what my problem is with relationships. It's that I can't stand being alone."

I stopped and stared at her. Elise didn't break her façade of invincibility very often, so when she did, one took notice. "Elise, nobody wants to be alone—"

"No, you don't understand," she said. "I can't be alone. I don't know how. It's like, I'm terrified that any second a guy is going to get sick of me and leave. So I don't let them get too close, and I always keep another guy in reserve. That way I can't get hurt. But with Owen, I really regretted it. Jean-Claude's kind of a douche."

"You think?" I said. "Look, if you never let anyone in, you're never going to experience anything close to love."

"Don't you think I know that?" she said. "Why do you think I'm fighting for Owen now? I want to fall in love, I do. But how can I believe in love when my own parents can't stand the sight of each other?"

"Just because your parents got it wrong doesn't mean you will."

She sighed and shook her head. "Sometimes, Emma, it's like I can feel myself becoming my mother. Did I tell you she cheated on my dad? I worry that I'm incapable of being faithful. What if I'm just like her?"

"Elise, that's ridiculous. The mere fact that you're worrying about it means you won't make the same mistakes she did," I said.

She smiled slightly. Once again, I was the one making her feel better instead of the other way around.

When I got back to my room, I was so exhausted I felt like I could have slept for a week. But even through my bleary eyes, I saw the thing I feared most. The mirror had been un-covered again. My mind immediately went to Monsieur Cres-peau, but he usually cleaned during the school week, and after the drama last night, chainsaw and all, I couldn't imag-ine he'd be making his rounds this morning.

Something in my gut told a darker story. I felt Gray's presence in the room, like that loneliness from earlier in the year but more visceral, and then he seemed to pass right through me like a cold chill. Fear was my first emotion, but it was quickly replaced by anger. Why was Gray haunting me like this? Why wouldn't he let me go?

"Someone could have died in that accident!" I said out loud. "Owen could have died. I could have died!"

I knew I sounded insane, but I also knew Gray could hear me. Whatever he was, it was no longer the loving and generous person I'd fallen in love with. He was something twisted and dangerous now. "Go away!" I shouted. "Leave me alone. I can't love you anymore. Not like this. You have to let me go so you can be free. And I can be free. You're killing me!"

I was nearly crying, torn apart by my emotions, which seemed to take form in the air, swirling around me in an ever-sickening vortex. "Let me go, Gray," I sobbed. "Let me remember you the way you were. So I don't have to fear you. So we can both move on."

I didn't understand how this mirror had come to be the portal through which we were able to cross into each other's worlds, but I knew it had to stop. And there was one way to make sure it never happened again.

I grabbed one of my black boots from the closet. "I'm sorry, Gray, but I can't do this anymore." I heaved the boot into the air and brought its heel down upon the mirror, cracking the glass right down the center. I struck it again and again, whaling away at the mirror until the surface was completely shattered into a spiderweb of fracture lines and shards of glass littered the floor. And then the room stilled, and I felt peace descend on me like a warm blanket. I took a deep breath and held it, listening intently, hearing nothing but my own heartbeat. I dropped the boot and shuffled to the bed, collapsing onto it like a stone.

A line from Tennyson's "The Lady of Shalott" echoed

through my head as I fell asleep that night: "The mirror crack'd from side to side."

Yes, it had. I had finally broken the love spell I'd recited and tossed into the Seine. But I had forgotten one thing about the Lady of Shalott.

It was only after the mirror broke that her true curse began.

CHAPTER 15

It was strange to have my family visiting in Paris, like my two worlds were colliding. Plus, it conferred on me the status of tour guide and default native of the group.

"Look at you," Barbara said as they met me in front of my school. "You look so grown-up and sophisticated."

"It's just the black dress and the scarf," I said. But I did feel older and more grown-up, like I'd matured several years in a matter of months.

As I led them past the Louvre and across the Pont du Carrousel, it was a gift to see all of them relaxing and enjoying themselves. My father and Barbara held hands as they walked, and at each new monument, my grandmother's eyes lit up like she was eighteen instead of eighty.

I'd never seen my father more in awe than when we entered the van Gogh gallery of the Musée d'Orsay. There in his signature bold colors and swirling brushstrokes were van Gogh's self-portrait, his bedroom, his *Starry Night Over the Rhone,* and my favorite, *The Church at Auvers.* I'd seen the painting in a textbook before, but the actual canvas seemed to glow with intensity and quiver with some kind of spiritual energy.

My father stood before it for at least ten minutes, his focus as intense as when he was reeling in a particularly intractable fish. We followed our museum tour with a simple café lunch of wine and cheese. Barbara squealed with happiness at the creamy richness of the Caprifeuille, a nutty goat cheese melted right onto fresh-out-of-the-oven baguettes. My grandma drank a bottle of Beaujolais all by herself, and the conversation flowed, too.

"So, how are your classes?" Grandma asked.

"Classes?" I said. "What classes?"

"Ha ha," my father said. "Seriously. How are you doing? Are your AP classes hard?"

"Killer," I said. "But I'm keeping up with the workload. And I love my opera class."

"Great," Dad said. "You're not going to major in opera now, are you?"

"No, but I'm writing one," I said.

"Really?" Barbara said. "That sounds fascinating. What's it about?"

I told them about the libretto contest and how we'd just advanced to round two and were going to perform our opera for the judges in April. "If we win, a professional opera company could perform our opera next year."

"Oh, Emma, that's wonderful," Grandma said.

Barbara touched my dad's arm. "Well, I for one can't wait to see it. John, can we come back to see the performance? Spend April in Paris?"

"I don't think we can afford two European vacations in one year," he said. "Plus, April's a bad month for me." In New England, April was when prime fishing season resumed. I knew my family wouldn't get to see us perform, and that actually relieved me.

After lunch, we took a leisurely stroll to the Eiffel Tower. My dad took the opportunity to grill me on my college selections. "Soooo," he said. "Is it going to be Hampshire or Amherst?"

"I haven't even gotten my acceptance letters yet," I said.

"Who knows? Maybe I'll stay in Paris and go to la Sorbonne."

"Did you apply there?" he said, looking alarmed.

"No, Dad. I'm only joking."

I didn't have the heart to tell him I'd applied to all those other schools. Once we were finished with our sightseeing, I tried to convince Barbara that the Métro was perfectly safe, but she insisted on finding a taxi stand, and I accompanied them back to their hotel in the Saint-Germain neighborhood. The plan was to let them get some rest and then meet up later for dinner.

Walking home from their hotel, a strange sense of calm overcame me—and not just the winter quiet of the meandering back streets, but an inner peace that suggested my obliteration of the mirror may have solved my problems. As relieved as I was, I also felt lonelier than ever. Here it was just days before Christmas with my family in town to see me, and I felt like I was completely alone in the universe. The presence that had haunted my steps for the past two months was gone. Gray's ghost, for all its destructive and dangerous impulses, was no longer a part of my world.

When I got back to my room, Monsieur Crespeau was waiting at my door, holding a large cardboard box.

"I hear you are in need of a new mirror," he said.

"Who told you?"

"Your friend Elise," he said. "I am sad to hear of the mirror's demise. You know how much I admired it."

"Well," I said as I opened the door, "its demise wasn't exactly an accident."

He followed me into the room and saw the devastation I'd wrought against the piece of glass. "I see what you mean," he said. "What did you do? Take a crowbar to it?"

"Something like that," I said. "I suppose I just got fed up."

"Half-sick of shadows?" he said, quoting Tennyson.

"Exactly."

"And has the curse befallen you?"

"You tell me. A giant Christmas tree just fell on me and my friends."

He smiled grimly. "Yes, how is your gentleman friend?"

"My gentleman friend is doing better. All but his rib has recovered, and that will heal in time."

"Yes, time heals all wounds eventually."

"Does it?" I said.

He raised an eyebrow mysteriously. "Have you told your friend how you feel about him?"

I looked up at him, surprised. "No."

"Why not?"

"I guess because I'm not sure how I feel."

"Oh, really?" he said. "When you two were dancing together, you did not look unsure."

"You saw us? I thought you were playing the piano."

"The music had ended, and you were still dancing. That's how I knew."

"Oh."

"What holds you back?" he said. "Is it the boy you saw in the mirror? Your Lancelot?"

"I don't know," I said.

"Emma, don't be like me, wasting your life on a romantic fantasy."

"But your life doesn't have to be that way."

"I'm afraid it does," he said.

"Why? Why can't you tell her how you feel?"

"I am too afraid of her response. The wrong one could kill me."

He strolled across the room and began taking out the screws holding the mirror in place. Why hadn't I thought of calling him before? It would have saved me a lot of angst. "I am not so good at the real world," he said. "This is enough for me. Seeing her? Looking out for her? It gives my life purpose."

I shook my head, frustrated. I didn't understand all this self-abnegation. "Can I ask you something?" I said.

"Oui."

"What are you doing for Christmas?"

But when I invited him to come out with us for Christmas dinner, he did me one better. He invited my family to dine with him at his place on Christmas Eve. And he told me I could bring Owen as well, winking at me in the way I imagined Santa Claus might wink.

Since he was playing the part of matchmaker, I figured I would return the favor. That afternoon, I called Mademoiselle Veilleux and invited her to come to Christmas Eve dinner. Unfortunately, she already had plans, but I asked if she might consider coming for dessert. "It would mean a lot to Monsieur Crespeau," I said, trying to give her the hint.

"You've become very fond of him, haven't you?" she said.

"Yes. He's a sweetheart. And kind of handsome in a rugged way, don't you think?"

She ignored my last comment. "I will see what I can do," was all she would promise.

My family was thrilled to be dining in an actual home, as Christmas just wasn't Christmas in a restaurant. Owen met me at my room so we could walk to Crespeau's house together. My heart jumped a little when I opened my door and saw him, still a little battered-looking, but cleaned up and looking sharp in a jacket and tie. My mind fled back to that unfulfilled kiss on the dance floor.

"Hey," I said. "You're early."

"I know," he said. "I couldn't wait."

"You look so much better," I said.

"Yeah, my face is no longer one giant bruise."

"I love your face, bruised or not," I said, my tongue getting away from me.

Owen blushed and came into the room, sitting on my bed while I finished getting ready in my new mirror—an ordinary rectangular one that had probably cost twenty euro at the department store. I could see Owen watching me as I applied my makeup and perfume. He was making me nervous.

I turned around, and Owen smiled. "You look beautiful," he said.

"Thank you, sir," I said, doing a dramatic twirl. I was wearing a black velvet dress cut on the bias, with black strappy shoes studded with rhinestones.

"I got you a little Christmas gift," he said, pulling out a package from his inner jacket pocket.

"Aw, Owen, I told you not to."

"I know, but I couldn't resist." I went over and sat next to him on the bed. "It's not a big deal. And it's as much for me as it is for you."

"Oh, really?" I said, digging into the shiny silver wrapping paper. Enclosed in a small flat box was a CD hand-labeled: *Emma's Phantom.*

"A friend from the hostel let me borrow his recording equipment, and I made a mock-up of the opera score. All the songs we wrote together are on this CD."

I reached out and pulled him close. "Owen, this is the best gift ever," I said.

When I pulled away, he was staring at me with this urgent, expectant look and I found myself wanting to pin him down on the bed. But instead I said, "We should probably go."

"I thought I was early."

"Yeah, but you promised to bring wine and I promised to bring dessert."

We stopped off at a bakery and wine shop on the way and still got to Crespeau's house about ten minutes before everyone else. Honestly, I had never pictured Crespeau anywhere other than in the halls of our school. His house was a tiny slate-roofed cottage in the heart of the Marais. But what really surprised me were the colors inside. Crespeau was one of the most understated people I knew. While he was hard to miss with his six-foot-three frame, he didn't like to call attention to himself and dressed in simple, neutral-colored clothing.

But as he gave us a tour of his home, I saw that he'd painted the walls of each room a different color: sunset orange for the living room, Provençal blue for the dining room, lemon yellow for the kitchen. I was reminded of van Gogh's paintings, the irrepressible joy and color in his canvases that belied the depression and madness of their creator.

It was no wonder Crespeau had loved the mirror in my room; it would have fit in perfectly here among all his antiques. A fire blazed in an old fireplace in the corner of the living room, classical Christmas music poured forth from his record player, and dozens of wineglasses and brandy snifters sat lined up on a sideboard waiting to be filled. It seemed Monsieur Crespeau was the perfect host.

My family arrived shortly after us, and we made the introductions, with Crespeau insisting everyone call him Nicholas. I hadn't even known his first name. Once everyone had drinks in hand, conversation began to flow. Barbara admired Crespeau's taste in stemware, my father commented on the delicious appetizers, and Grandma commented on the brandy. Well, mostly she drank the brandy. And then she started flirting.

"So I see you like antiques," she said to Monsieur Crespeau. "I've always found that the older something is, the more value it has."

"Yes, that has been my experience, too," Crespeau said, going along with the joke. Too bad she was at least thirty years too old for him.

For dinner, Crespeau had cooked duck in wine and herbs, and we had all pitched in on the sides. My dad and Barbara brought oysters and foie gras, my grandmother brought truffles and champagne, Owen brought wine and cheese, and I brought a rich chocolate cake drizzled with cranberry ganache.

"So you live here all alone?" Barbara said during dinner.

"Oui," he said.

"What a pity," Barbara said. "This place could use a woman's touch."

"Barbara," I said. "This house is perfect. I want to live here!"

"It is lovely," Barbara conceded, "but a woman would hang lace curtains in these windows to catch the light, and she'd have flowers on the table."

"Oh, I did forgot the flowers," Crespeau said, winking at me.

"And I could polish up this silver for you in no time," she said.

"Oh my God," I muttered to Owen, who squeezed my thigh under the table.

Barbara rambled on about the feminine improvements to be wrought by some imaginary girlfriend, but all I could think about was Owen's hand on my thigh. Had he meant to squeeze my hand instead? I wanted to sneak a look at him, but I didn't dare.

"What do you think of these oysters?" my dad asked.

"They are very good," said Crespeau.

My father made a satisfied groan. "They're different from the ones we get at home. Better."

"Yes, each region produces its own distinct oyster," Crespeau said. "Do you know much about seafood?"

"Oh yes," my dad said, laughing. "I'm a fisherman."

"Emma did not tell me," Crespeau said. "What kind of fish?"

Then the two of them were talking about trout and carp and grayling and the best places to fish in Normandy and the Dordogne.

You're interested in fishing, Emma. Get into the conversation.

But I was still distracted by that hand on my thigh. Crespeau got up and refilled my grandma's champagne glass and then mine, which I downed rather quickly.

After dinner, Owen and I cleared dishes, and I brought out the cake while Crespeau made some strong French press coffee. We were all sitting down to dessert when someone knocked on the door.

"No, don't get up," I said. "I'll get it."

I opened the door to see Mademoiselle Veilleux. "You came!" I said, perhaps a bit giddy from the champagne. I took from her yet another bottle of wine and helped her off with her coat. She looked radiant in a form-fitting raspberry dress with an exquisite silk scarf of Chinese characters. She'd worn her hair down for a change, and it looked rich and lush against the delicate material of the dress.

I felt a presence looming behind me and saw Mademoiselle's eyes go soft and glassy. When I turned around, Crespeau stood staring at Mademoiselle Veilleux in wide-eyed awe. It was as if all the music and chatter and clinking of silverware fell away, and they were the only two people in the universe. Except for me, of course, standing right between them.

I took a step back, and Crespeau gave me a brief questioning glance before we all realized we'd better introduce Mademoiselle to the rest of the party. I took my seat next to Owen.

Crespeau introduced everyone, and I leaned over to Owen and said, "Flynn will be devastated."

"How about your grandmother?" he said, grinning.

I turned to look at Grandma, knowing she'd never be jealous. In fact, she looked apple-cheeked and young again, happy to be here on Christmas Eve instead of in our somber house back home, where memories choked us.

"Emma, can I talk to you for a moment outside?" my grandmother said rather suddenly.

I didn't know what this was all about, but we got up from the table, Crespeau rushing to my grandmother's side to help her out of her chair. He led us into the kitchen and showed us the door that led out to his small garden courtyard.

Before we went out, my grandmother said, "Nicholas, do

you happen to have a cigarette? I don't normally smoke, but I like to on special occasions."

"Of course," he said, retrieving a pack and handing her a narrow cigarette and lighting it for her.

Then we stepped out into the cold night air. The sky was clear and flush with luminescence from the city's twinkling lights.

"Well, I'm having a splendid time," she said. "What's wrong with you? You've been acting like you've seen a ghost."

"I don't know," I said, shivering a little in my short sleeves.

"Owen's in love with you," she said. "Just as sure as that man in there is in love with Mademoiselle Veilleux." I looked guiltily at my grandma, then dropped my eyes. "Look," she said, taking a quick puff of her cigarette, "I know we haven't had much chance to talk lately. It's hard to get a word in edgewise when Barbara's around. But I know how tough this year has been on you. You've suffered more losses than anyone your age should have to. Which means, you have to find happiness where you can."

My grandmother had always had this ability to see right through me. She was highly intuitive that way.

"It's just . . . I feel like I can't . . . I can't . . ."

"Get over Gray?" she said. I felt tears begin to well in my eyes. "I know, sweetheart. Gray's disappearance devastated us all. And your father's been so worried about you. It was all I could do to stop him from coming here months ago and moving in with you at your dorm." I cracked a tiny smile. "But all of us are amazed at how well you're doing here. You're really thriving. And you seem so mature and independent. And now, there's this opera with Owen. You've always been so creative. You take after your mother that way." She stopped talking, but I could hear her swallow the lump in her throat. "Your mother would be . . . so proud of you. I just know she's up there somewhere looking down at you, and she wants so badly for you to be happy. We all do." A tear rolled warmly down my cheek. "And Gray would want you to be happy, too."

"Would he?" I said, beginning to sob.

"Of course, Emma. Why would you ever doubt that?"

"It's just, I've had these dreams, Grandma. These horrible dreams and Gray is in them, and he's so different—angry and mean and jealous."

"They're just nightmares, Emma," she said. "Your fears playing out in your head. You've always been prone to them. Well, ever since that damn lightning strike. How I wish that had never happened to you."

"You and me both," I said.

"But you've got to do away with dreams and nightmares for a change and embrace your real life. Start over again. And I think Owen could help you do that."

"I know," I said, feeling so much better now that my grandmother had given me her blessing to move on. Maybe that's what I'd been looking for all along. A sign that I didn't have to save myself for Gray anymore, even though I'd made a promise that now lay at the bottom of the Seine. "Thank you, Grandma," I said, throwing my arms around her and giving her a huge hug. She felt smaller to me and more fragile physically even though mentally she was still tough as nails. "You've always understood me best," I said.

"You too, kid," she said. "You know I love you."

"I love you, too."

"Merry Christmas."

"Joyeux Noël."

When we went back inside, the mood seemed to have changed radically. Crespeau and Mademoiselle Veilleux were standing to the side, stunned to silence by something, and everyone else was gathered around my father, who was uncharacteristically staring down at his cell phone with tears in his eyes.

"What happened here?" my grandmother said, and I got a sinking feeling that someone had died.

My dad looked straight at me, and I saw his lips moving but was unable to hear what he said. A strange ringing had begun in my ears, and my legs were trembling.

Owen came toward me and put his arm around me, repeating what my father had just said.

"Emma, Gray's been found."

CHAPTER 16

I hadn't wanted to go home. I had tried to avoid it. But something or someone had wanted me there.

Because of the holidays, we couldn't get a flight out of Paris until the twenty-ninth, and the wait was torture. I did talk to Gray's mother, Simona, and his sister, Anna, both of whom confirmed what my father and Owen had told me on Christmas Eve night. That Gray had been found alive in the middle of the Atlantic.

He was recuperating in the hospital and unable to talk to anyone, except apparently a reporter who had written this "feel good" piece for the *Miami Herald*:

BERMUDA TRIANGLE MIRACLE:
MISSING COAST GUARD SWIMMER
FOUND AFTER 61 DAYS AT SEA

Miracle is not a word often associated with the Bermuda Triangle, the triangular swath of the Atlantic Ocean off the southeastern coast of the United States, known for its treacherous weather conditions and mysterious maritime disappearances. But *miracle* is the only word to describe the rescue of Gray Newman, a Coast

Guard swimmer missing since October 23, who was found alive in a life raft on the western edge of the Sargasso Sea 61 days after he went missing during a rescue operation.

"It's karma," said Coast Guard pilot Sheldon Boyers. "He saved eight people; it's only fitting that we save him."

Newman had been the first rescue swimmer on the scene when the windjammer *The Lady Rose* began capsizing off the Florida coastline during a hurricane. While Newman was able to secure all eight passengers, the crewmembers were still in the water when Boyers made the difficult decision to leave them in Newman's care while he went to refuel the chopper.

But as Newman went to retrieve the life raft, a rogue wave overtook him, separating him from the crew of *The Lady Rose*. When Boyers returned with a second rescue swimmer, they found no trace of Newman or the life raft.

All life rafts are equipped with EPIRBs, or Emergency Position Indicating Radio Beacons, but no signal was retrieved in the days following Newman's disappearance, leading the Coast Guard to assume Newman had perished.

But late Friday afternoon, the Coast Guard received word that an EPIRB had been activated in an area 500 miles off the coast in the middle of the Sargasso Sea. They immediately sent Boyers's unit and two others out in search of their missing swimmer.

"We were skeptical," said Lt. Cmdr. Marcus Shilling of the U.S. Coast Guard's Miami base. "After all that time, we knew there was a good chance Newman was no longer with the raft.

And even if he was, there was a good chance he hadn't survived. But at least we had a signal. We were no longer looking for a needle in a haystack."

Boyers and his team were astounded to come upon Newman's life raft still intact, with Newman alive and safely inside it, although he was severely malnourished and dehydrated. Marine biologist Sidney Barrow said Newman was lucky he ended up in the Sargasso Sea. "The warm waters of the Gulf Stream allowed him to survive the winter, and he was able to subsist on the bitter sargassum weed that's so plentiful there, along with a variety of fish."

His doctor was quick to point out that Newman's ordeal isn't over yet. "He has a long road to recovery ahead of him," said Dr. Michael Vargus. "He's very weak, he's lost a lot of weight, and he may have lost some functionality in his legs. He was very disoriented when we found him and seems to have experienced some temporary memory loss. We're still putting the pieces together to understand how he was able to survive all that time. It truly does seem like a miracle."

But Newman's friend and the flight mechanic for his unit, Evan Wheeler, doesn't agree. "It's no miracle. It's just Gray. The kid is so tough. He knew exactly how to survive in those conditions. He's a hero. And he's going to make a speedy recovery, I have no doubt."

Speedy recovery or not, Newman is happy to be alive and back on dry land. When asked if he was going to continue swimming for the Coast

Guard after his recovery, Newman was resolute.

"Of course," he said. "It's what I do."

Hero, indeed.

Tears were streaming down my cheeks as I finished the article. I hadn't really believed it until I'd seen it in print. But there was no doubt about it now. Gray was alive. And I was heading home to see him.

The relief I felt for Gray was immense, yet there was something preventing me from being heady with joy, like I ought to have been. Gray had been missing for two months, and I had mourned him. I had said good-bye to the man I loved. And now he was back.

But when someone came back from the dead, he wasn't the same person, was he? And that was what I was most afraid of.

In order to get a flight home during the busy holiday week, my family and I flew out of Paris on a rainy Sunday morning, so early it was still dark when we took off. With the six-hour time difference, it was almost like time stood still, with the sun just rising over Boston as we landed.

After a short pit stop home to freshen up and change, my dad and I headed over to the hospital. Gray was asleep when we arrived at his room. I felt a whoosh of emotion when I saw him, like all of the love and regret and sorrow and fear I'd stored up over the past few months had unleashed itself and was conspiring to choke the breath out of me. Even more terrifying was that the man lying in the hospital bed looked like the Gray from my dreams. His normally trim dark hair was long and scraggy and bleached blond, and his full lips were brittle, chewed away by salt and sun. His skin was brown as a walnut, and his face was all sharpness and hollows, his cheekbones protruding like wings.

My father's hands gripped my shoulders to steady me. I

hadn't realized I was shaking. But I was staring at someone who, until a few days ago, I'd thought was dead. That would shake anyone.

Sitting at the chair by his bedside, I grabbed his hand because I still worried this could all be a dream, that it wasn't real. Even though his hand was thin and dry, it was warm. Blood ran through his veins, and a pulse beat at his wrist. Everyone and everything in the room disappeared as I leaned in to hear his heart beat, and for a moment we were back on our own island, the only two people in the universe.

Two years ago when I'd been struck by lightning and fallen into a coma, Gray had been the one to pull me back from the brink. Now I was the one pulling him out, calling him back.

"Gray," I said softly, feeling no self-consciousness at my father's eyes on me. "It's me. Emma."

Even though I'd thought him unconscious, he stirred at my words. His eyes fluttered open, and they were Gray's eyes—hazel, sad, but older and wiser, too. They were as familiar to me as my own eyes. And in their depths was none of the fear or dread I'd felt when we'd met on that nightmare shore. Here was solace and relief and love reclaimed.

"Gray, I'm here," I said. I wanted him to know as I did that this was real. I had no idea if he remembered any of our visits through the mirror, or if he did, if he'd perceived them in the same way I had.

"Emma," his voice croaked as he squeezed my hand with what little strength he had.

"He's awake," I said, turning to my dad with tears in my eyes.

"Yes, Emma," my dad said, affirming what I still doubted.

A doctor came into the room, looking very brisk and efficient in his white coat with his clipboard. "Is he okay?" I asked him, so thankful to have someone here who could answer the thousand questions swirling in my head.

"He's much better than when he first came in," the doctor said. "We've got him on fluids, and he's slowly regaining his strength. He's going to be fine. He's a fighter. I'm Dr. Sorentino."

After shaking the doctor's hand, I laced my fingers with Gray's again, and I thought I saw him smile. And in that moment, he was my Gray again. The world made sense.

Shortly afterward, Gray fell asleep, heavily medicated as he was. But we stayed for over an hour until Gray's parents and Anna showed up. I broke down at the sight of Anna, who'd believed all along that Gray was still alive. She had kept her faith while mine had faltered.

Simona hugged me like I was the one who'd come home after being lost at sea. And in a way, I had been lost. I had struggled to reestablish my place in a world without Gray. And I had found it. Now that he was back, I wasn't sure where this left me.

My dad and I finally left the hospital, promising to return the next day. As anxious as I was to see Gray again, I worried about what we would say to each other. How would we acknowledge the seismic shift that had taken place inside both of us and between us?

When we got home, my father shut off the ignition and turned to me. "Why don't you stay?" he said.

"Where else would I go?"

"No, I mean stay here and not go back to Paris," he said. "With Gray home again, it just seems to make sense for you to stay and finish your semester here."

"But, Dad," I said, "I've got to go back. We have the opera contest. And I'm already registered for all my courses. I'm doing really well there."

"I know you are. But you'll do well here, too," he said. "You can take all your AP courses at Lockwood. And it won't be such a hassle to take the exams. And the opera contest . . . well, it's a wonderful honor, of course, but your friends can continue without you, can't they? It's not like you've ever had ambitions to study music seriously. It's . . . an extracurricular." A distraction, is what he meant. "It just seems to me that nothing could be as important as the fact that Gray is back. Don't you want to be here for him?"

"Of course I do," I said.

"Emma, everyone would understand, given the circumstances."

"It's not that," I said.

"Then what? How can you think of going back now that Gray's here? I also think you need your family and friends around you now. This can't be easy for you, all this shock. It's been so nice having you home. Grandma's sort of bereft without you, and she's not going to be around forever—"

"Dad, stop it!" I said.

"Stop what?"

"Giving me a guilt trip. What if I *want* to go back to Paris? Would that be so horrible?"

"To be honest, Emma? Yeah, it would be. I just don't understand what could be so important that it would mean leaving us. You got to go away and study abroad. Now you should end your senior year here at home where you belong."

How could I tell him? How to explain that from the moment I'd stepped off the plane in Boston, I'd felt that I no longer belonged here at all.

Maybe I would feel different in a few months or a few years. But right now, I belonged in Paris. I wasn't sure why. Was it the opera contest, the promise of my words being sung onstage and possibly performed professionally next year? Was it Owen? Or was it simply that I wanted to finish the journey I'd started and see where it led me?

"Can we talk about this later?" I said. "I'm supposed to meet Michelle and Jess in less than an hour."

So far, Michelle and Jess had been the only relationship to weather the turbulence of this year. Elise and Owen hadn't lasted. And Gray and me? For now, we were an unsolved equation.

I was meeting them at eight o'clock at Melville's, the local beach seafood shack. It was a dive, but it had sentimental value. My friends arrived in the orange Volvo station wagon I'd lent Michelle for the year I was away. The sight of Michelle and Jess emerging from my orange boat of a vehicle and clasping their hands as they crossed the street toward me was one of the happiest moments I'd experienced in a long time.

They attacked me in a group hug, showering me with overblown words of affection.

"Emma, we missed you so much!" "You look great!" "How are you, our frog-leg-loving, horse-meat-eating, scarf-wearing friend?"

By the time we entered the restaurant, I was laughing so hard I was crying. We sat at our favorite booth, the one with the mural of Ahab harpooning a whale that looked far too chipper about the ordeal, and ordered a feast of fried seafood that came to our table in red plastic baskets with wax paper.

"Oh, how I missed clam strips," I said.

We dug into the food, and I got caught up on all things Lockwood before Michelle brought up the giant elephant in the room.

"How is Gray?" she asked, grabbing my forearm for emphasis.

"He's okay," I said. "We didn't get to talk. He was sleeping most of the time."

"I still can't believe he's alive," she said.

"Was it weird seeing him?" Jess asked.

"Yes and no. It was a little surreal after thinking he was gone, but at the same time . . ."

I told them about my dreams and admitted that a part of me had never really accepted that he was dead.

"You and Gray have always had that psychic connection," Michelle said. "It makes sense that you'd get a feeling he was still alive. Because . . . he was. It really is a kind of miracle."

"I don't know about that," I said.

"What do you mean?"

"Don't get mad," I said. "But . . . I did a spell."

"Darlene's spell?" Michelle asked. "Damn, I knew that's what was in the gift bag. I told you not to mess with that voodoo stuff, Emma."

"I know," I said. "But I was desperate."

I couldn't help remembering a story we'd read in middle school called "The Monkey's Paw," about an old couple that makes a wish on a cursed monkey's paw to bring their dead son back to life, only to realize that their wish would be granted at a terrible price.

"How long are you home for?" Michelle asked, bringing me back to reality.

"Just a few more days," I said.

"Aw, you can't stay longer?" Jess said.

"No, the second semester starts next week, and we have to get working on our opera." I told them all about the competition at school and how we'd advanced to the second round and would perform our opera in April.

"We?" Michelle said. "Is that you and Elise?"

"Sort of," I said. "She was working with another team, but she came back to ours when her relationship with the writer went sour."

"Same old Elise," Jess said.

Michelle raised an eyebrow. "So she and Owen are . . ."

"Over," I said. "I think."

"Hmmm."

"What?" I said.

"I'm getting the feeling that there's more to this story," she said.

"Like what?" Jess asked, her eyes hungry for gossip. "Oh, don't tell me you and Owen are . . . complicated again."

"Complicated doesn't begin to cover it," I said. And then I sighed and told them about the past few months—the singing lessons, the almost-kiss in Arles, the masquerade ball.

"I always thought you'd be great together," Michelle said. "Well, once I stopped dating him."

"Ha," Jess said. "Once you came to your senses, you mean."

"Exactly," Michelle said, leaning in to give Jess a kiss.

"Do you have feelings for him?" Jess asked.

"Of course," I said. "He's one of my best friends. And lately, he's been so there for me, but sometimes I wonder whether . . . Oh, I don't know what to think."

Both of them looked at me sympathetically but with that air of detachment of people who no longer have to worry about their love lives. "What are you going to tell Gray?" Michelle asked.

I dropped a clam strip back on my plate, no longer hungry. "I don't know," I said. "I really don't."

CHAPTER 17

Michelle's question weighed on me all night as I tried to sleep, thoughts of Owen and Gray swirling through my head with all the accompanying guilt and turmoil.

When my dad and I got to the hospital the next day, Gray was awake, sitting up, even. He had some color in his cheeks and looked so much more alive than before. I smiled at him, and the smile he returned nearly undid me since I hadn't seen it in so long.

My dad gave him an uncharacteristic hug, and they managed to have a stilted conversation that never even hinted at the nightmare Gray had endured. Then my dad made some obvious excuse to leave the room so we could be alone, and I sat down beside Gray like I had yesterday. His hand reached for mine this time, and I was surprised how much force was in his squeeze.

"You seem better today," I said. "Stronger."

"I want to kiss you so bad," he said, ignoring my observation. "If only I wasn't hooked up to this contraption." A nasogastric tube was feeding him a constant stream of liquids and nutrients to compensate for months of dehydration and malnutrition.

"I know," I said, touching his cheek. "It's not fair."

He must have sensed some hesitation in my voice because he asked me, "Do I look horrible?"

"No," I said. "Just thinner. And tanner."

"Tanner?" he said. "My skin's like shoe leather. And what about this hair? The first thing I want to do when I get out of here, other than kiss you, is get a haircut."

"Why wait? Give me a razor, and I'll shear it off now," I said, reaching out to touch his new curls. He laughed a little but it seemed to pain him somewhere in his ribs. "Are you okay?"

"Yeah. Come here," he said, his voice soft and husky.

He patted the spot next to him on the bed, and I timidly crawled in beside him. There was barely room for me there, so I had to cling to his body to balance myself, but I was afraid of hurting him. I was also nervous being this close to him. We hadn't been this intimate since the beginning of last summer before he left for his EMT training.

I nuzzled his neck like I used to do, trying to recapture some of the familiarity and comfort I used to feel around Gray. I had always loved this part of him—that hollow between his head and shoulder blade that smelled of his cologne, like the beach at nighttime. But he smelled different now. It made sense; he had been out on the ocean for two months with little water or nourishment and had survived an ordeal beyond my comprehension. In a sense, he was a different person. But it didn't make it any less disconcerting that I felt ill at ease with him, like I was cuddling with a stranger.

I was trying hard not to let my discomfort show, but Gray was intuitive like that, especially with me. "You're not the same with me," he said.

"What do you mean?"

"I don't know. Just . . . this feels different."

"It's because you're so much thinner," I said. "I guess I'm being careful with you."

"Because I've grown so weak," he said. "And you're so much stronger. I must disgust you now."

"No, Gray. Why would you say that?" I said, feeling unsettled by the similarity between this conversation and the one we'd had on the beach in my nightmares.

"Why wouldn't you be? I mean, look at me. I'm a shell of a man, and you—you're so beautiful. And you've been in Paris, learning new things and meeting new people. I bet you can't wait to get back."

"No, it isn't like that," I said. "I'm glad to be here with you right now. You have no idea how much I missed you. I'm strong because I had to be strong to live without you. But I never stopped loving you. I never stopped hoping you were alive."

He turned his head away. "That's not entirely true, is it?"

"What do you mean?"

"Just . . . it's stupid, really. But I could have sworn you were there with me. Out on that life raft. Making sure I held on. But sometimes I felt you letting go. Giving up. Like I said, it's stupid. I'm sure I was just hallucinating."

"No, Gray, it was more than that, and you know it. I was there for you. I was strong for you."

"But you must have had moments when you doubted. When you thought I was gone. It would make sense that you'd move on."

"But I never did, Gray," I said. "I waited for you. It's always been me and you. Nothing could change that."

I'd known Gray since we were little kids. We had a history together. A connection that went beyond time and space, maybe even beyond death. I had to believe Gray had come back to me for a reason.

"The Coast Guard is giving me a few months' leave to recuperate," he said. "They'll be keeping close tabs on me to make sure I'm ready to return to service. But I want to come visit you in Paris once I'm strong enough. The Coast Guard will pay for the trip. I mean, if you want me to come."

"Of course I do," I said. "Oh, Gray, I'm so glad you're back." I curled against his body, trying to summon the muscle memory of this act, to remember how good it used to feel to have our bodies pressed against each other, so close we almost merged into one. But now lying right beside him, I couldn't have felt more far away. What was keeping me so detached? The fact that I was leaving in a few days?

I pulled away and stared into his eyes, trying to find that warm place again, that frisson that drew us helplessly toward each other and made every moment feel electric.

"I never thought I'd see you again," he said.

"I know." I felt the tears pooling in my eyes. "It's so strange having you right here under my fingertips. I keep wanting to pinch you."

"It's strange for me, too," he said. "I wake up in a cold sweat sometimes, and I'm back in the life raft, cold and wet, and the currents are making me sick to my stomach and the sharks are nosing at my legs from beneath the raft, and I'm so thirsty I think about killing myself just so I won't feel that hunger anymore, and then I open my eyes and I see you and I hear your voice, and I think it's the most miraculous thing that I'm alive."

I reached over and stopped a tear from falling down his cheek and then I kissed the same place, right below his temple, tasting the salt of his tears, imagining that he still carried the scent of the sea on him.

This has to be right, I thought. *I wished for this. I did a spell. And the universe gave Gray back to me. I have to be grateful and do whatever I can to deserve this gift. And maybe that means staying.*

*   *   *

As my dad and I left the hospital together, I felt frustrated that I couldn't talk to him about my dilemma. I already knew where he stood. He wanted me to stay in Hull's Cove, finish my senior year at Lockwood, and get back together with Gray as if nothing had changed.

But something had changed. I had changed.

I thought about the Scorpio dog tag, how I'd lost it in Arles. I hadn't had the heart to tell Gray. But it seemed significant somehow.

I wished I could talk to my mother. She had appeared to me many times in my dreams, and I knew I could call on her when I needed to. But I wasn't sure if the voice whispering back to me was really her or just my own subconscious telling me what I knew to be true.

The next day was New Year's Eve. I spent most of the afternoon with Gray, planning our itinerary for when he came to Paris. I didn't let on that I was considering not going back because it might give him false hopes that would make my decision that much harder.

My dad had actually called Lockwood to ask about the possibility of me returning for second semester. Elise's father had taken over as interim headmaster when our old headmaster resigned, and with my father so adept at expressing his fatherly concern for my best interests, Mr. Fairchild didn't see any problems with me finishing my year at Lockwood.

The one person I hadn't talked to about all of this was Owen. I'd been texting him the entire trip, giving him updates on Gray's condition, but I'd avoided talking to him on the phone, precisely because I knew how much his opinion meant to me. But today being New Year's Eve, I couldn't help but think about last year when we'd spent New Year's together and had almost kissed on the beach. The entire history of our relationship seemed to consist of a series of almosts.

That night, my dad and Barbara went into Boston for a

New Year's bash like they always did, and Grandma and I were on our own, with no particular plans to celebrate. We should have been partying wildly. This past year had been pretty grim; the next one couldn't help but be better, right?

Grandma was watching a backlog of digitally recorded episodes of her favorite soap opera, *Salem General*, about a hospital beset not only by the usual medical maladies and melodrama but also by a bevy of witches and ghosts. I only watched it every now and then and always with my grandma, but it was pretty easy to get caught up on the story line.

"Oh my God, is that Dr. Melbourne?" I said. "I thought he was dead. He hasn't been on the show in, like, three years."

"They wanted to bring him back for the final season," my grandma explained. "It turned out he was in Haiti during the earthquake and got amnesia and didn't remember who he was. But he recalled all of his medical training, so he started working at a clinic there until, one day, he finds this shell on the beach, just like the shell he wore around his neck. And suddenly he remembers all about Megan and their kids and about his job at Salem General."

"Deus ex machina saves the day," I said.

"What?"

"Oh, it's this term I learned in AP English. It's when a conflict gets resolved by divine intervention."

"Oh," she said, turning the TV to mute as the credits rolled. "Like a miracle."

"Yeah."

"Well, his resurrection wasn't exactly a miracle," she said. "Because the reason he is suddenly back from the dead is that's he's a zombie now."

"You're kidding."

"This is *Salem General*, you know? Where Soap Meets Scares. Speaking of which, any chance of *scaring* up some champagne around here?"

I laughed. "I don't think so, but I can put some seltzer in your chardonnay."

"Good enough," she said.

I went and retrieved us some champagne flutes, thinking about the concept of deus ex machina. In literature, it was often seen as a cop-out, an easy way for the author to get the protagonist out of a sticky situation. But here I'd experienced my own real-life intervention.

Sometimes I wished I believed in God in that unequivocal way others did. While I did believe in a cosmic force that had played some role in our creation, I had no idea what form it took or how much it actually intervened in human endeavors.

Maybe the return of Gray was just the natural order of things, not the answer to a prayer to Saint Anthony or the consequence of some voodoo spell. Gray was a highly trained Coast Guard rescue swimmer who had secured a life raft before he'd disappeared. Was it really so miraculous that he had survived? Or was it just Gray's stubborn will to live?

"Grandma," I said, handing her a glass. "Do you think Gray's return is a miracle?"

"A miracle," she repeated. "Maybe. Who knows? If you figure out the ways of the universe, let me know, will you?"

I sat beside her, and we clinked our glasses to a happier new year.

"What's wrong?" she said, reading my thoughts.

"Nothing," I lied.

"Emma, I know you. And you have those little frown lines forming on your forehead. Spill it."

"I don't know, Grandma," I said. "I'm confused. Dad thinks I should stay here for the rest of my senior year now that Gray is back."

"And not go back to Paris?"

"Exactly."

"Hmmm," she said.

"He even played the 'Grandma won't be around forever' card."

"He did not!" she said. "Now I'm offended. I actually did plan on hanging around forever." She smirked at me, and I laughed. "Well, what do you want to do, Emma? What's your heart telling you?"

"That's just it," I said. "My heart is torn. On the one hand, I don't want to give up Paris and the opera and all I've worked so hard to accomplish. But on the other hand, there's Gray. I wished and prayed so hard for this, for Gray to come back to me, and now that he has, I can't abandon him, can I?"

She took a long sip of her drink, then set the glass down. "Wishes and prayers are important, Emma. They express what we want, or at least what we think we want. But it's our actions that define us. You've got to decide how you want to define yourself. By making other people happy? Or by making yourself happy."

I sighed. "I've always been a people pleaser," I said.

"I know. But doing something for yourself doesn't make you a bad person. In fact, it can be the best course of action to prevent people from getting hurt in the future."

"What do you mean?"

"You forget, I was young once, too. And I was a lot like you. I ended up marrying my high school sweetheart, and we loved each other very much."

"I wish I had known Grandpa," I said.

"I wish you had, too," she said. "He was a good man, and we had a good marriage. But I always wondered what could have been. I never allowed myself to explore other options, to go down other paths. I wasn't as brave as you."

"Brave? I'm not brave."

"Sure you are. Going to Paris by yourself? That took guts. And living through this nightmare with Gray? Emma, you've been so strong, much stronger than I would have been. And now you have to make a decision that is going to hurt someone. You can't avoid it. And it takes strength to realize that and do it anyway. I know you'll make the right decision, whatever you choose." She held up her empty glass and shook it. "Refill?"

"You bet. Hey, it's almost midnight," I said when I saw the kitchen clock.

"Let's break out the noisemakers."

I was gathering the pots and pans when my phone rang. I pulled it out of my pocket and looked at the display, grinning stupidly. "Owen!"

"Happy New Year!" he said.

And then it occurred to me that it was just before six A.M. in Paris. He had woken himself up early so he could call me at midnight here.

"I can't believe you remembered, time change and all," I said.

"How could I forget you on New Year's Eve?" he said. "It's a tradition."

"Oh, so two years in a row, and we have a tradition now?"

"That's how traditions start," he said.

I loved hearing his voice. At that moment I wanted to be wherever he was. We caught each other up on the past few days we'd spent apart, feeling like it was much longer than it had been.

"I'm sorry I didn't call you at midnight there," I said. "I was still at the hospital."

"Of course you were," he said. "How was Gray today?"

"Better," I said. "He thinks he might come to Paris when he's feeling a little stronger."

"Really?" Owen said. Immediately, I was sorry I'd told him. His buoyant tone deflated in an instant.

"Owen, I really miss you," I said, trying to make up for the mood shift.

"I know," he said. "I didn't want to call because I knew

you'd be busy. But I hadn't realized how much I'd gotten used to hearing your voice every day."

"My voice?" I said, doing a terrible falsetto.

"Still you joke," he said. "But secretly you know you want to belt out an aria onstage. You're a closet diva."

"Oh, right," I said. "I think one diva is enough for this show."

"Do you mean Elise or Flynn?"

"Good point," I said.

"Flynn's already shopping for his costume. He said he wants his Phantom to be 'wicked sexy,' not a 'foppish tool in a tux and tails,' his words, not mine."

I laughed. "It sounds like everyone is in usual form."

"Except me," he said.

"Why not you?"

"Because Raoul is without his Christine."

"But I'm not Christine anymore, remember?"

"You are to me," he said.

And three days later, I boarded a plane back to Paris.

CHAPTER 18

When I arrived at the airport, I had this foolish fantasy that Owen would be waiting for me at baggage claim. I knew it wouldn't happen, but I hoped.

Elise was back a few days early, too, but she was miserable. Over the break, she'd found out that she got wait-listed at Berklee. You would have thought her life was over.

"Elise, you got wait-listed," I said. "That's incredible."

"It's humiliating," she said. "I might as well go to community college."

"Don't you think you're being a bit dramatic?"

"Hello," she said, gesturing to herself as a reminder that drama was what she was good at.

"Being wait-listed means they're still considering you, and besides, you're probably going to get into all your other schools."

"But I don't want to go to any other school," she said. "Berklee was the one."

"How do you know?" I said. "Maybe the universe is trying to tell you that you belong somewhere else. Or that there are infinite places you could belong. With all the stuff going on with your parents, I would have thought you'd welcome the opportunity to go far away for school."

"Stop making such sense," she said, continuing to pout even though I thought I saw the glimmer of a smile. "What about you? Are you thinking it's going to be Miami now that Gray is back?"

"I don't know," I said. "There's a lot to consider."

"Like what?"

Ugh. How could I explain this to her without sounding like a horrible person? *Well, even though my boyfriend survived a treacherous two months at sea during which his only thought was of me, all I can think about now is Owen.*

"Things with Gray are complicated. This whole experience has been surreal. We need to take a few steps back and make sure we're in this for the right reasons."

"Huh," she said, looking shocked.

"What?"

"I just always thought you considered him your *soul mate* or something. Does Gray know you feel this way?"

"Um . . . I don't know."

"Well, maybe you should tell him before he flies more than three thousand miles to see you."

Elise wasn't assuaging my feelings of guilt one bit. But she did remind me that I had to talk to Mademoiselle Veilleux to make sure that if Gray did visit, it was okay for him to stay here. My stomach lurched a little at the thought of him staying in my room for several weeks. Maybe that was exactly what we needed. Maybe the only problem was that we'd been apart for so long and needed time to reconnect and remember how good we were together.

After lunch, I walked over to Mademoiselle Veilleux's office. As usual, she was dressed impeccably in a sheer blouse over a camisole and black wide-leg trousers, her hair twisted into a chignon.

"Emma, chère," she said, standing to hug me. "How is your boyfriend doing?"

"Better, thanks," I said.

"I was thinking about you over break. What a miracle."

"I know," I said. "I did say a prayer to Saint Anthony."

"Ah, so perhaps it was fate that you ended up here at Saint-Antoine. Meant to be."

Meant to be. The universe and everyone in it seemed to want me and Gray together forever.

"I actually have a favor to ask," I said. "The Coast Guard agreed to send Gray wherever he wants while he recuperates. Sort of a hard-earned vacation. And he wants to come here."

"Of course he does!" she said. "How romantic."

"Yeah," I said, feeling my palms begin to sweat. "I was wondering if it would be okay if . . . if he stayed here at the dorm."

"Bien sûr," she said. "Of course, he will have to stay with one of the male students. Then again, these are coed dorms, and you are eighteen."

Was she giving me carte blanche to stay with my boyfriend?

"I'll ask Georges or Louis," I said. "But thank you for letting him stay. I appreciate it."

"Anything for *l'amour,*" she said. "Oh, how are rehearsals coming for your *Phantom*?"

"We haven't started yet," I said. "We won't be able to use the Studio space at the opera until their Debussy series closes. We're not really sure where to rehearse."

"I have just the place," she said. "The chapel."

"The chapel? Here?"

"I know it's small, but it is soundproofed, and it has a surprisingly good sound system. Plus, no one's ever there." She laughed. "You'll have plenty of privacy."

"But . . . what about God?"

"I do not think God will mind some beautiful music in his house."

I smiled.

I was about to leave when I thought about Crespeau and all the years he'd invested in his unrequited love for Mademoiselle Veilleux. My well-intentioned matchmaking on Christmas Eve hadn't done the trick. But I wasn't out of ideas yet. "Mademoiselle, can I ask you a question?"

"Oui."

"Monsieur Crespeau has been here for a long time, right?"

"Many years."

"Did you ever wonder why he stays here?" I asked. "I mean, he's intelligent and talented and kind. He could be so much more than a handyman."

"Oh, Emma," she sighed. "He was broken after his parents died. He couldn't move on. And when I got hired as headmistress, I thought I was doing him a favor by giving him a permanent job."

"How do you mean?"

"In high school, I knew he was in love with me. And I loved him, too. Just not in the way he did. But I liked knowing he would always be there for me. I didn't realize how much I was hurting him until that day when I went away with my boyfriend, and he tried to come to the train station to stop us. I've always felt partially responsible for what happened to his parents. Like I owed him something. But I wonder if it kills him to be so close to me."

"I think it does," I said. "But he doesn't blame you. He only blames himself."

"I know, Emma, because that's the kind of man he is. The world is a sad, strange place."

"It is, isn't it?"

I left her office, feeling overwhelmed by emotion. I owed it to Gray to give us another chance, to try to recapture what we'd once had.

*   *   *

Over the next few weeks, Gray and I began Skyping again. Slowly, our former dynamic resumed, complete with our requisite sign-off of "I love you" followed by "I know." But in a way that I didn't want to admit to myself, we were playing old roles, delivering lines memorized so long ago they had almost lost their meaning.

As the new semester got underway, academics took a backseat to rehearsals for our Phantom opera. My applications and transcripts had been sent to my schools long ago, so grades hardly mattered anymore. And I was barely worried about my performance on the AP exams. The only class I really cared about was Opera II, taught by Luke again. Since our school had two teams that had advanced in the competition, Luke took a more active role in advising us as we blocked out scenes, revised the librettos, and rehearsed the songs.

First, we had to scale back our cast list, since we only had three solid performers. Having been replaced by Elise, I took over the role of director. But things got off to a rocky start. For one thing, Owen was being rather cold toward me since he'd discovered Gray was coming to visit. I understood why, but I didn't know what to do to change our dynamic. He would dutifully listen to my notes after each rehearsal, but I no longer felt like we were collaborating as we had during the fall. He was merely doing his time.

The other difficult part was that he and Elise seemed to be getting close again. I knew it was probably just the intensity of their roles and having to perform together each day as Raoul and Christine. They had acted together in last year's production of *The Crucible,* and their chemistry onstage had been palpable. At least I hoped it was just stage chemistry. But for a moment, I couldn't help wishing that I was playing Christine again. Dark thoughts occasionally blindsided me—

visions of Elise croaking like Carlotta in the original *Phantom,* losing her voice so I would have to replace her.

Of course, since Mademoiselle Veilleux had given us permission to use the chapel, she'd extended the same offer to Jean-Claude's group. We negotiated a rehearsal schedule, and Jean-Claude, Georges, and Yseult claimed the time slot before us. But they would always stay over their time. Not to mention, the chapel would reek of smoke after they left.

I tried to put these tensions out of my head and focus on Gray's impending visit at the end of the month. A voice inside me kept telling me what I was doing wasn't fair, that I should tell him not to come. But each time I imagined letting him go and moving on without him, guilt rose up in me again, that feeling of obligation to the gods or saints or forces that had reunited us.

On the day his flight arrived, I met him at the airport. He walked into the baggage area, looking very tired but a little more like his old self. His hair had been trimmed and he'd gained some weight and some color in his cheeks. And when I hugged him, I could no longer feel his ribs.

"I've missed you so much," he said, clinging to me like he was afraid I wasn't real.

"I can't believe you're really here," I said, as we wheeled his bags to the taxi stand. "I have to keep pinching myself."

He reached over and pinched me playfully, like the old Gray. I smiled, and he let his bag drop to the ground so he could kiss me.

It should have been terribly romantic. Then why was I dissecting everything and feeling a little uncomfortable around him? Gray kept finding excuses to touch me on the ride home, and after all this time apart, his touch should have been welcome. But I kept fidgeting, feeling like the taxi doors were closing in on me.

Finally, we got back to my room, and I was relieved when Gray asked if he could take a shower. I needed some time to get my thoughts together, to moderate my feelings so my discomfort didn't show plainly on my face. But I was also worried.

When Gray came out of that bathroom, he would want what any red-blooded nineteen-year-old would want after being separated from his girlfriend for six months. And that terrified me.

He came out ten minutes later with a towel wrapped around his waist. I don't know why this surprised me, but a jolt of adrenaline raced through my limbs. He was still pretty thin and his skin was tanned in a way that looked almost permanent. But his eyes had a spark of life in them again. I burned with nostalgic longing and threw my arms around him, shocked to find that I was crying.

"What's wrong?" he said, pulling back so he could wipe the tears from my eyes.

"I'm just so happy you're here," I said.

"I am," he said, placing his hands on my waist. "I'm really here."

And then I broke down again, unrepentantly sobbing. Once I started, I couldn't stop.

Gray led me to the bed and rubbed my back until I had calmed myself. I took a wad of tissues and wiped off my face, and Gray traced a line of tearstain down my cheek. Then he placed both of his hands on my cheeks and stared into my eyes with an intensity that made my insides twirl.

He leaned in to kiss me, and some familiar ache drew me toward him. His lips pressed on mine, and for a moment, we were back—Emma and Gray, meant to be—our kiss petal-soft and sweet. His palm cradled my neck, and then he was guiding me to the bed, the weight of his body so thrilling and right. I kissed him back a little harder, and we switched places so I was on top, removing his towel while he removed my shirt, my bra, my jeans.

Then he pushed me away suddenly, jerking back toward the headboard.

"What's wrong?" I asked.

"The scorpion tag. Where is it?"

"Gray, I was going to tell you. I just forgot, with all the craziness of the past few weeks . . . I lost the necklace."

"You lost it? What the hell, Emma?"

I stood up, hiking my jeans back on. Gray pulled the sheets up to cover himself. "Look," I said, "I didn't do it on purpose. I was walking around one day, and when I got back, it was gone."

"Were you with him?"

"With who?" I said, but I could feel my cheeks burning.

"You know who," he said.

"Gray, why are you acting like this?"

"Because I know something's going on between you two."

"Why would you say that?"

"Because of the grasshopper!" he said. My insides froze.

How could he know? I'd hidden it away in a drawer.

"Gray, what are you talking about?"

"I'm . . . starting to remember something . . . but, I definitely saw you with a grasshopper pin. And Owen gave it to you, didn't he? Emma, you know what I'm talking about. Don't pretend you don't."

So Gray'd had the dreams, too. I stood with my mouth open, trying to think what to say.

"You make me sick," he said suddenly, leaping off the bed, grabbing his clothes, and locking himself in the bathroom.

I heard him hastily get dressed, then he came out and grabbed his bag, heading toward the door. "Gray, where are you going?" I asked.

"Out."

"You just got here. Let's talk about this."

"I'm afraid of what I'll do to you if I stay," he said, flashing me a look that horrified me. Then he left and slammed the door behind him, so hard that the new mirror Crespeau had installed came crashing to the floor.

CHAPTER 19

When Gray came back three hours later, he was remorseful. He knelt down in front of me where I sat on the bed and gripped my legs, laying his head in my lap and begging forgiveness.

"Where did you go?" I asked.

"I went running."

"For three hours?"

"Well, I stopped now and then and walked around the sights. I was trying to calm myself down. I hate when I get like that."

"Does it happen often?" I said.

"More lately," he said. "I don't know why. I'm starting to remember what happened on that life raft. I must have blocked it out. But being here with you is triggering something in me. It scares me."

"What does it feel like?"

"Like something's raging inside me, and I have to run to get rid of the bad energy. And then after a few hours I'm fine again."

He dropped his head into my lap, and I ran my fingers through his hair, hoping it would soothe him.

"It wasn't just the grasshopper pin that set me off," he said.

"No?"

"Since I've been back, I can't seem to . . . I can't . . . well, you know."

"No, I don't. What is it?"

"Don't make me say it, Emma," he said.

And then I understood. "Oh." He looked up at me, shame in his eyes. "Gray, it's understandable. What you've been through was so traumatic. Give yourself a break."

I pulled him up so he was sitting next to me on the bed and propped myself on my knees to face him. "It's going to take some time, but you will be able to . . . feel again." And suddenly, it became a challenge to me. I wanted to be the one to make him feel again. "Besides, we can have fun trying."

I crawled onto his lap and ran my fingers across his scalp, leaning in to kiss his neck, feeling him squirm beneath my touch. "Emma, don't," he said.

"Why?"

"It just makes me feel damaged, because I know I won't feel anything."

"How do you know?"

"I just do."

"Okay then," I said, moving off him and getting off the bed.

"This was what I was afraid of."

"Then let's get out of here and not think about it," I said. "Let's do something." The truth was, I was starting to feel claustrophobic again.

"I'm too tired."

"I guess you would be after running for three hours," I said. "You mind if I go out for just a little bit? I need some air."

"When will you be back?" he said.

"I don't know. I won't be long."

I felt such a welcome sense of relief when I emerged from the stifling hot dorm into the cold winter air outside. What I really wanted was to find Owen, but I knew that wasn't the best idea.

So I walked to Pont des Arts, the bridge where I had secured the padlock. I had a strange desire to see if it had changed or fallen off, to find some outward sign of what I was feeling inside: scared, confused, guilty. But the padlock looked exactly the same.

When I got back to my room, Gray was asleep. But his sleep looked restless and haunted. He jerked awake when a floorboard creaked, sitting upright. For a moment, he was stuck in some liminal space between slumber and wakefulness, screaming at something from his nightmare and scratching the air as if batting demons away.

"Gray, it's okay. Wake up," I said, trying to still his arms.

He finally woke, staring at me as if he had no idea where he was. After two months on a life raft, I imagined that happened a lot.

"What's wrong?" he said.

"You were having a nightmare."

"Yeah, I get those now." He was breathless and sweaty.

"How often?"

"A few times a night."

"A few times a night?" I said. "Isn't there anything you can take? Sleeping pills or something?"

"I don't think they would work," he said.

"Why don't you ask your doctor?"

"I can't tell my doctor."

"Why?"

"Because the Coast Guard won't let me back if they find out I've lost it."

"Gray, you haven't lost it. I'm sure they'd understand a few nightmares considering what you've been through."

"Emma, you don't know what the Coast Guard is like. You can't show any signs of weakness."

"Well, you can in front of me," I said.

But he just turned over in the bed, exhausted, and fell back to sleep in a matter of minutes. I crept around my room, trying not to make any noise. But it was difficult getting anything done without disturbing him.

Gray slept a lot during those first weeks. And he often woke in the middle of the night, sometimes crying out as if in pain. But when I'd ask about the nightmares, he'd shut me out and tell me everything was fine.

I didn't try to seduce him again, so our nights were spent next to each other physically but as far away emotionally as possible. And yet, every time I came home from classes or rehearsals, Gray grilled me on my whereabouts, acting more possessive than he'd ever been before. But he refused to come out with me and my friends, telling me he wasn't ready to see anyone. Elise and Owen and Flynn kept asking for him, and I had to keep making excuses for his absence.

And then one day, he showed up at the chapel during one of our rehearsals. Elise was practicing the song Christine first sings after visiting the Phantom's lair. I didn't even know Gray was there until I saw Owen's jaw drop and then harden into stone.

I turned around, and Gray was standing at the back of the chapel with his arms folded across his chest, like we were supposed to carry on as usual even though this was the first time he'd shown his face outside my dorm room. Elise stopped singing, then stepped offstage and ran toward him. I was shocked when, without a word, she threw her arms around him. Gray seemed taken aback as well, even more so by the fact that Elise was crying. But they had dated for six months during our sophomore year. It was totally normal for her to be relieved that he was safe and standing in front of us now, apparently healthy and intact.

"Gray, it's so good to see you," she said.

"Thanks. It's good to be here," he choked out. I knew it was a lie, a politeness that no longer came naturally to Gray.

Owen and Flynn were a little more wary around him. Flynn shook his hand and made a few offhand remarks about him being "a tough son of a bitch." Owen shook his hand out of obligation, but it was clear there was no love lost between them.

"I'm so glad you decided to come watch our rehearsal," I said.

"Oh, is he staying?" Owen asked.

"Um, I don't know. Gray, are you staying?" I asked. He shrugged. "You're welcome to. Right, guys?"

"Of course," Elise said.

Flynn and Owen muttered some lukewarm affirmations, and it occurred to me that I was treating Gray with kid gloves. Everyone else was following my lead.

Gray took a seat in one of the pews, and I attempted to resume my directorial duties even though the atmosphere in the room had become thick with tension, like someone had swung an incense censer around.

Elise picked up where she'd left off, singing the lines:

> *I'll be your guardian angel*
> *If you'll be my tragic muse.*
> *Between this world and yours,*
> *I have no will to choose.*
>
> *Take me in your arms,*
> *Don't let me answer no.*
> *And when I say I love you,*
> *Tell me that you know.*

Gray had never heard these lines before, but he must have recognized us in the song, must have noticed how I'd incorporated our tortured meetings in the dreamscape into the lyrics. It took all my resolve not to turn around to see his response.

"Okay," I said when she'd finished. "That was great. Now let's try the duet between Christine and Raoul."

Owen ascended the altar, and Flynn cued up the sound track. This was the song Owen and I had written together, and it occurred to me now how much we'd based Raoul and Christine's relationship on our own conflicted friendship.

Owen began singing:

> *Come away from the darkness;*
> *Let me make you whole again.*
> *I'm the one who's at your side,*
> *As your lover and your friend.*
>
> *Whatever you need from me,*
> *I can be that man.*
> *The one who makes you smile,*
> *The one who holds your hand.*

And then Elise responded:

> *I want to let you in;*
> *I want the day not night.*
> *The darkness is my prison;*
> *My salvation is your light.*
>
> *But fear holds me in shackles.*
> *I'm afraid to take your hand.*
> *A dark force haunts and holds me.*
> *It will not let me stand.*

The more lines they sang, the more uncomfortable I became, fearing what Gray would think if he recognized the parallels.

Everyone seemed on edge that day, and none of us was at the top of our game. Elise left with Owen and Flynn to grab some lunch, but Gray said he wasn't hungry so we ended up walking back to the dorm ourselves.

Finally, I decided to confront the silence head-on. "So what did you think?"

"About what?" he said.

"About the rehearsal? The songs."

"They were . . . good. Your friends can sing."

He wasn't making this easy. "So what do you want to do now?" I said. "You're not hungry. And you seem in no mood to talk."

"Sorry, I'm just a little tired."

"It's okay," I said. "We can go back to the room if you want."

"No." He stopped walking.

"Okay . . . well, what then?"

"I don't know, but I don't want to go back there. I feel like you want to hide me away so I don't embarrass you."

"Gray, what are you talking about? It's you who hasn't wanted to come out. I've been begging you to come say hi to everyone. But you weren't ready, and I didn't want to pressure you."

"The only reason I didn't want to see anyone was because I knew how you felt."

"Gray, you're acting paranoid."

"Great," he said. "Now you're psychoanalyzing me?"

"No, I'm not psychoanalyzing you. I'm saying you're paranoid if you think I didn't want you to come out with my friends. Because that's not how I feel at all."

"I just want things to go back to the way they were. When everything was easy. Just you and me against the world."

He stared off into the distance like he was trying to conjure some wisp of a dream of how things used to be. So much had happened to him over the past few months that I wondered if he was remembering clearly or if he was romanticizing our past.

"Gray, I want that, too. But you're here now, and we can

create new memories. I don't want to go backward. I want to go forward."

"And that's just the trouble, isn't it?"

"What do you mean?"

"I'm your past. And everyone here is your present."

"And you're here now, too, so you're a part of my present. So what's the problem?"

"I don't know. I feel stuck. Like I can't get out from under this . . . suffocating tangle. And the more I try to free myself, the more tangled up I get."

"You're still working through everything that happened to you," I said, trying to take his hand. He flinched. "You have to give it time."

"Time," he said. "I don't have time."

"What do you mean?"

"I mean, I go back to the States in four weeks, and if I pass the physical, they ship me back to Miami, and I go far away from you, and I lose you all over again."

"Gray, that's ridiculous. Think of the summer, how often we Skyped. We don't need to be together to stay connected, remember? We've got this."

I made a fist and pounded my heart, then pounded his, recalling a line from *Jane Eyre,* in which Rochester tells Jane: *It feels as though I had a string tied here under my left rib where my heart is, tightly knotted to you in a similar fashion. And when you go . . . with all that distance between us, I am afraid that this cord will be snapped, and I shall bleed inwardly.*

And yet Jane had returned to her Rochester and promised to love him even when she found him blind and enfeebled. Rochester could hardly believe she had returned to him or that she would devote her life to someone so damaged.

In many ways, my life was coming full circle now. I had lost myself in *Jane Eyre* two years ago when I first fell for Gray, who, like Rochester, had been a cocky young man haunted by his past. And now just like Rochester, Gray was broken and doubted my devotion. In a place very dark and hidden inside me, I doubted it, too.

"Let's go away," he said suddenly, a faint gleam returning to his eyes.

"Away?"

"Just you and me. I think that's the problem. Since I've come, you're always with other people. You and I are best when it's just the two of us. Let's go somewhere and try to find ourselves again."

"I do have the winter holiday coming up."

"When? Because I want to go now."

"February fifteenth."

"All right, we'll go then. You think you can take off the day before? I'd like to be away for Valentine's Day."

"I think so," I said, smiling at this touch of the old romantic Gray. "I only have Opera and French on Fridays. I can probably skip. Where do you want to go?"

He told me he'd always wanted to visit Dunkirk, the site of a WWII battle in which over 350,000 British and French soldiers had gotten trapped on the beaches. The British wanted to evacuate them by sea, thinking they'd only be able to save a fraction of them, but the navy called on civilians to help. For ten days straight, ordinary citizens in small fishing boats began arriving to evacuate the soldiers, even though the Germans were shelling the area the entire time. Many civilians lost their lives, but in the end almost all of the men were saved. People called it "the Miracle at Dunkirk."

"Dunkirk is supposed to be a pretty seaside town," he said. "We could get a hotel on the beach."

"Gray, it's February."

"So? We used to walk the beach at Hull's Cove in the winter."

"That's true."

"It'll be like old times."

I smiled, feeling a little relieved by Gray's change of mood and heart. But also a little apprehensive about going away with him. It was one thing to be stuck together in my room, surrounded by other students on all sides, and quite another thing to spend the Valentine's Day weekend with him in a hotel room overlooking the ocean.

That next week with our romantic holiday on the horizon, Gray's spirits seemed to lift. He let me go to my rehearsals without giving me the third degree and even joined us at the dining hall a few times. Sophie and Yseult eyed him with interest from the table across from us, and I couldn't help but beam with pride that Gray was mine. That he had chosen me.

But despite the miracle that had happened to Gray on that stormy sea, we had a tempest brewing in a Bermuda Triangle of our own. Owen and Gray couldn't be in each other's company for more than a half hour before things got awkward and tense. It was uncharacteristic of Owen to act cold and hostile, but he could barely make eye contact with Gray, and every time he looked at me with those puppy-dog eyes, I felt like the most fickle and disloyal person ever.

Worse, I had to face him at rehearsals and hear my own words being sung to me, hear how his voice caught at certain lines. I wanted to talk to him, to explain my behavior, but as soon as rehearsals ended Owen would gather up his things and take off before I could reach him.

And then things started to go missing. A mask we'd taken from the masquerade ball to use for the Phantom. A page from my libretto with the duet between Erik and Christine. And then the sound track CD Owen had spent hours recording in his friend's studio for me. We asked Jean-Claude if he had seen any of the items.

"No," he said. "It must be the curse of the Phantom."

"Shut the hell up, dude," Flynn said, looking like he was at his breaking point. "I'm the Phantom, and I'm anything but cursed."

"I am not talking about your Phantom," Jean-Claude said. "I am talking about the Bastille Ghost."

"Not this again," I said.

"What? You still don't believe me?" he said. "Even after a Christmas tree almost killed your boyfriend?"

I didn't bother to correct him. "Why would the Bastille Ghost care about our production?" I asked.

"Imagine you were imprisoned without trial in the Bastille," Jean-Claude said. "You waste away in a filthy cell as the Revolution rages outside. No one will listen to your pleas. No one sees you weeping at night. You have no touch of tenderness, no hope for love. And you die there, cold and alone. And in death, you are cursed to wander that place for eternity. One hundred years later, they build a school where the prison once stood. Young people move here and there, beautiful and carefree and in love, and you know you can never be a part of that world again. So you grow bitter. You come to loathe the sight of lovers kissing. You begin by taking their things, just to prove you're there, that you exist. But then your anger rises, and sometimes, it gets the better of you, and you can't help but lash out."

"That's bullshit," Flynn said.

"I don't know," Yseult said. "There was that fire in your room, Emma. Well, Mademoiselle Veilleux's room."

"It's an old building," Owen said. "She probably used too many extension cords or something."

"Believe what you like," Jean-Claude said. "But don't say we didn't warn you."

They left the chapel finally, leaving us to begin our rehearsal. It didn't go well. Flynn and Owen were both on edge, and Elise was distracted and couldn't hit her notes. Then she beat herself up about it and sulked.

"Are you letting Jean-Claude get to you?" I asked.

"No," she said. "Well, maybe. I just have a bad feeling about this."

"Don't let him get inside your head," Owen said. "That's exactly what he wants to do. Psych us out."

"Well, it's working," she said.

By the time Valentine's Day weekend arrived, I was looking forward to a break from school and people as much as Gray was. I had done a little research on Dunkirk and found that there wasn't much to see beyond the beach where the evacuation had taken place. I convinced Gray that after our historical research trip to Dunkirk, we'd drive on another hour to Bruges, a Belgian town that boasted quaint medieval streets, charming canals, and Belgian chocolate. It seemed the ideal destination for Valentine's Day.

We rented a Peugeot that Gray drove, since my manual transmission skills were a bit rusty. But I noticed he wasn't quite as adept at navigating as I'd remembered. A few times, he nearly drove off the road, distracted by the sights. I also noticed his hands trembling as he shifted gears, like he was nervous. The word that came to my mind as I watched him drive was *shell-shocked.*

We drove to the nearby suburb of Dunkirk called Malo-les-Bains so Gray could see the beach where the evacuation had occurred, now covered in a thick blanket of snow. The landscape reminded me a lot of the New England coastline. Gray walked me through the entire mission as I scanned the harbor, the white beach a blank canvas on which I could almost imagine the hordes of exhausted soldiers, piles of dead horses, rusting artillery, and the armada of little ships filled with ordinary heroes.

I volunteered to drive the hour to Bruges to give Gray a break, and we arrived just a little before dark. We had booked a room at a charming red-and-white-brick guesthouse with a tiny orangerie in the back. Our room was at the top of the house and had sloped ceilings, a fireplace, and a skylight that caught the snow. It was small but cozy.

We settled in, changed into warmer clothes, then walked

around in search of a place to eat. At night, the town looked like something out of *Harry Potter*. The narrow, gingerbread-cute houses along the canal were lit warmly from within, shining their reflections onto the waterways. Rowboats were moored in front of the houses like cars parked on a curb.

We found a casual café off the market square that sold the Belgian specialty *moules-frites,* mussels with fries dipped in mayonnaise. Along with a couple beers, the meal ran us over 40 euros. Bruges was every bit as expensive as Paris.

After dinner, we strolled the canals, climbing up and down the ubiquitous stone bridges and watching flurries fall in lazy swirls to the water. As we were climbing one bridge with a striking view of the cathedral spire, Gray grabbed my arm and pulled me toward the edge.

"We've known each other our whole lives, right?" he said.

"Right," I answered, shivering. The North Sea air was bitter cold.

"We have a past together. I know it's been rocky at times, but you don't just throw away years of history."

"Of course not," I said.

He looked down at the river, like he was trying to channel some of its momentum. "I know I haven't been easy to deal with since I got here," he said. "Part of it is jealousy. I'm so in love with you it's hard to see you happy without me. Because I can't be happy without you. I need you."

"Oh, Gray. I need you, too."

"No, that's just it. You don't anymore. And that's okay. I want you to be independent. I want you to be happy on your own. I'm glad you have good friends to watch over you when I can't be here," he said, with his hands in his pockets. "Like you said before, we have our past together, and your friends claim your present. But I want to claim your future. Will you marry me, Emma?"

He opened a clamshell box to reveal what looked very much like a diamond engagement ring. And even though this was the appropriate thing to be holding given what he'd just asked me, my cold-addled brain wasn't connecting the dots.

A funny thing happens to a girl when she hears this particular question. No matter how many objections float around in the rational part of her brain, there's another part of her that's been fed such a steady diet of fairy tales and romantic movies that her knee-jerk reaction is to say yes, not to ruin the moment with practical concerns like age or readiness or even whether she truly wants to spend the rest of her life with this person.

And yet, some tiny gnawing in my gut gave me pause, just enough pause for Gray's face to fall. His change in mood was so profound that I knew no amount of belated enthusiasm on my part could have brought him back from that ledge of disappointment.

"Your answer's no, isn't it?"

"No," I said. "I mean, it's no answer yet. I need time, Gray. We're so young. What's the rush? We love each other. We don't have to make this decision right now, do we?" I was rambling, not wanting to stop talking for fear of what Gray might say or do. What he did say surprised me.

"Here, I want you to have it anyway," he said, foisting the ring on me. "You don't have to wear it, but I want you to keep it with you while you consider."

"Gray, I can't."

"Emma, please do this for me. It's all I ask."

I took the ring and slid it into my coat pocket, where I imagined it burning a hole of guilt into my chest.

Even though Bruges was a perfect town to explore over a snowy winter weekend, it was clear that my non-answer had succeeded in sucking all the romance out of it. I tried to explain later, even less articulately, why I couldn't give him an immediate answer, how I needed a few days—a week at most—but by the time we got back to the guesthouse, Gray no longer wanted to talk about it. In fact, he didn't seem to want to talk, period.

So Valentine's Day ended in romantic disaster, with a failed proposal from Gray and a sleepless night for me. In the morning, Gray was fast asleep, so I snuck out and asked the hostess if it would be too much trouble to bring our breakfast to the room. It was a conciliatory gesture—breakfast in bed—but I knew it would do little to assuage the pain of my implied rejection.

Because that's exactly what it had been. I couldn't agree to marry Gray. Not now when I doubted his mental soundness. When I doubted my own feelings for him. It wasn't a few days I needed. It was more like a few years.

But how could I tell him that in a way he would understand? After the horrific nightmare he'd endured at sea, he wanted things settled. He wanted the rest of his life to be a safe trajectory of events in which he could control all the elements. My saying no had not been a part of his plan.

I could see all of this plainly, but it didn't make it any easier to explain it to him. He would have to be patient, to trust that events would unfold according to their own plan, and perhaps to accept the possibility that despite our earlier romantic sentiments, we weren't destined to be together after all.

I tried to salvage the rest of the weekend with an itinerary that included a chocolate shop and a brewery (both with free samples), a trip to the Groeninge Museum, and finally, a stop at one of Bruges's famous "discussion cafés," where guests could sit around for hours listening to jazz and talking politics over beakers of cherry lambic.

But at night, we slept facing away from each other, and everything felt tainted. Church bells ushered us home on Sunday morning. My heart felt heavy as we drove back to Paris, like we'd come to the end of an era together. Like nothing could ever return to the way it had been.

When we got back, Gray grew even more withdrawn. He'd been holding on to that trip as our possible means of salvation, and now that it was over, he had nothing to look forward to. And we still had a week of holiday to endure before I'd have an excuse to go to classes and get away from his brooding. I was surprised Gray didn't opt to go home early, and, I'm ashamed to admit, a little disappointed. Since he'd arrived, my life had not been my own. And I was in a constant state of emotional upheaval, like that saint in that painting we'd seen at the museum, drawn and quartered by four horses pulling him in opposite directions.

I needed to talk to someone objective, someone who might have some idea of what I was going through. One day while Gray was napping, I went in search of Crespeau and found him in the administrative building, waxing the floors of the lobby where the masquerade ball had been. The room looked so plain and ordinary now without the velvet fabric, the Christmas tree, and sparkly lights.

"Hey," I said, waving to him over the noise of the buffer.

When he saw me, he shut off the machine. "Emma, this is a pleasant surprise. How are you?"

"I've been better," I said. "Gray and I are . . . struggling. Rehearsals are going terribly. And some ghost is stealing our things."

"A ghost?"

"Yeah," I said, laughing at how silly it sounded. "Monsieur Crespeau, have you ever heard of the Bastille Ghost?"

"Hmm?"

"Some of the kids told me about him when I first arrived here. Apparently, he wanders this neighborhood where the Bastille once stood, a shell of his former self, his life stolen because of a mistake he made long ago. Now he haunts these hallways to remind himself what it feels like to be young and alive. And I think he's been stealing our stuff."

Monsieur Crespeau chuckled. "Le fantôme? C'est moi."

"What?"

"I am your ghost. I clean up after you in the chapel and sometimes I pick up a memento or two. I must confess I listened to your CD and forgot to return it."

"I'm so relieved," I said.

"Your songs are beautiful. Heartbreaking and beautiful. He inspired you, no doubt, your Gray."

I frowned, knowing it was true. "Why can't we let go of our first loves?" I asked suddenly.

He sighed, surely thinking of his long-burning flame for Mademoiselle Veilleux. "I don't know. They take hold of our hearts, don't they?"

"Exactly. And just when we think we're ready to move on, we freeze."

"I know," he said. "I've been frozen here for twenty years."

"Oh, Monsieur Crespeau."

He smiled sadly. "Do you still love him?"

"I think a part of me always will. But it was a different girl who fell in love with Gray. I'm ready to move on, but I'm afraid of hurting him."

"It will hurt more the longer you wait. Trust me on this. You must tell him."

"Then why haven't you ever told Mademoiselle Veilleux how you feel? I mean, I know you're afraid of her response, but come on, it's been years. Why can't you—"

"Because," he shouted, "that's exactly what I'd been about to do when . . ." He thrust a hand over his eyes.

"When the car crashed," I said, my heart breaking for him. "Oh, Monsieur Crespeau, I'm so sorry I pushed."

He wiped his brow and looked at me. "It is all right," he said. "But I can't help thinking I was punished for my selfishness."

"Your selfishness? How could you be selfish for loving someone?"

"I wanted too much. I was not good enough for her. I never deserved her."

"That's not true!" I said.

"Oh, Emma, you should have heard her sing *La Bohème*. She was exquisite. I used to hide in the back of the theater listening to her and watching her, mesmerized. I taught myself to play piano and to dance because I thought it would impress her. But she never noticed."

"How do you know?"

"Emma, you see her going out with a different young man every week. How can I compete with that?"

"Did you ever think that the reason she does that is she's just as lonely as you are? Maybe she's been waiting for you, too."

"No, it is too late for us," he said. "If it were going to happen, it would have by now. The stars do not align for us."

"The stars don't control your fate, Monsieur Crespeau. You do. If you want something, you've got to make it happen." I thought about my grandma's reminder that our actions define us.

"Says the girl who refuses to tell her boyfriend the truth," he said. "Aren't we a pair?"

"Yes, we are," I said. "You know, I always thought Gray and I were soul mates, that we were 'destined' to be together forever. I even put a padlock on the bridge at Pont des Arts. If I break up with Gray, it feels like I'll be breaking some cosmic promise I made."

"The padlock is only a symbol," Crespeau said. "It is not reality. You must not be a slave to your first love like I have been."

"I know; it's just so difficult."

"Come with me," he said. "I have just the thing you need."

"What?"

"You'll see."

I followed Monsieur Crespeau outside to his toolshed,

where he found a pair of bolt cutters and wielded them in front of me.

"Seriously?" I said.

"You begin moving forward with one step," he said. "Or one cut, in your case."

"No, I couldn't."

"Then I will help you," he said. "As you've tried to help me."

We walked together through the city, chatting about life and love, until we came to the Pont des Arts. The man selling the padlocks eyed us suspiciously, but Crespeau looked so resolute that the man didn't question us.

When we found my padlock, Crespeau handed the bolt cutters to me and gave me a brief demo on how to use them.

"Emma," he said. "This is just one symbol of your past with Gray, but you must say good-bye in small increments. It is the only way to mourn your losses without losing yourself."

The bolt cutters were heavy in my hands, but I knew Crespeau was right. I pulled apart the blades and snipped down on the padlock, watching it drop into the Seine, feeling a sharp pain inside, like a part of me was breaking off with it. But the pain was followed by a slackening in my chest, like maybe this had been the first step in setting my heart free.

CHAPTER 20

Ipretended everything was fine as I tried to work up the nerve to tell Gray the truth. The worst part was that Gray seemed a little better over the next few days—less brooding and more optimistic. It gutted me to think of breaking his heart. But I had to do it in order to salvage my own. I didn't want to end up like Crespeau, letting nostalgia for a past love freeze me in place, never allowing me to experience a possible different future.

One night, I asked Gray to take a walk with me, as I didn't want to have this talk in my room with all its disturbing associations. We strolled through the cobblestoned streets of the Marais, silent except for our footsteps. It was already dark out, and the air was cold but held a promise of spring.

"This feels like a walk with a purpose," Gray said. "Yet you haven't said anything."

"I know," I said. "I'm trying to find the right words."

"Then it must be the answer to my question."

"Yes," I said, noticing a temporary brightening in Gray's eyes. We were in a quaint little alley in the Jewish quarter, and I reached out to grab his hand. "Gray, I think you've known my answer since Bruges. But I owe it to you to explain why . . . why I have to say no."

He pulled his hand away and grew rigid, moving slightly

away from me and leaning against the wall of a bakery, long since closed for the night.

"I know you're upset," I said. "But you have to understand, I'm eighteen years old. And we've both been through so much this year. I think we need to slow things down and . . ."

"Slow things down? Emma, it sounds like you're breaking up with me."

"No. I mean, I don't know, Gray. I didn't even know you were alive two months ago. Now you're asking me to spend the rest of my life with you. And I'm not even sure you really mean it. This could just be fear talking. You're scared of things changing. But things need to change. People need to change, or they die."

He moved away angrily. "I get it, Emma. You're ready to move on. You and Grasshopper Boy want to hop off into the sunset."

"Gray, it's not like that. I told you before this isn't about Owen."

"Oh no? Emma, it's no accident that you lost my scorpion. You wanted to lose it."

"Gray, that's ridiculous. And I don't want to lose you. You've been a part of my life since I was four years old. You're my oldest, dearest friend."

"Friend? You think when I was stuck on that life raft for sixty-one days that what kept me alive was the thought of being your friend? Do you have any idea what kind of hell I went through?"

"No, I don't," I said. "But do you know what kind of hell it was for me to think you were dead? To mourn you and accept that I wasn't ever going to see you again?"

"I wish I had died out there," he said. His breathing had grown shallow and erratic.

"Don't say that."

"Why? What do you care? You wish I'd never come back."

"That's not true. I wished every day for you to come back."

"So what happened, Emma? Now I am back. Why can't you be happy? Why can't it be like it was before?" The vein in his forehead was throbbing, and the intensity in his eyes was beginning to frighten me.

"Because I'm not the person I was!" I said, feeling desperate. "Losing you made me face my worst fears, but I came out stronger on the other side. And so did you. You might not believe it now, but you're different, too."

"No, Emma, I'm the same. And so are you. We can be like we were before." He gripped my arm and pulled me toward him.

"Gray, you're hurting me."

"Well, you're not listening. I have to make you listen. Think of what you're giving up." He pressed his body against mine, pinning me to the wall.

"Gray, stop! What's happened to you?"

"You know what fucking happened to me!" he said. "And the only thing I want right now is you. Is that too much to ask? Don't I deserve to get what I want after everything I've been through?"

"Not if it means hurting me," I said. "Gray, we were good together once because we both wanted each other. I still love you, but I want new things in my life, new experiences."

"So you get what you want, and I lose everything. You said you still loved me. You're such a liar!" He pounded his fist against the wall just above my head.

I cowered from him, something I'd never done in my life. "Gray, I never meant to hurt you."

"Whatever. I'm going to make things easy for you, Emma," he said. "I'm going to leave. For good this time."

"Gray, don't leave things like this."

"Like what? Horrible and depressing as hell?" He tore off his Virgo angel pendant and threw it at the wall, nearly missing my head. "My guardian angel? What a joke."

"Gray, it was never a joke."

"Well, love is. The fairy tales tell you otherwise, but it's all bullshit. Happily ever after is a fucking lie. People break your heart. That's the real end of the story."

"Gray, I'm so sorry," I muttered, wiping tears from my face.

But Gray just gave me a devastating stare and said, "You're not sorry, Emma. But you will be."

Then he turned and fled the alley, leaving me a quivering wreck against the wall.

My first thoughts ran to Owen. In Gray's state, I had no idea where he might go or what he might do. He seemed to hold Owen responsible for all of this. At this time of night, Owen would probably be at the hostel or maybe at a café with Flynn. If Gray managed to find him, at least he wouldn't be alone.

But I felt compelled to check on him anyway. I pulled out my cell phone and dialed his number.

"Hey, Emma, where have you been? We're at Opéra Bastille. We got the go-ahead to move rehearsals into the Studio space, and it's amazing. Do you believe Jean-Claude and Yseult beat us here? Bastards!"

"So you're not alone?" I asked.

"No, Flynn and Elise are with me. We've been calling you for hours."

"Sorry," I said. "I've been a little preoccupied. Gray and I . . . we just broke up."

"Oh." Silence radiated across the phone line.

"Do you mind if I check out the space tomorrow?" I said.

"Emma, are you okay?" he asked, nothing but kindness in his voice. "Why don't I take you out somewhere so we can talk?"

"No, I'm not really in the mood to talk," I said. And the last thing I needed was for Gray to stumble upon me and Owen together. "I'll call you tomorrow."

After we hung up, I picked up the Virgo pendant from the ground and put it in my pocket, then set off in search of Gray. I ducked into a few of the cafés Gray and I had gone to together, checked the park where he went running, and ended up back at the school, hoping he might be in my room.

But as I was heading up the stairs, I ran into Monsieur Crespeau.

"Emma, I just saw your friend. He had his bags packed. I asked him where he was going, but he wouldn't answer me."

"Oh, God," I said, feeling a tiny twinge of relief. Maybe he'd decided to get a flight home. Even though I hated the way things had ended between us, this scenario was a lot better than the alternatives.

"You told him?" he said.

"Yes. And he didn't take it well."

"You did the right thing, Emma."

"I'm not so sure. I feel terrible."

"Of course you do. You didn't want to hurt him. But dragging things out indefinitely wouldn't help him move on. Or you. It was time."

He reassured me again and again that I'd made the right decision, but somewhere in my gut, I still feared the consequences.

That night I had a horrible nightmare in which Gray had Owen trapped in a tank that was rapidly filling with water. Owen was gasping for breath, flailing as the tank filled, and Gray stood by watching and doing nothing. Gray, who had the power to rescue him, was so enflamed with jealousy that all he did was watch Owen die.

And I stood helpless, frozen in place, unable to save either one of them.

CHAPTER 21

Two weeks went by with no word from Gray. I went to classes in a fog of distraction, worrying every second that Gray had done something awful. It was possible he'd just flown home, but I didn't want to call his parents and risk alarming them if Gray wasn't there. Or perhaps he had gone traveling to blow off some steam. Something in my gut told me neither of these possibilities was likely.

Meanwhile, as my thoughts became darker and more disturbing, the weather got more springlike and intoxicating with each passing day. Owen began spending more time with me, trying to take my mind off things. We'd walk all over the city or go sit in a park, relishing the sunshine that seemed to be out in full force.

"Are you holding it together?" he asked as we lazed on a blanket at Parc de Bercy on an unseasonably warm afternoon.

"As much as can be expected."

"You don't have any idea where Gray is?"

"I really don't," I said. "And it's driving me insane. I don't know what to do."

"There's nothing you can do but wait."

"I feel like that's all I ever do with Gray," I said. "I don't mean to sound uncaring, but this is so selfish of him. Leaving like this without a word after what I went through last fall."

Owen didn't say anything, perhaps not thinking it was his right to criticize. But I knew where he stood on the subject of Gray.

"I don't really want to talk about Gray anymore," I said. I'd had enough of him monopolizing my every waking thought and even my non-waking ones. Gray had brought me nothing but grief all year, and I was so exhausted. So ready to feel something good again.

Owen gave me a surprised look. "Fine by me," he said. "So . . . in another few weeks, you'll be getting your acceptance letters. Any idea where you're going to school next year?"

"Well, first I have to see if I get in."

"Oh, you know you're going to get in."

"Not necessarily."

"You're being modest," he said, smiling, "and that's cute. But let's just say, for argument's sake, that you get into all your schools. Where do you want to go?"

There was the question again, and I still didn't have the answer. "I don't know," I said, flopping onto his shoulder. I wanted to bury my head in his neck and stay there forever, not have to think about some future that loomed before me, immense and terrifying.

"Well, let me propose an alternative, just for fun. What if you took a gap year?" he said.

"A gap year? You mean, not go to college in the fall? I think my father might have something to say about that."

"Emma, you're eighteen. I think your father gave up a long time ago trying to control your life."

"I'm not so sure about that," I said. "When I was home, he tried to convince me to stay and finish my senior year at Lockwood."

"But he didn't succeed. Look where you are now," he said, squeezing my arm.

"So what do you suggest? That I bum around Europe like you?"

"How about you bum around Europe *with* me?" he said.

I fell silent, not sure if he was serious but also trying to quell the excitement his suggestion had generated in me. "Very funny," I said.

"I'm not joking. Travel is the best education. It helps you figure out who you are and what you want to do. College will still be there waiting for you at the end of the year."

"So you're not planning to go back home and try college?" I said. "You're going to stay in Europe?"

"I don't know what I'm going to do," he said, "but the longer I'm away from traditional school, the less I want to go. If I went to college now, I'd only be wasting my father's money."

He had a point. Not everyone was ready to begin planning for their future at the age of eighteen or nineteen. Society told us we should be, but this was the reason so many thirty-year-olds were camped out in their parents' basements playing video games while their expensive business degrees went unused.

"What are you going to do with your life?" I heard myself asking, horrified by the scolding, motherly tone of it.

"I don't know. Play music. Backpack. Maybe write a little."

"And for money?"

"Staying at hostels is cheap, and I can get a temporary work visa, maybe wait tables. Become a tour guide. Flynn and I can arrange some more gigs and make a little money that way. I'm not worried."

An ugly thought shot through my head: *It's easy not to worry when you come from money; there will always be someone to bail you out.*

"My situation's not the same as yours," I said. "I don't have money saved up, and my dad isn't going to give me a cent if I don't go to college. I've got a good shot at getting a scholarship somewhere. I don't want to jeopardize that by deferring enrollment." But I felt myself softening ever so slightly to the idea of blowing off college, just for a year, so I could do what Owen said: travel and figure out what I really wanted out of life. "Why do they make us decide so early?" I asked. "Choose a major, apply for internships, commit yourself to one path when there are infinite paths to go down."

"Exactly," Owen said, his face glowing. "Now you're seeing the light."

"But my dad—"

"Your dad will love you and support you no matter what."

"But I don't want to disappoint him."

"What about disappointing me?" he said, contorting his face into a doleful puppy pout.

"Well, we wouldn't want that," I said, laughing. "Let me think about it."

When the heat of the afternoon grew too oppressive, we ducked into the Musée des Arts Forains, a quirky collection of fairground art with antique carousels, swings, billiards, and an automatic orchestra that played creepy organ music. There, we took a ride on the gondola merry-go-round. The eerie organ music made it feel like we were in a haunted house and that the spirits of old clowns and circus freaks were hiding in the shadows watching us. I was actually a little relieved when we stepped outside and back into the sunshine.

When we said good-bye later that night, Owen leaned in and kissed me on the cheek, lingering there so I could feel the heat of his breath on my skin. I walked up to my room in a bit of a daze, wondering how I would ever sleep that night.

We had only three weeks until the opera competition, so rehearsals kicked into high gear. But after that kiss, I could barely focus as I watched Owen perform on the Studio stage, jealousy burning through me as he touched Elise's arm or gave her a smoldering stage glance. But when we'd pause to go over my director's notes, Owen would give me a real stare that made my insides melt.

Meanwhile, Elise was getting more and more obsessive as our deadline loomed. She began staying at the Studio long after everyone else had left, singing and re-singing her songs and beating herself up every time she made a mistake. This wasn't like her. Elise usually exuded confidence; to let her vulnerable side show was a rarity.

"I'm just not satisfied yet," she said. "I've got to keep practicing."

Flynn sighed, irritable from hunger or boredom. "I feel like we're at that point where any more rehearsal is going to make me so sick of the material, it's going to take away from my performance," he said.

"Yeah, we want a little rawness," I agreed.

"I don't want to sound raw," Elise said. "It's got to be perfect. You guys can take off, but I'm going to stay a little longer. I want to run through my solo one more time."

I had a feeling this perfectionism had something to do with her being wait-listed at Berklee. Elise rarely suffered rejection, so this relentless drive to excel was her attempt to compensate for her feelings of inadequacy.

We left Elise at the Studio, and Flynn went to meet some girl at a bar, giving us a knowing wink before heading off. I was starving so Owen and I decided to take the Métro to our favorite dim sum restaurant in Chinatown. The hostess sat us at a tiny table toward the back beside an intricate carved wooden screen.

"I think this might be my favorite place in all of Paris," Owen said as he poured us tea.

"Really? Not the café with the amazing foie gras? Not the brasserie with the to-die-for coq au vin?"

"Nope. This little Chinese restaurant with its cheesy red silk chairs and bad lighting. This is my favorite."

"Why?"

"Because it reminds me of you."

I blushed and looked down at my plate, took a sip of my too-hot tea. Something was happening to me—to us—and it frightened me, perhaps because I hadn't planned on it. And I was used to planning my life rather carefully.

We ate a huge platter of dim sum, sharing the ones we liked and stopping just short of feeding each other. Even so, the meal felt like some elaborate form of culinary foreplay. It was exciting to talk and eat with my friend Owen but imagine that afterward, we might go back to my room and become something different.

After dessert, our waitress returned with more tea and two fortune cookies.

"Choose," Owen said, holding out his palm.

I reached out and grabbed the closest one, cracking it open and pulling out the little strip of paper.

"Don't let heartbreak stop you on your quest for true love," I read aloud.

"Smart cookie," Owen said, making me smile.

"Now read yours," I said.

Owen looked down at his fortune and read, "Love is friendship set to music." Then his face broke into his trademark dimples.

"That's kind of beautiful." I felt a jangle of nerves that made me start babbling. "Don't you think it's strange when horoscopes or fortunes are so dead-on like that? I mean, you and I have been working on this musical and we're friends—"

He stopped my mouth with his, and suddenly we were kissing, really kissing this time with no interruptions or reservations. I forgot we were in a public place, dazed by the feel of his tongue in my mouth, dizzy from the sheer cinematic splendor of it. We pulled away a few seconds later, breathless, and he took my hand. His face was full of heartbreaking vulnerability.

"What's going on here?" I said.

"I don't know," Owen said, "but I like it." He ran his fingers along my arm, sending chills through every limb of my body.

"Want to get out of here?" I said, feeling reckless and excited.

He nodded quickly. "Uh-huh."

We quickly paid our bill and left the restaurant, surprised to find it was raining. On the subway back to Bastille, neither of us said anything out of fear of ruining the moment. We had waited so long for it. When we finally got off at the station, it was raining even harder, so we ran the entire way back to my dorm, racing each other up the steps to my room.

Once inside, Owen's face grew very serious as he dripped rainwater onto the floor. My room felt completely isolated from the rest of the world, the only dry place in the universe.

"I'm nervous," I said. "I've never felt nervous with you."

"That's a good thing," he said, moving toward me.

I had no idea what to expect but I knew it was somehow inevitable. This had been building for three years now. Owen stood before me and ran a hand through his wet hair, sending a thrill through me. For a moment, I felt paralyzed by the old fears. In some ways, I'd died on that ocean right along with Gray. Even once he'd returned, I'd still hovered in limbo, unable to feel anything but guilt and fear. But now every nerve felt alive and my body tingled with electricity and anticipation.

Owen remained in place, his face flushed and expectant. It was my turn to take a step forward, to lift up the anchor that had weighed me down for so long, unleash the moorings, and let sail my heart.

I began slowly, taking a few tentative steps toward him and draping my arms over his shoulders, feeling the strange dissonance of friendship crashing into unfamiliar romantic territory. Owen helped me adjust, grabbing my waist and pulling me toward him, then backing me up toward the bed. I didn't think, just acted and reacted, falling backward and feeling an immense sense of trust combined with overwhelming need. Owen was kissing my lips, my cheeks, my hair. I was a puddle of sensation, letting his mouth crash over me like a tide.

I hadn't known it could be like this with Owen, had never allowed myself to imagine it, which made the reality all the sweeter. We didn't actually have sex—neither of us had prepared for this—but it didn't matter. The end result felt the same as we lay in bed next to each other, nearly naked and spent, feeling desire twine through our limbs. We stayed up late talking in bed, and I tried to memorize the intense and intimate way it felt as we talked in hushed whispers and shared our most private hopes and fears.

"So that was . . . unexpected," he said. I gave a shy smile. "Do you regret it?"

"Not at all," I said. "Why would you ask that?"

"I don't know. It's just, everything going on with Gray . . ."

"I know it's been complicated," I said, taking his hand. "And I'm sorry. For so long, I was living in the past or waiting for some future I thought was going to happen. And when that future disappeared, I felt lost. But for the first time, I feel like I could have a different future. I can't quite see what it looks like yet, and that's kind of thrilling. I'm enjoying living in the moment. With you." I leaned over and kissed him on the mouth, feeling almost euphoric.

"You're incredible," he said.

"And you're wonderful."

He laced his fingers through mine and pulled me close. "It's about time you noticed," he said, and my heart flew right out of my chest.

CHAPTER 22

I woke early, surprised to find Owen in my bed. He looked so young and adorable with his head smushed into the pillow that I leaned over and kissed him softly on the temple. He stirred.

"Hey," he said, reaching out to grab my hand. "Good morning."

"Yes, it is," I said.

He pulled me against him, and I nestled into the curve of his body. "I could get used to this," he said.

And I felt a surge of emotion so overpowering that it made me say something completely bold and unplanned. "I want to do it," I said.

"Right now?" he said. "Give me a few minutes to wake up."

"No, not that," I said, laughing. "I want to stay in Europe with you."

He pulled away and sat up in the bed. "Really?" he said. "You mean it? You're not just teasing me?"

"No, I'm not teasing you. What's one year, right? I have my whole life to work hard, but I may not get an opportunity like this again. And I want to be with you."

"With me?" he said. "Like really with me?"

"Like really," I said.

"Can I call you my girlfriend?" he said, smiling shyly.

"I think that would be appropriate," I said. "So long as you don't come up with any stupid pet names for me."

"Aw, no Pookie? No Pumpkin or Honeybunch? No Dumpling?"

"Definitely not Dumpling," I said.

"How about my little Dim Sum?"

"Now you're pushing it."

"Oh, am I?" he said, grabbing me around the waist and pulling me on top of him.

"Owen, this feels amazing, but I have to go to class."

"Oh shit, it's Thursday, isn't it? It feels like the weekend."

"Everything feels like the weekend to you," I said.

"And it will to you, too, as soon as you finish this semester," he said. "We can do whatever we want, go wherever we want, stay as long as we want."

"Mmmm, that sounds wonderful."

I kissed him, then reluctantly extracted myself from his embrace and headed toward the bathroom. On my way there, I saw something glinting on the floor and leaned down to pick it up. My blood ran cold.

"Oh my God."

"What?" Owen asked, propping himself up.

"Gray's scorpion. I thought I lost it in Arles. How could it be here?"

Owen hopped out of bed and came over to inspect the pendant. "Obviously, you only thought you lost it. But it must have been here all the time. Maybe one of us kicked it into view last night."

"I don't know," I said. "This seems weird." I turned it over just to make sure it was the real pendant, the one etched with the inscription: *To Emma, the only antidote to my sting.*

"What's so weird about it?" Owen said.

"Me finding it this morning just after I made this decision to be with you? Doesn't it seem a little uncanny?"

"I think you're looking for omens where none exist. It's just a coincidence."

"Can I admit something to you?" I said. "All this time Gray's been gone, I've had this feeling that he's still been here. I didn't want to say anything because I thought it made me sound paranoid. But sometimes when you and I are together, I get the sense that he's watching us."

"That's just your guilty conscience," Owen said, getting abruptly out of bed, his mood completely soured.

"What do you mean?" I said.

"You're never going to be over him, Emma. I don't know why it's taken me this long to realize it. Every time I feel you and me making some progress, suddenly Gray pops up again. He's never going to go away. He's everywhere because he's a part of you. In a way I never could be."

I went over and touched Owen's shoulder. "He's a part of my past," I said. "You're my future."

"Are you sure about that? You told me last night you couldn't see your future, so how do you know, Emma?"

The way he said my name, laced with bitterness, killed me.

"Where are you going?" I said, watching Owen gather his things and move toward the door.

"I'm leaving," he said. "You have to get to class, and I need a shower."

"You can shower here," I said. "I'll be back from class by eleven. We can talk then."

"I don't want to talk anymore," he said. "Especially not about you and Gray."

And then he left, shutting the door with a sad finality.

I felt hurt and deflated, but I couldn't blame Owen for using my own words against me. In a way he was right. Gray did keep coming back. Perhaps I hadn't cut him as loose as I'd thought. And if I still had unresolved feelings for Gray, I needed to sort them out before I could truly give my heart to Owen.

I lay the scorpion tag on the vanity and searched through my jewelry box for Owen's grasshopper pin, placing them side by side. These gifts seemed to embody the qualities that drew me to each of them.

Gray was the scorpion—intense, competitive, dangerous. A survivor.

Owen was the grasshopper—soulful, laid-back, joyful. An idealist.

They couldn't have been more different. And yet I loved them both.

Reluctantly, I got dressed and made my way to class, knowing I wouldn't remember a thing from today's lessons. I felt so drained when I got back to my room that I fell asleep doing my homework and woke up only to realize I was a half hour late to rehearsal. Owen was already angry with me; now he was going to be furious. Throwing my matted hair up into a ponytail, I headed to the Opera House.

I smelled something first, an acrid odor that pinched my nose and made my stomach tighten. Sirens blared from a distance, and the roar of panicked people intensified as I neared the scene. I picked up my pace and turned the corner by the Bastille to see fire engines and emergency vehicles surrounding the Opera House. The flashing lights reflected on its mirrored exterior made the building look like some sickening carnival ride. People swarmed the streets, and smoke billowed from the back of the Opera, where most of the commotion seemed to be taking place.

I pushed my way through the throng, covering my face to shield myself from the smoke. Firefighters ran to and fro, assisting people out of the smoldering building. It seemed the fire had been extinguished, but everyone still stood gaping at the wreckage, coughing and commiserating about what had caused it.

I almost lost it when I spotted Owen standing by the back exit of the Opera House. I called out to him, but he was too far away to hear me. His face looked stricken. Flynn was there too, looking just as stunned as Owen, and staring at something outside my line of vision.

Finally, I ducked down and crawled under arms and legs and torsos to make my way across the street. There I saw what had been commanding Owen and Flynn's attention: Elise was being wheeled away from the building on a gurney. Her nose and mouth were covered by an oxygen mask, and two medics were at her side, volleying instructions back and forth in rapid-fire French. I watched as they transferred her into an ambulance and Owen and Flynn hopped in behind her.

Before I could get my bearings, one of the medics shut the door to the ambulance and ran around to jump in the driver's seat. The siren began shrieking, and then they disappeared through a haze of smoke and ash.

I whipped out my cell and texted Owen to find out which hospital they were headed to, but he must not have heard his phone amid all the chaos. After wandering helplessly for a few minutes waiting for a response, I decided to try to get into the Opera House and ask what had happened. But they weren't letting anyone in.

And then I saw him in the crowd. He was dressed all in black with a baseball cap partially obscuring his face. But it looked just like Gray.

At least I thought it looked like Gray. But the entire area was filled with people and smoke, and the noise and flashing lights had disoriented me. Even so, my gut seized with a wrenching cramp, like it knew something I didn't.

Finally, Owen texted me back with the name of the hospital, but the fire had brought the neighborhood to a standstill and I had to wait thirty minutes for a cab. As the taxi driver made his circuitous way to the hospital, I fretted about what could have started the fire. How serious were Elise's injuries? Would she be okay?

My friends and I had spent more than our share of time in

hospitals over the past few years. You could say we were accident-prone, but the truth was: I was a danger magnet. Trouble tended to find me wherever I was. And my friends ended up being endangered by association.

When I arrived at the emergency room, I stopped at the front desk to ask where Elise was, and the nurse gave me a room number. I made my way through the labyrinth of the hospital to find Elise lying in a bed, pale and visibly shaken but conscious.

Owen and Flynn still seemed a bit in shock, barely registering my presence.

I grabbed Elise's arm and squeezed. "I'm so glad you're okay," I said. "And I'm so sorry I wasn't there." I turned to Owen. "What happened? How did the fire start?"

"I don't know," he said breathlessly. "Flynn and I were late, too. But I know it started in the Studio. Elise was the only one there."

Flynn snorted. "Yeah, because Jean-Claude hightailed it out of there so he wouldn't be a suspect. I bet he started it with one of his pretentious Gauloises."

"We'll have to ask Elise once they take the oxygen mask off," Owen said.

But the doctor told us she probably wouldn't be able to speak for a while since the smoke had swollen her respiratory tract.

We were huddled around, speculating about what had happened, when Jean-Claude burst into the room.

"Elise, darling," he said. "Are you okay?" He wedged himself between us so he was standing right next to her, like he'd suddenly decided to be her boyfriend again.

"What the hell are you doing here?" Flynn asked.

"I heard the news, and I came right away," he said.

"And I'll ask you again. What the hell are you doing here?" Flynn said.

"Making sure she's all right. We may have broken up, but I still care about her."

"Oh, you care about her?" Flynn said. "So much that you dropped your damn cigarette and started the fire that landed her here?"

Jean-Claude looked genuinely flabbergasted at the accusation. "No, you are mistaken," he said. "The fire was an accident."

"Well, I don't believe in accidents," Flynn said. "Maybe you and Yseult were trying to get rid of the competition."

"Flynn," Owen said, grabbing him by the arms. "That's enough. You're upsetting Elise."

"No, *he's* upsetting Elise," Flynn said. "I'm sick of this asshat toying with her emotions."

"I'm not *toying* with anyone," Jean-Claude said.

"Ladies and gentlemen," the doctor said, "I really must insist you leave. Elise needs her rest. I have your contact number. I'll call you with any news."

Reluctantly, we filed out of the room, and Owen and I had to hold Flynn back to prevent him from coming to blows with Jean-Claude.

When we exited the hospital, Jean-Claude turned to me and said, "I am sorry things are so . . . ugly between us. It was not my intention. Believe me, I had nothing to do with the fire. I am not a monster."

"No, just a douche bag," Flynn said.

"Enough," I said. "Jean-Claude, I think you'd better go. I'll call if we learn anything."

"Don't call that son of a—"

"Flynn!" Owen and I both shouted at the same time.

After Jean-Claude left, the three of us walked back toward school, trying to make sense of the accident. "It's obvious they started the fire," Flynn said.

Owen shook his head. "I hate him as much as you do, but I can't see him doing something so . . . evil."

"I agree," I said. "But they may have started the fire accidentally. They are a bit careless about their smoking."

"I think we should call the police," Flynn said, "and tell them what we know."

"We don't know anything," I said. "Let's just cool off and think about this tomorrow after we've all calmed down."

When we reached their hostel, I said good-bye and we went our separate ways. But my sighting of Gray still nagged at me. Could I have just imagined him there?

I reached campus and went through the main building, hoping to find Monsieur Crespeau. I needed to tell someone what I'd seen. What I was really hoping for was someone to tell me I was mistaken.

I found Crespeau in the courtyard, trimming hedges. When he saw me, he shut off the trimmer and ran toward me, which was somewhat alarming given his limp. "Emma, I've been hoping to find you. I must talk to you."

"And I have to talk to you. You're never going to believe what happened."

I told him all about the fire and Elise and watched his face grow more concerned with each revelation. "But she's fine," I said. "The doctor said she's going to need a few weeks of recuperation, and she may not be able to talk for a while. She couldn't even tell us how the fire started." And then I told him about Gray. Because somewhere in my mind, those two ideas were linked. "You don't think it could have been him, do you? My mind is just preoccupied with him, so I imagined him there, right?"

Crespeau took my hand. "Emma, you'd better come with me. I need to show you something."

I followed him into the administrative building and up the stairs to the chapel, where we walked the tiny aisle to the first pew, on which sat a blanket, a knapsack, and some toiletries.

"What's going on?" I asked.

"It's Gray. He never left."

"What do you mean?"

"I found him camped out here this morning, and before I could get any answers from him, he ran away."

"So he's been here the whole time?" I said. "I knew it!"

"But, Emma, do you realize what this means?"

"No," I said.

"You did see him at the fire," he said. "It seems like a co-incidence, no?"

"What are you implying?"

"People do awful things when they're emotionally scarred like Gray is. I think he may be suffering from post-traumatic stress."

"Post-traumatic stress?" I said. "Gray?"

He nodded. "I know a thing or two about it."

"Oh, you had it? After your parents' accident?"

He sat down on the pew and stared at the floor. Eventually, I sat down next to him, sensing there was more to the story. "Emma, I am telling you this in confidence," he said. "Nobody knows about this."

I nodded and gave him my word that I'd never tell a soul.

He took a deep breath. "It was a year after the accident, the anniversary of my parents' death. I still hadn't told Claire how I felt about her, and the pain was eating through me like poison. We were seniors then, and she was leaving to go to the university. I knew I had to tell her before she left, but I didn't think I was brave enough. So I went to a café and had a few drinks. Too many drinks.

"When I got to Claire's room, I paused at her door and that's when I heard two voices. Claire was with another man. I couldn't hear what they were saying but knew from their tone exactly what they were doing, and something exploded inside me. The next few hours are a blank in my memory. I didn't know myself. All I remember is waking up in my room to the blare of the fire alarm. The hallways were full of smoke, students running and screaming, trying to get out of the building. I ran to Claire's room, and when I got to her door, I suddenly remembered that I was the one who had started the fire."

"You?" I said. "But why would you do that? You loved her."

"When you're sick like I was, there is no why. Maybe, subconsciously, I set the fire so I could rescue her, to show her that she needed me."

"And did you? Rescue her?"

"No, her boyfriend helped her escape." He laughed bitterly. "When I think what could have happened to her, or to anyone . . ." He fell silent, unable to go on.

So the rumors swirling around Saint-Antoine at the beginning of the year had been true after all. I glanced up at the chapel altar, realizing this was the perfect place for Crespeau to make his confession.

"Mademoiselle Veilleux still doesn't know you set the fire?" I said.

"Do you think she would have hired me and let me stay all these years if she knew?"

"I guess not," I said. "But no one got hurt. And you're okay now, right? You're not sick anymore?"

He shook his head. "After the fire, I disappeared for a while. And I sought help from a therapist. Eventually, I healed from my parents' death and felt ready to live again. But I couldn't stop myself from returning to Saint-Antoine years later when I heard that Claire had become the headmistress. And when she offered me a job, I thought I'd found the answer to all my problems. I would be near her for the rest of my life, even if I couldn't have her. I thought it would be enough.

"On my first day back, I went into the maintenance closet and saw the mirror that had been in Claire's room, soot-covered from the fire but still intact. I couldn't believe it. So I cleaned it off lovingly and hung it back in her room, to remind myself of what I had done. What I was capable of and what I could never do again."

So that was why he loved the mirror. And I had broken it, but I hadn't broken the spell. Crespeau was still stuck here, watching life from the sidelines rather than embracing it fully.

I thought about Gray and what he had endured in his nineteen years. Watching a girl drown and not being able to save her. Being marooned on a life raft for sixty-one days. And now, learning that the person he thought was his soul mate was in love with someone else. All of that could drive any person insane.

"So you're wondering if maybe Gray set the fire himself?" I said.

"I'm only saying it's a possibility," he said.

"Well, we have to find him."

"Yes."

"And I have to call Gray's parents. They should know what's going on."

Monsieur Crespeau agreed.

Making the call to Gray's parents was one of the most agonizing things I'd ever done. At first Simona was so filled with relief at the news that Gray was okay that she barely listened as I explained about the fire.

"He's been hiding out in the chapel at my school like some fugitive. Acting crazy and making threats. And now this fire . . . I mean, I don't know if he set it or not, but I think he's suffering from post-traumatic stress."

Simona paused. "And just what do you know about post-traumatic stress, Emma?" An icy chill ran down my spine at her tone. Simona used to love me almost as her own daughter, and now she seemed to find me reprehensible.

"I only know that Gray isn't himself and he hasn't been since he was rescued from that life raft. I don't think he ever dealt with what happened to him out on the ocean. And I think it's time we notify the Coast Guard. Gray needs help."

Simona grunted in disgust. "Do you know what will happen if we notify the Coast Guard? Gray will be subject to psychological testing, and if they uncover anything out of the ordinary, he could be discharged. The Coast Guard is the only thing Gray has left now that you have abandoned him."

So Simona knew about our breakup. "I didn't abandon him," I said. "Why do you think I'm calling you? I still care about him so much. I'm trying to help him."

"Emma, your help only hurts. Don't ruin his life."

We argued back and forth for another ten minutes, but there was no convincing her. Which meant the responsibility of notifying the Coast Guard would fall on me. And I didn't want it.

I had no reason to think Gray would start a fire except for Crespeau's story. If Gray was as traumatized as Crespeau had been, he might have done something terrible without even knowing what he was doing. Especially if he thought I was in the Studio that day.

But it seemed unlikely Gray could have gotten into the Studio without authorization. Then again, he'd been camping out for weeks in our school's chapel without anyone knowing. It was almost like he'd become a sort of phantom himself.

CHAPTER 23

I held off contacting the Coast Guard as I tried to make up my mind about the best course of action. I saw no reason to come forward until we knew something definitive about the cause of the fire.

On the day Elise was released from the hospital, we took her out for a celebratory lunch, where she gorged herself on wine, cheese, and pastries. I'd never seen Elise scarf food down like that before. I guess the hospital cuisine had been disappointing.

Flynn was trying to convince us all to come forward with the information about Jean-Claude's team smoking in the Studio space prior to our rehearsals. He figured it might even disqualify them from the competition, pushing our opera into first place and securing the production in next fall's season. But then Elise spoke up, as best as she could with her limited vocal capacities.

"Emma," she whispered, "do you remember the fire in the stables during our sophomore year?"

"The fire that nearly killed me?" I said. "Yeah, I have a vague recollection." Ironically, Gray had rescued me from that fire. It never would have occurred to me then that he could have started it. What had changed to allow me to believe such an awful thing about my boyfriend?

"Then you remember the investigation when you and Michelle tried to pin the fire on me," she said.

"Well, you guys were smoking pot," I said, feeling defensive. "And then you tried to pin it on Michelle."

"I know," Elise said, her voice hoarse. "And that was wrong. Maybe Jess and I did cause the fire that night. Who knows? But what good would have come from proving that?"

"Stop making the girl talk," Flynn said. "She sounds like the Godfather, for God's sake."

All similarities to Marlon Brando aside, Elise was right. Maybe she would have been expelled, but more than likely her father would have gotten her off the hook and nothing would have changed. No lesson would have been learned. It had all been a game of one-upsmanship, each of us trying to get the upper hand in our petty high school battle.

The same thing was going on now between Flynn and Jean-Claude. And the last thing I wanted was to tie up our competition in a legal battle with the Opera House and jeopardize the final outcome. If we were going to beat Jean-Claude and Yseult, I wanted it to be on our own merits and not because of a technicality

"You're right," I said. "And I'm willing to drop it if Flynn is. Besides, if Jean-Claude is found responsible, the liability might fall on the school, and that would only hurt Mademoiselle Veilleux."

"Yeah," Owen said. "You wouldn't want that, would you, Flynn?"

Owen smiled at me, the first time I'd seen those dimples since our fight in my bedroom that morning. It felt like the sun coming out after days of rain.

Flynn grudgingly relented, and we decided to drop our plan for revenge.

But even after we resolved that issue, I had so many things left to worry about: Gray; my relationship with Owen; and, of course, what I was going to do with my life after this year. My college acceptance letters had finally arrived. I had gotten in everywhere except Johns Hopkins, but this barely made a dent in my somber mood. The thought of going to Amherst or Hampshire left me cold after imagining myself in Budapest or Berlin with Owen.

I called Michelle to get some much-needed perspective and told her all about the drama of the last few weeks. But I didn't tell her Crespeau's suspicions about the fire because I wasn't quite ready to accept that Gray was capable of something like that.

"So how are you and Jess?" I asked after I'd finished with my rant. "I miss you guys so much."

"We're good. Great, really. She's going to Emerson next year so she can be near me at MIT."

"Oh, Michelle that's wonderful!"

"Yeah, we're both really excited," she said. "What about you? Did you hear from your schools yet?"

Okay, this was my rehearsal for telling my father. Michelle's reaction would pale in comparison to my dad's, but I had a feeling she would still disapprove. She'd had her college plans mapped out since she was eight years old.

"Yeah, but actually, I'm thinking of taking a year off."

There was silence on the other end. Finally, she said, "Miss SAT and AP Prep is thinking of blowing off college for a year? Why?"

"Because Owen asked me to stay in Europe with him."

"Oh, really?" she said. "There's more to this story than I thought. Spill!"

I told her all about the complications in my love life, most notably that I was in love with two men at the same time. "Do you think that's possible?" I asked.

"I don't know," Michelle said. "I think you can love two people at the same time but you can only be in love with one of them. Does that make any sense?"

"Perfect sense," I said. Because that was exactly it. I loved Gray, but I wasn't in love with him anymore. And I wasn't sure how I felt about Owen.

"So what would you and Owen do together in Europe, or is that too personal?"

"Oh, shut up," I said. "We'd travel. See parts of the world I'd never get to see otherwise. I may never get another chance like this again."

"Of course you will," she said. "Emma, you're going to college, not joining a nunnery. Why risk everything you've worked so hard for?"

"I don't think it's a risk," I said. "I'll just defer enrollment for a year."

"A year is a long time," she said. "A lot could happen to change your mind. And just what does John have to say about this?"

Michelle had taken to calling my father by his first name, which I found rather cheeky and amusing. "I haven't told him yet," I said.

"Why am I not surprised? Look, Emma, you know I'll support you no matter what, but I think this is a mistake. But it's your life. You have to decide what's best for you."

Yes, it *was* my life.

But when I got off the phone with Michelle, I thought about how little control we often had over our own lives. They were hopelessly entangled with everyone else's lives. I couldn't make a single decision without worrying how it would impact my dad, or Owen, or Gray, or the dozens of other people I loved and cared about. How did we ever create our own story if we were constantly revising it to suit other people's expectations?

I held off telling my father about Europe even though I knew he'd be asking for my decision any day now, and in fact, so would the colleges. Most schools wanted a decision by May first.

The one bright spot in my week was when I met Flynn and Owen at Café Rabelais so Flynn could give us some good news. And good news was something we all sorely needed.

"The competition is on again," Flynn said, saddling up to the bar with a huge, self-satisfied smile.

"How?" I said.

"Because I'm a genius with connections."

It turned out that he and Mademoiselle Veilleux had grown rather close over the past few months—I didn't want to know how close—and when Flynn told her about the fire at the Studio, she called in a favor with an old friend, the manager of La Péniche Opéra, where she used to perform. The company was on a short hiatus, but because the manager adored Claire, he was going to allow us to have our competition on his barge! His captain was even going to cruise us down the Seine as we performed, ending with the dramatic finale of sailing through the tunnel that ran beneath the Bastille.

"That's incredible!" I said. "But aren't you forgetting about the other tiny problem?"

"What's that?" Flynn said.

"Our lead singer can barely speak, let alone sing."

Flynn frowned into his wineglass, but now it was Owen's turn to be the hero. "You know the solution, Emma," he said. "You've always known it."

Flynn's eyes popped wide open. "Dude, you're right. I can't believe I didn't see it."

"What are you guys talking about?" I said.

Owen turned to me and smiled. "Emma, you're going to be my Christine after all."

CHAPTER 24

Not too long ago, those words had frozen me, had given me a cramp in the stomach tight enough to paralyze me. But this time, all I felt was a thrill so expansive and intense I could barely wait to get onstage. I don't know what exactly accounted for the change—let's call it *je ne sais quoi*—but suddenly I felt supremely confident, ready to face a sea of critics if it meant I'd finally get the chance to sing my own songs.

With the show back on, Owen, Flynn, and I spent every spare moment in the chapel rehearsing since the Studio space was out of commission. Elise, mostly recovered but still hoarse, came and watched us sulkily. I felt pangs of guilt about usurping her role. Then again, it had rightfully been mine until she had taken it from me back in December.

Rehearsing with Owen made me realize how easy it would be for an actress to fall in love with her leading man. Or maybe I really was falling in love with Owen. My feelings for him had been growing and evolving so slowly and for so long that I no longer knew how to define them. And maybe I didn't have to.

"Can I tell you something?" Owen said after rehearsal one day.

"Sure."

"You're the perfect Christine," he said. "I mean, Elise has a flawless voice. But you have a sweetness and vulnerability that Christine should have. That selfless love that saves the Phantom. Elise could never pull that off."

I felt a swell of affection for him and wished, once again, that I could give Owen my heart freely. "Owen, that's one of the nicest things anyone's ever said to me." Happiness washed over me, but it couldn't sweep away the tiny pit of guilt still lodged in my gut. Because I hadn't saved my Phantom yet. And I didn't know if I could.

That night alone in my room, I sat at the vanity, staring at the place where the mirror had been and replaying all of those dreams of Gray in that nightmare world of black sand and silver water.

In *The Phantom of the Opera,* what finally frees Christine from the Phantom's torment is her love. When she kisses the Phantom for the first time, Erik is so overcome at the purity of that kiss that he relents and allows Christine to leave with Raoul.

I'd thought my opera was complete, but now I realized it needed one more song. In my version, Christine sings a duet with Raoul, but she never sings one with the Phantom. She never tells him that she loves him, and he never sets her free.

I began scrawling in my notebook, and before I knew it I had a draft of what would become the final song in the opera. If Owen could set it to music with the same passion and talent he'd brought to my other poems, this would be the song to bring the house down.

I called it "Last Good-bye."

Just a few days before the competition, I was on my way home from a café, where I'd had dinner with Owen, and was coming down the alley to the back gate when I got the sensation of someone following me. It was the same feeling I'd gotten that night last fall. But when I turned around, no one was there.

I was searching for my keys and laughing at myself for still believing some silly story about a Bastille ghost when I felt a cold hand grip my arm. I whipped around and saw Gray standing there, pale as a specter. He was gaunt, like he hadn't eaten in days, and he was shivering, though it was easily 70 degrees out.

"Oh my God, you scared me," I said, trying to slow my breathing. Even though I was immensely relieved to see him, I was angry more than anything else. "Where have you been? I've been worried sick!"

"I've been running," he said.

"What do you mean? You've been gone for weeks."

"Well, I was hiding out in the chapel at night, but mostly I've been running through the city."

"Running? But why?"

"Because I didn't know what else to do."

"Oh, Gray." I hadn't intended to do it, but I reached out to hug him. He flinched for a moment and then collapsed onto my shoulder, sobbing. "Let's go up to my room," I said. "You're trembling."

He followed me into the dorm, his arms dangling by his sides like someone who'd forgotten how to walk. When we got to my room, I led him to the bed and sat beside him, stroking his back.

"Gray, what is it? Tell me what's wrong?"

He looked at me, his eyes haunted and sad. "I keep thinking I'm going to come back one of these times, and I'm going to look in your eyes and see myself reflected in them again. But now when I look at you, all I see is you, stronger than you ever were with me."

I pulled away, forcing him to support his own weight. "I am stronger," I said. "And that's a good thing. In time, you'll be stronger, too."

He shook his head. "No, I've lost it. And I can't get it back," he said.

"Can't get what back?"

"That will to be strong for someone else. That ability to save someone. And if I can't save anyone, I might as well . . ."

His voice trailed off, and I felt a sinking in my stomach. "Gray, I have to ask you something. Did you have anything to do with the fire?"

His head shot up, his eyes flaring. "What?"

"Don't get offended," I said. "It's just, there's been some talk about how the fire started and . . . well, I thought I saw you there."

"Yeah, I was there because I thought I might be able to help," he said, his face a mask of hurt. "Emma, please tell me you don't think I could have started that fire. You think I'm capable of that?"

"Well, the last time I saw you, you threatened me. You told me I'd be sorry. What was I supposed to think?"

"I don't know, Emma, but I'd hope not that. My God, you think I'm a monster."

"No, Gray," I said, grabbing his arm. "I think you need help."

He looked crushed by my suspicions. "Emma, I've only ever wanted to help people. The only person I even thought about hurting was myself. What I meant when I said you'd be sorry is that you'd miss me when I was gone."

"Is that why you left? So I could realize what I'd lost?"

"No, I left because I thought everyone would be better off without me. I wanted to disappear. And running made me feel like maybe I might."

"Gray, that's ridiculous," I said. "You have a gift. A talent for saving people. You've saved my life more than once. So many people rely on you. But more than that, so many people love you. You can't just disappear. Think about your parents and Anna and all of your friends. Think of me. We all love you and want you to be happy."

"I'm afraid that's not possible," he said.

Owen had said something to me once, and I hadn't believed him. But now I knew it was true. "Gray, you will be happy again," I said. "I promise you."

"I just don't know how to do this," he said.

"Do what?"

"Live. Without you."

"Gray, you don't have to," I said. "I'm here for you."

"No, you're not," he said. "You love someone else."

"You know what, Gray? You're right. But I love you, too, just not in the way you want me to. But you'll move on, you'll love again, and you'll be happier than you could ever have imagined."

He was shaking his head, giving up. I went over to the vanity and picked up the scorpion dog tag, my Virgo angel, and the engagement ring. I handed him his scorpion first.

"The Gray I knew was a survivor," I said. "A fighter. He wouldn't back down from a few blows. He would get back up and come out swinging even harder."

"That's because I had you watching over me," he said, taking the Virgo angel from my hand.

"No, that's because of who you are. You have everything you need to save yourself. I'm only here because I want to be, not because you need me. I care about you so much, but I can't marry you, Gray." And then, I placed the engagement ring in his palm and closed his fingers around it. I hoped he would give it to someone else someday. Someone who could make his heart race but who could also calm the raging sea inside him.

"I love you, Gray," I said, leaning in to kiss him on his cheek. When I pulled away, he had tears in his eyes.

"I love you, too, Emma." It was the first time he hadn't responded with the Han Solo punch line.

"I know you probably won't take me up on this," I said, "but I would really love it if you'd come see our opera. It would mean so much to me."

He wiped his cheeks and turned his face to the wall, as if he could hide the fact that he'd been crying. "I don't know, Emma. It might kill me to see you with him."

"But it might not," I said. "What doesn't kill you . . ."

"Makes you stronger," he said, his mouth breaking into a half smile.

We decided that Gray shouldn't stay in my room, so I told Monsieur Crespeau that Gray needed a place to stay, preferably not the chapel, since that was our rehearsal space now. Crespeau agreed to turn his maintenance closet into a temporary bedroom with a cot and everything. In fact, that next week Crespeau took Gray under his wing and spent a lot of time nurturing him, slowly trying to get him to admit he needed help. I suspect Crespeau saw a bit of his younger self in Gray, and Gray found a wise and compassionate mentor in Crespeau.

The investigation into the Studio fire yielded few definitive answers, but they did rule out arson, saying that most likely our costumes or the drapes had gotten too close to the hot stage lights, igniting the blaze. However, as the Opera House's fire extinguishers had failed to respond in a timely manner, the school would not be held liable for the fire.

So the show would go on.

We were able to get on board the barge for one dress rehearsal the day before the show. Mademoiselle Veilleux introduced us to Thierry Roland, the opera manager, who led us onto the boat and showed us the "backstage" area, a windowless, beamed cabin that would be hidden from the audience by an enormous curtain. The stage area was very small compared to the Studio space, so we had to run through our blocking carefully to adjust to the new dimensions. What little furniture and stage props we'd acquired had gone up in smoke during the fire, so our set design would be minimalist, to say the least. Although we ran through our lines one more time, we didn't sing the songs, not wanting to risk blowing out our voices the day before the competition.

The next morning dawned stormy and gray. Owen, Flynn, Elise, and I met in the chapel for one final pep talk. At this point, more rehearsal wasn't going to do us any good. We'd sung these songs backward and forward, had run lines and blocked scenes until we were practically keeling over, and now was the do-or-die moment. Adrenaline pumped through my limbs, making me feel wired and terrified but more alive than I'd felt in months.

Around six o'clock, we packed our costumes and equipment into Monsieur Crespeau's van and he drove us to Canal Saint-Martin, where our operatic cruise would begin. The barge was moored in front of a scenic footbridge on the Seine, the lit-up houses along the river casting their glimmering reflections in the water. Jean-Claude, Yseult, and Georges were already there, but Thierry had divided the backstage area with a large screen so each team would have at least the illusion of privacy.

Jean-Claude's *Cyrano* would be performed first, which made my nerves kick into overdrive. It was scary enough to perform in front of a live audience for the first time, but to have to sit through our competitor's performance and rein in all of my nervous energy seemed like torture. Owen could sense my mood and came over to calm me down.

"Emma, you've rehearsed and rehearsed. You know every line as your own because every line is your own. It's going to be amazing."

I rested my head on his chest, hoping the sound of his heartbeat might slow down my own. "I know; I just wish we could get it over with."

"You say that now," he said, "but the minute it's over, you're going to want to do it all over again."

"Really?"

"Really. Emma, I'm so proud to be a part of this." His arms came around me tightly, and I squeezed him back as hard as I could. This was a moment I was never going to forget as long as I lived. "I have a little surprise for you," he said once we'd pulled out of our hug. "Follow me."

He took my hand and led me through the main curtain to the small stage area. In front of the stage, Thierry had laid out rows of chairs for the audience and had strung up gaudy colored lights along the walls so the interior of the barge looked as festive and magical as a circus. Even with the lights, the theater space was dim and I could barely see as Owen led me down the center aisle toward the door that led to the outer deck. Someone hovered by the exit, but it wasn't until we had reached the door that I recognized him.

"Dad?"

"Surprise!" he said, extending his arms for a hug.

"Oh my God, Owen, I can't believe you didn't tell me!"

I threw my arms around my dad and he lifted me off the ground so I was suspended and weightless, carefree as a little girl. Even though I'd been standing on my own all semester, it felt good to surrender myself for just a moment in my daddy's arms, to put my trust so completely in another person. I knew at that moment that no matter what I decided to do about college and my future, my father would love and support me.

"I can't believe you came!" I said.

"I wouldn't miss my little girl's debut. Even if the ticket did cost me an arm and a leg. And the first week of the fishing season."

"Oh, Dad, you didn't miss it just for me, did you?"

"I missed it for me," he said. "Nothing could make me happier than this moment. Not even fishing."

His presence soothed me and gave me the final surge of confidence I needed. Over the next hour, audience members began trickling in until the boat was at full capacity. We stood out on the deck for a brief cocktail hour as the motor revved and the barge slowly departed from the dock. Our opera teacher, Luke, was there, looking very proud of his young protégés. I couldn't believe I had known nothing about opera at the beginning of this year, and now I had written my own libretto.

Just as a misty rain began to fall, the lights along the outside of the cabin began to flicker, signaling that the guests should take their seats. Monsieur Crespeau stood at the back of the theater, playing the part of usher. My father and friends and I walked down to the front row, where seats had been reserved for us with a white ribbon.

Mademoiselle Veilleux took the stage. "Good evening, ladies and gentlemen, and welcome to a special, one-night-only performance of L'Opéra Bastille's Young Artists' competition featuring original librettos by two students from Lycée Saint-Antoine: Monsieur Jean-Claude Bourret and Mademoiselle Emma Townsend."

The crowd applauded, and for the first time, I felt so impressed by what I had accomplished, not just because everyone kept telling me how proud they were but because I was proud of myself for having had the courage to put myself out there and make myself vulnerable. I felt like a real artist now.

Even once the other team began performing their version of *Cyrano,* I no longer felt jealous or nervous; in fact, I was thrilled to be a part of the project and so awed by the talent displayed by my rivals that I didn't care who won or lost tonight.

Jean-Claude was commanding as Cyrano, singing his solos with poignancy and strength. And Yseult, for all her mean-girl bravado, displayed a sweetness and vulnerability as Roxanne that I wasn't expecting. The songs they had written blended operatic melodies with punk rhythms and rawness.

The ending was heartbreaking. Fifteen years after Cyrano's

club was forced to close in financial ruin, Roxanne is still mourning the loss of rock star Christian, who died of a drug overdose years ago. Cyrano is now himself dying of lung cancer, but he visits Roxanne faithfully every day, never revealing that he was the one who penned all the love letters she thought were from Christian. On Cyrano's last visit, Roxanne asks him to read the final letter she received from Christian before he died, and Cyrano sings her the words, so sincerely and passionately that Roxanne finally knows the truth. In the final aria—a fusion of Joni Mitchell soulfulness and Kate Bush sweetness—Roxanne tells Cyrano that she has always loved him, and he is able to die with the knowledge that he did not live in vain, that someone loved him despite his flaws.

As the crowd began to clap, I was a weeping mess, not sure how I was going to pull myself together in time to perform our show. That final scene reminded me so much of Crespeau, who had dedicated his life to serving a woman who had never returned his love. I turned toward the back of the theater, searching for Crespeau by the door, but someone else stood in his place. Even though it was dark, I knew it was Gray. But he no longer looked pale and ghostly, like the frightening specter from my nightmares.

He looked strong and handsome and capable. And I knew his goodness had returned to him, since he'd come to my show simply because I had asked him to.

The lights rose slowly, and Mademoiselle Veilleux announced that there would be an intermission to allow the second team to prepare for their performance. The audience filed outside as my team headed toward the backstage area, but as we began changing, I could hear the winds picking up above deck and the rain pattering harder on the roof.

Elise, still bereft of her full vocal capacity, served as our costume-and-makeup person, dashing around to make a tuck here, swipe some blush there, fasten a clasp here. Once I was dressed, I sat in front of the mirror for one final check. Since we'd lost the few costumes we'd had, I was wearing the red velvet dress from the masquerade ball. My hair was pinned up with loose curls falling around my face, which Elise had made up with porcelain foundation and a deep red lip stain. As I stared into the mirror, all of the chaos going on behind me faded so all I could see was my own reflection staring back at me.

But my reflection no longer seemed like a stranger to me. The mirror didn't lie, and it didn't fill me with dread or fear. It just showed me myself as I truly was: strong, confident, and ready for my solo.

There was one moment after I took the stage but before the curtain was drawn aside when the entire house was silent but for the rain beating on the roof. I took a deep breath and drew up my courage from some well deep inside me. And then the curtain parted, but I didn't even look out at the audience. For the next hour or so, I was Christine Daaé, the promising singer whom everyone had discounted until she got her chance to shine in the spotlight.

Owen and Flynn and I sang our hearts out, and by the last aria I felt as emotionally spent as if I had just lived through all the heartbreak and fear and longing and guilt that Christine had endured. And in a way, I had.

For the final scene, I was alone onstage, locked in Erik's penthouse apartment during the final round of the singing competition. But Raoul had sacrificed his chance at stardom to come and save me. However, this had been part of the Phantom's plan all along. Erik had never left his apartment and had been using me as bait so he could trap and kill Raoul.

But when he sees Raoul's reaction at finding me alive, the Phantom softens and realizes that Raoul and Christine truly love each other. He is torn over whether to exact his revenge or to let Christine go. Feeling a surge of pity and love for him, Christine sings her part of the duet, "Last Good-bye," in which she sets him free with her words, and Erik weeps because he knows their story has come to an end.

During the last moments of my part, the noise of the rain ceased and the acoustics made the room a temporary echo chamber, signaling that we were going through the Bastille tunnel. This was my big finale, the moment the audience had been waiting for.

Christine is so moved by the Phantom's tears that she sings the words—"I will love you always, but my heart must be free"—and the two are so overcome by emotion that they're brought to their knees. The Phantom takes Christine's hand, and she pulls him toward her one last time and kisses him so tenderly that he rises from the floor and opens the door for her.

At this point, Owen reached for my hand, and together we walked through the door and offstage, leaving Flynn alone for his final scene and the second part of the duet.

Suddenly, the rain began beating on the roof again, and the acoustics shifted back to normal. Flynn's voice rang out with brilliant clarity, "It is over; you are no longer with me. My heart forever chained to yours must be set free," and he climbed atop the wooden frame meant to be a window overlooking the Seine. Just as he was about to leap through it in his final suicidal flight, we saw a flash of lightning outside and felt a lurching of the boat as if someone had jammed on the brakes. And then the stage went dark.

In fact, the room was plunged into a darkness so total that the audience gasped. There was a brief moment of silence before the house erupted into applause. They thought this was part of the show. But then when the lights didn't return, the audience began to murmur.

Before anyone could panic, Mademoiselle Veilleux took the stage and made an announcement. "Please do not be alarmed. The engine seems to have malfunctioned, but the captain is working to restore power. Just remain in your seats, and we'll have you all safely back on dry land in no time. The judges will have their verdict momentarily."

She kept her placid demeanor in front of the audience, but as soon as she came backstage I could tell something was very, very wrong. Owen, Flynn, Elise, and I were huddled there, wondering what to do.

"I'm afraid we struck something," she told us, her forehead knotted in worry.

"Or something struck us," I said, thinking of that lightning bolt. It seemed somehow appropriate that my supernatural adventures had begun with a lightning strike and might end with one.

"How can I help?" Flynn asked.

"Yeah, what can we do?" Owen said.

"Come above deck with me," she said. "I'm worried because I can't find Nicholas."

We took the rickety staircase from the cabin up to the deck of the barge, which was slick with rain. We could barely walk without sliding toward the edge, as the boat seemed to be listing slightly to one side.

Thierry was already on deck with another man, presumably the captain, and they were both looking at something in the river. I watched the captain toss a life preserver over the railing.

"Mon dieu!" Mademoiselle Veilleux cried, racing over to the edge. "It's Nicholas. He's fallen overboard."

Before I could even think, I was racing back toward the cabin to find Gray. He was still standing by the exit door, so I grabbed his arm and yanked him outside before anyone else could hear the panic in my voice.

"It's Monsieur Crespeau," I said. "He's fallen overboard. He's got a bad back. I'm not sure he can swim."

I began running toward the stern of the barge, and Gray followed until we saw everyone braced against the railing, peering into the river at a dark spot churning in the water below. The life preserver was floating several yards away from Crespeau, and I doubted he'd be able to get to it in the churlish waters.

Gray tore off his jacket and shirt and kicked off his shoes, then flung himself over the railing and dove into the river. Mademoiselle Veilleux screamed at the unexpectedness of it, and we all watched helplessly as he swam out to Monsieur Crespeau. The captain had tossed a rope ladder over the side, and Gray was able to pull Crespeau close to the boat, but Crespeau was too weak to get a foothold on the ladder, and Gray seemed to be struggling under his weight. As heroic as his instincts had been, Gray wasn't strong enough to have attempted this rescue.

After several anguished minutes of treading water and grappling for purchase, Gray eventually secured Crespeau onto his back and began mounting the rope ladder himself. Both Thierry and the captain leaned overboard while Owen and Flynn helped ground them on the boat. Together, they were able to grab Gray and hoist him and Crespeau up and over the railing, where they both collapsed in a soaking heap on the deck.

I ran over to Gray and grabbed his hand while Mademoiselle Veilleux knelt at Crespeau's side. Crespeau was coughing violently, spurting up water from his lungs. Wet hair was shellacked to his face, and his lips were blue. Gray looked a little better but his teeth were chattering and his face was pale.

"Gray, are you okay?" I asked.

"Uh-huh," he muttered breathlessly. "Worry about him. I'm fine."

I glanced over at Crespeau, who was sitting up in Veilleux's arms now, shivering uncontrollably, his right hand clutching his left arm. "Nicholas, I'm here," Mademoiselle Veilleux said, stroking his face. "Nothing bad is going to happen. You're with me now."

He turned his head to look at her and with the utmost effort said, "I've always . . . been . . . with you."

He coughed and sputtered again, and she gripped his face with both of her hands. "Shhh, I know, I know," she said. "You've always been with me. Which means you can't leave now. Please don't leave, Nicholas. I love you."

His face, which had been contorted in pain and exertion, finally surrendered to some greater power. "I know," he said, his mouth curling into a peaceful smile just before he passed out.

CHAPTER 25

Crespeau never regained consciousness. He died of heart failure later that evening, with Mademoiselle by his side. She leaned over and kissed him tenderly, but it was too late. His cheek was already cold.

So Nicholas Crespeau, who had lived a life of pure love and selfless devotion, died without ever having felt the lips of his beloved.

His funeral was held on the barge where he'd died. I asked Mademoiselle Veilleux if I could read something during his service, choosing a passage from Tennyson's "The Lady of Shalott." As I read, my mouth was dry, but my eyes were not:

> *Lying, robed in snowy white*
> *That loosely flew to left and right—*
> *The leaves upon her falling light—*
> *Thro' the noises of the night*
> *She floated down to Camelot;*
> *And as the boat-head wound along*
> *The willowy hills and fields among,*
> *They heard her singing her last song,*
> *The Lady of Shalott.*

* * *

Heard a carol, mournful, holy,
Chanted loudly, chanted lowly,
Till her blood was frozen slowly,
And her eyes were darken'd wholly,
Turn'd to tower'd Camelot.
For ere she reach'd upon the tide
The first house by the water-side,
Singing in her song she died,
The Lady of Shalott.

Mademoiselle Veilleux sang "Sono Andati?" from *La Bohème,* and I thought my heart would burst. Her voice was tremulous as she told Monsieur Crespeau what she should have told him in life:

I have so many things I want to tell you,
or only one thing, but as huge as the ocean,
deep and infinite as the sea.
You are my love and my whole life. . . .

The service concluded with Jean-Claude playing Beethoven's Moonlight Sonata, the song Crespeau had played so beautifully the night of the masquerade ball. As Jean-Claude played, the barge passed through the Bastille tunnel before emerging once again into the sunshine.

Gray stood next to me on the deck as Mademoiselle tossed Crespeau's ashes into the Seine, where I imagined them flowing all the way to the English Channel, or perhaps to Camelot. Gray leaned over to me, his cheeks stained with tears.

"I'm so sorry," he said. "I wasn't strong enough."

"Gray," I said. "You were stronger than anyone else there. When you saw him in the water, you didn't even hesitate. You dove right in, despite all the risks. And you hardly even knew him. That's why you're in the Coast Guard."

"But I couldn't save him," he said.

"But don't you see, you did save him," I said. "You gave him the chance to say good-bye to Mademoiselle Veilleux."

I thought back to that conversation I'd had with Crespeau about the Lady of Shalott and his theory that she'd turned around purposefully because she was ready to die.

Why had Crespeau been out on the deck in the middle of the storm? Had he simply been investigating why the motor had shut off? Or had he finally turned from his world of shadows and embraced the real world with all its risks and heartbreak?

Gray grabbed my hand as we disembarked from the barge, and I squeezed as hard as I could, trying to show him how much he meant to me. Because love was a complicated thing. There were so many ways to define it. Mademoiselle Veilleux had loved Crespeau—perhaps not in the way he had wanted—but purely and deeply. Her words at the end had set him free, just as Roxanne's had done for Cyrano. Just as Christine's had for the Phantom. Crespeau's life had not been in vain because someone had loved him.

Perhaps somewhere out beyond the boundary between life and death, Crespeau had felt that final kiss on his cheek and it had given him the strength to take a step forward into the light. He was no longer the Bastille Ghost, trapped in the past and doomed to tread those hallways alone and unloved. He had finally found a place where his parents still smiled, where he walked without a limp, and where forgiveness wasn't necessary because love was stronger than death.

I imagined his heaven bursting with gleaming stars and swirling skies, a world of van Gogh colors such as his enormous heart deserved.

CHAPTER 26

Just as the show must go on, *life* must go on.

About a week after Crespeau's funeral, the opera company selected Jean-Claude's modern *Cyrano* to be performed next fall on the main stage of L'Opéra Bastille. I was disappointed but not unhappy. Jean-Claude's opera was beautiful and haunting and it had moved me. It deserved to be seen by a larger audience.

For me, the only audience I cared about was my father and Gray. And after everything I'd accomplished, suffered, and endured this year, I was ready to go home.

Graduation Day was bittersweet as I found myself reunited with my dear friends Michelle and Jess, and saw my loved ones all gathered in one place in honor of me. My dad. Grandma. Barbara. Michelle's aunt Darlene. Even Gray and his family.

Elise had been named valedictorian, no shock there. But her speech did surprise me. It was very personal, vulnerable, and heartfelt. She explained how disappointed she'd been when she didn't get into Berklee, her first choice of college. For someone like Elise, accustomed as she was to getting her own way, this rejection had been humiliating and devastating. Until she'd had time to reflect on what it might mean for her future.

"No, I didn't get into Berklee," she said, "but I did get into UCLA, which has one of the top vocal programs in classical and opera in the country. And I realized I'd been too fixated on defining my life by these narrow definitions of success or these promises that one school held the key to my happiness. Once I mourned the loss of that dream, I opened myself up to new possibilities. Who knows where my life will go from here, what connections I might make out in California, what opportunities I might encounter or make for myself? Because life isn't a script to be followed; it's a novel to be written."

I thought about her words as I mingled with my classmates and family at the reception. Gray approached me with his parents and Anna, who hugged me so hard I couldn't feel my legs afterward. Simona also hugged me, without any words, but transmitted through her embrace all of the regret she felt at that awful conversation we'd had on the phone. I was sorry, too. Gray was her little boy, and she'd only wanted what was best for him. And in the end, she'd been right.

I never contacted the Coast Guard after all. Gray had done it himself.

He told me later that day once we were alone. "After my ordeal," he said, "I was so messed up and lost that I wasn't in control of myself. But I was scared of what might happen if I admitted this to anyone, showed any sign of weakness. Now I'm working with the Coast Guard's Employee Assistance Program, and they're providing counseling until I'm back in fighting shape."

"Which will be in no time, I'm sure," I said.

"And I'm not going to be discharged," he said. "In fact, they're giving me a commendation for my role in *The Lady Rose* rescue."

"Gray, that's wonderful. Congratulations!"

"Thanks, Emma, for believing in me even when I was so awful to you."

"I just wanted you to realize how strong you were so you'd go back to doing what you love most."

He smiled. "Speaking of things I love doing," he said, "I, uh . . . got my feelings back."

"You got your . . . oh!" I said, realizing what he meant. "Gray, that's fantastic! I'm so happy for you."

"Me too," he said, and we both laughed in the way two friends might when reuniting after a long separation.

I knew that someday we really would be friends again. We'd forge something new out of the wreckage of our failed relationship. I realized that all that time I'd spent grieving for Gray wasn't in vain. The Gray I knew and loved really had died out there on that ocean. But this new Gray would endure his losses and become stronger, just like I had, and one day he would move on and find the next love of his life.

Because there wasn't one person out there for each of us, one soul mate who held all the answers to our problems. Even after heartbreak, we could find love again if we were brave enough to open our hearts to someone new. It was scary, leaving the familiar and the safe for the unknown, but what we found on the other side might be exactly what we were looking for.

Although I no longer believed in Darlene's voodoo spells, I did believe the universe wanted us to be happy. But we couldn't wait for happiness to come to us. We had to go out and find it.

So in late August the day before my nineteenth birthday, I got off a train and walked through the station toward the streets of an unfamiliar city. I stood on the corner amid tourists and businessmen and artsy teenagers, wondering how I'd ever find my place amid all this foreignness and bustling energy. Looking down at my map, I found the café, turned down a side street, and picked up my pace. He would be expecting me any minute.

I'd spoken to him on the phone only yesterday, but it was so different seeing him in person. I saw him seated at a table by the window, sipping a latte and reading a book. My heart beat wildly.

Dr. Goldman, Ph.D., author of five works of fiction and two volumes of poetry and head of creative writing at NYU, had agreed to meet me to go over my course selections. This was such a New York moment, and right then, I didn't wish to be anywhere else in the world.

While I still craved knowledge and experience, I'd had enough traveling for a while, and what I really needed was to find myself at college. Owen was searching for his true self in Australia this year. He promised to come home for winter break, and I planned to visit him next summer if I could save up the money. Before we went our separate ways, we said *I love you,* but we made no claims on each other's futures. We'd have to wait and see where our hearts led us.

Because life was an adventure—sometimes tragic, sometimes transcendent. But it would change us if we let it. I was pretty sure that was the point of it all.

Dr. Goldman spotted me at the entrance and waved. I waved back and felt a tremor in my chest. I took a deep breath and opened the door. My life, which for so long had relied on other people's stories to give it meaning, was finally opening to a fresh new chapter.

I couldn't wait to start writing.

CREATING EMMA'S PARIS:
ON MEMORY AND THE MAGIC OF GOOGLE EARTH

You could say I had a one-night stand with Paris. Not that I've ever had a one-night stand, but if I had, I imagine it would have been like my trip to Paris: brief, intense, and memorable. I was there only once, many years ago in what feels like a different lifetime, and I stayed for a brief three days that feels much longer in my memory.

And ever since I selected *The Phantom of the Opera* as the inspiration for the final book in this trilogy, I have been fantasizing about going back to Paris. Unfortunately, timing and finances prevented a return visit, which means that when I sat down to write the book, I was summoning memories that were almost two decades old. Had Paris changed much since I'd been there? And were my memories too clouded by nostalgia?

As the book began to come together, I realized that what mattered more than the authenticity of locations or even of my own recollections was the spirit of my time spent in Paris, that joy and wonder I felt at discovering a city I could fall in love with. So I channeled my inner twentysomething and tried to infuse the novel with the same *joie de vivre* and romance that characterized my first trip there.

But in my short stay, I hadn't been able to visit so many of the sights and landmarks that are iconic in Paris's history. How would I make those places come alive for the reader? Or for Emma?

It was then that I discovered Google Earth, which allowed me to "wander" the streets of Paris from the comfort of my living room couch, taking in museums, cathedrals, rivers, bridges, restaurants, cafés, even the tiny back alleyways of Paris. As I researched various places for the book and took virtual strolls through the city, I found myself falling in love all over again.

These are just a few of the locations that were special to me when I visited Paris or that are crucial to Emma's story as she begins her own romance with the City of Light:

La Bastille: Emma's school in Paris stands on the grounds of the old Bastille, the fortress stormed during the French Revolution and, later, the prison where Louis XIV detained enemies of the state without trial. I wanted Emma's environs to have a dark historic past, to play up her fear of ghosts and the supernatural. The Bastille seemed one of the likeliest places in Paris to be rife with restless spirits seeking redress for past grievances.

Saint-Antoine: This is the neighborhood where Emma's school is located and also the school's namesake. The district was immortalized by Dickens in *A Tale of Two Cities* when he described: "The wine was red wine, and had stained the ground of the narrow street in the suburb of Saint Antoine, in Paris, where it was spilled. It had stained many hands, too, and many faces, and many naked feet, and many wooden shoes. The hands of the man who sawed the wood, left red marks on the billets; and the forehead of the woman who nursed her baby, was stained with the stain of the old rag she wound about her head again." See how he creates a metaphor for the blood spilled during the Revolution? Brilliant.

Not only did this "colorful" locale suit my dramatic purposes, but Saint Antoine (Saint Anthony) is also the patron saint of lost things, which ends up being relevant to a major plot point in the book.

Le Marais: This is the neighborhood where I stayed during my visit to Paris, and thus it is my favorite. Whether meandering its narrow medieval streets or trying delicate pastries from a bakery in the Jewish quarter or traipsing through the trendy bars and cafés, this is a neighborhood for the young and fashionable. Ironically, its aesthetic is more Old World than hipster, boasting cobblestoned streets, ivy-covered buildings, and hidden courtyards. Its network of streets has been described as "dizzying," and I can testify to that. One night, I wandered for an hour trying to relocate a bar I had visited the night before, only to conclude that it must have disappeared overnight. *Midnight in Paris,* anyone?

Belleville and Chinatown: I never got to Belleville during my stay in Paris, but I stumbled upon the area while researching Paris's Chinatown, where several important scenes in my book take place. Belleville was an independent commune during the revolution of 1848 and was known for its leftist politics. It's safe to say that blood ran through its streets, just as it did through the streets of Saint-Antoine nearly sixty years before. In more recent years, Belleville has become home to a diverse and bohemian crowd, as well as lively outdoor markets, ethnic restaurants, and artists' studios. Edith Piaf grew up there and performed at the cabarets.

Père Lachaise Cemetery: This was another destination I regretfully never made it to, but I had so much fun looking up photos of the various graves, tombs, and crypts. It's a creepy, fascinating place that's home to the bodies of literary and artistic geniuses such as Victor Hugo, Molière, Edith Piaf, Gertrude Stein, Chopin, Colette, Oscar Wilde, and (if we're playing "Which of these things doesn't belong?") Jim Morrison.

Notre Dame Cathedral: Built in the French Gothic style and boasting flourishes like flying buttresses, gargoyles, and a show-stopping stained-glass rose window, this cathedral is even more impressive in person than you've imagined. Watching it emerge through the treetops as I walked along the left bank of the Seine was one of the most stunning experiences of my travels.

Shakespeare and Company: For any bibliophile, this bookstore is a must-stop. With its iconic green-and-yellow exterior and its cozy, dusty interior bursting at the seams with books going every which way, this was the quintessential independent bookstore before indies were cool. Set on Paris's famed Left Bank, the shop was a favorite haunt of literary giants like Ernest Hemingway, F. Scott Fitzgerald, Gertrude Stein, and James Joyce.

Musée d'Orsay: While my mention of the museum in the book is brief, Musée d'Orsay was one of my favorite places in all of Paris. Housed in a defunct turn-of-the-century railway station, the museum is now home to the largest collection of Impressionist and Postimpressionist art in the world. When I saw van Gogh's *The Church at Auvers* from three feet away, I felt like I was standing in the presence of God.

L'Opéra Bastille: I remember stumbling upon L'Opéra Bastille and having the same reaction Emma has when she first sees it: "*That* is the Opera House?" Anyone familiar with *The Phantom of the Opera* has come to expect a magnificent columned building with a green dome and golden statuary, not an ugly round building covered in mirrored tiles. (My apologies to the architect.) Aesthetics aside, this modern opera house is now the main facility for the Paris National Opera after President Mitterrand green-lighted its construction to compensate for the limitations of the old Palais Garnier. Thus, L'Opéra Bastille became the host to my fictional Young Artists' competition in the book.

Le Palais Garnier: What better testament to the power of place in fiction than the brilliant depiction of the Paris Opera House in Gaston Leroux's *The Phantom of the Opera*. While I never got to enter the opera's illumined doorways or climb its golden stairwell or watch an opera from its opulent gallery, the mystique Leroux created of a place steeped in music, tragedy, and romance provided all the inspiration I needed. The scene in which Emma, Owen, Elise, and Flynn attend *Orphée et Eurydice* at the Opera House was based half on inspiration, half on imagination, and was pure fun to write.

See how Emma's adventures in love and literature
first began in Eve Marie Mont's

A BREATH OF EYRE

Emma Townsend has always believed in stories—the ones
she reads voraciously, and the ones she creates. Perhaps it's
because she feels like an outsider at her exclusive prep
school, or because her stepmother doesn't come close to filling the void left by her mother's death. And her only romantic prospect—apart from a crush on her English teacher—is
Gray Newman, a longtime friend, who just adds to Emma's
confusion. But escape soon arrives in an old leather-bound
copy of *Jane Eyre.* . . .

Reading of Jane's isolation sparks a deep sense of kinship.
Then fate takes things a leap farther when a lightning storm
catapults Emma right into Jane's body and her nineteenth-
century world. As governess at Thornfield, Emma has a sense
of belonging she's never known—and an attraction to the
brooding Mr. Rochester. Now, moving between her two real-
ities and uncovering secrets in both, Emma must decide
whether her destiny lies in the pages of Jane's story or in the
unwritten chapters of her own. . . .

Turn the page for a special excerpt!

A K Teen / Kensington trade paperback on sale now

CHAPTER 1

There was no possibility of taking a swim that day. My stepmother had planned a sweet sixteen party, and the guests were about to arrive. I'd told Barbara at least a dozen times that I didn't want a party, but she insisted, saying if I didn't have one, I'd regret it later. And now that the day was here, setting a record for heat and humidity that summer, the only thing I regretted was that we didn't have central air-conditioning. That voice inside my head began to call me, that invisible cord tugging at my chest, drawing me to the ocean. But it was almost noon. The swim would have to wait.

Reluctantly, I threw on a tank top, cut-off shorts, and flip-flops and headed downstairs. The first thing Barbara said when she saw my outfit was, "You're not wearing that, are you?"

I looked down at myself. "It would appear that I am."

"No, that won't do," she said, clicking her tongue and studying me as if I was beyond hope. "Go upstairs, honey, and change into something pretty."

I raised my eyebrow at her, taking in the sight of her dramatic eye makeup and her piles of well-sprayed blond hair. Barbara had been raised in the rich and fertile soil of Georgia, fed a steady diet of debutante balls, diamond jewelry, and Dolly Parton hair. Her favorite color was yellow because "it's the color of sunshiiiine!"

"I'm perfectly comfortable in this," I said. "Besides, it's, like, a gazillion degrees in here."

"Honey, you don't know heat till you've been to Savannah in summertime. Anyway, that's even more reason to dress in something that'll make you feel pretty." Pretty being the end-all-be-all of life. "Gray Newman's going to be here," she sang.

Oh God. Gray Newman was coming to my party. Gray of the soulful hazel eyes that fooled me into thinking he had hidden depths, when really he was just a spoiled rich kid who spent his summers lifeguarding and seducing the sorority girls. At least, that's what I'd heard; we didn't exactly travel in the same circles.

His mother, Simona, had been my mom's roommate in college and later became my godmother, so Gray and I had been thrown together a lot as kids. Since my mom died, we only saw each other once or twice a year when we got dragged to each other's milestone events. The fact that he was going to be here in my house for my party mortified me. I didn't want him to see what a loser I was, to know that I had no friends, that I wasn't popular like he was. The urge to cut and run grew so strong I could feel it in my bones.

Reluctantly, I went back upstairs to change. On a whim, I put on my bathing suit underneath the green-and-white summer dress I'd chosen. I glanced at myself in the mirror and made a quick assessment. Face: too pointy. Hair: too flyaway, and not at all helped by this humidity. Body: too pathetic. I pulled my hair off my neck and scooped it into a ponytail, partly because it was too hot to wear down and partly because I knew it would annoy Barbara. "Ponytails are for horses," she'd say, or some other ridiculous gem of Southern wisdom.

When I got back downstairs, I saw that Aunt Trish, my cousins, and Grandma Mackie had all arrived together. Next came the neighbors, Bill and Rita, followed by Cassie, a woman I'd made friends with at the real estate office this summer. And yep, that was it. Saddest sweet sixteen party in history.

I went around saying hellos and collecting presents and cards, beginning to hold out hope that the Newmans weren't going to come. But around 12:30, their oatmeal-colored Subaru pulled up in front of our house, and my stomach fell. I watched Gray get out of the car, pick up his little sister Anna, and give her a piggyback ride to the door. Mr. Newman came in carrying an organically grown zucchini the size of a small infant, and Simona held out my present, which appeared to be wrapped in tree bark. They both hugged me, Simona clutching me for so long it was uncomfortable.

"Happy birthday, Emma," she said, tears welling up in her eyes. "You look more like Laura every day." I never knew what to say to this.

Gray squatted down so Anna could dismount, then gave me a slow, uncomfortable perusal, glancing briefly down at my chest, I suppose to see if anything interesting was happening there. It wasn't. Despite nightly pleas to a God I only half believed in, I remained a disappointing five foot three with barely any curves. Gray was even taller than the last time I'd seen him, and he'd definitely filled out. With his close-cropped hair and slightly broken-looking nose, he looked hard and proud, but also sort of haunted—like a medieval saint trapped in the body of a Marine.

Anna ran into me, hugging my legs so I was staring down at her long red hair. "Hey, beautiful!" I said. "You're getting so big."

"I just turned seven," she said.

"And I just turned sixteen."

"I *know*," she said. "Gray told me, like, a million times."

"So give Emma her present," Gray reminded her.

His voice was deeper than I remembered. A few years at a private school had chipped away at his Boston accent, but a hint of it remained. I found it irritatingly sexy.

Anna handed me a small package and demanded that I open it immediately. "Okay, okay," I said, laughing and making a small tear in one corner. When I pulled off the last of the wrapping paper, I was holding a turquoise leather journal inscribed with my initials. "Wow," I said.

"Do you like it?"

"I love it!"

She broke into an embarrassed smile, and then, mission accomplished, went running off to see if there was anyone to play with. I must have looked a little stunned because Gray felt it necessary to add, "Before you go getting all touched, it was my mom's idea. She remembered you used to write."

"Oh," I said, wanting to slam him into something sharp and hard. Why did guys have to be like this? Was it possible for them to admit they had any feelings other than the sports-induced grunting variety?

"So," he said, "are you still?"

"Still what?"

"Writing?"

"Not so much."

"Why not?"

"I don't know. I guess I haven't been inspired. What about you? Are you still lifeguarding?"

"No."

"Too busy doing keg stands and scoring with fraternity chicks?"

He glared at me, and for a moment, I thought he was going to punch the wall. "I don't do that anymore, Townsend."

"Which one?"

"Either."

I studied his face for traces of sarcasm. Even if he was being sincere, it was sort of an unwritten rule that Gray and I had to give each other a hard time. When I was five years old and he was seven, I kissed him under the apple tree in our backyard. He responded by giving me a bloody nose. We'd been sparring ever since.

After a few seconds of awkwardly staring at each other, I rolled my eyes and went to join the rest of the party in the kitchen. Everyone was hovering by the whining air conditioner except my poor dad, who stood outside on the deck in front of a hot grill. Why Barbara had planned a cookout for the middle of a heat wave, I had no idea. Grandma Mackie was sitting at the table, sipping her old-fashioned, content to be ignored even though she was probably the most interesting person there. I noticed her drink was getting low, and Grandma didn't like her drinks getting low.

"Can I make you another?" I said.

"A small one," she said. "Just tickle the glass."

"I think you've had enough, Elspeth," Barbara drawled. My grandma was eighty-three years old and had been drinking old-fashioneds since practically World War II. I didn't think one more was going to kill her. "And Emma, you know I don't like you making alcoholic drinks for your grandmother. It isn't appropriate."

"Dad always lets me make them," I said, playing the "real parent" card.

"I know, but he shouldn't. Elspeth, let me get you a nice sweet tea."

"If I wanted tea," Grandma said, "I'd go to the Four Seasons. Right now, I'd like to have a drink at my granddaughter's birthday party." She winked at me, then made a waving motion with her hand, ushering me down to her level. "Who's the David?"

"Who?"

"That beautiful Michelangelo statue," she said, pointing at Gray.

I covered her finger with my hand. "That's Gray Newman, Grandma. You remember. Mom's godson?"

"I don't remember him looking like that," she said, polishing off her old-fashioned. "Delicious." I didn't know if she was talking about her drink or Gray Newman.

My cousins were eyeing him with interest, too. Ashley and Devin were thirteen-year-old twins who resembled the creepy sisters from *The Shining* movie, especially as my aunt insisted they dress in the same outfits. I shuddered to myself and went into the den to make my grandmother's drink. Gray followed me in and watched me from behind, presumably with the intention of making me nervous.

"Quite a party you've got here, Townsend," he said. He always called me Townsend, like I was one of his swim team buddies. "Your parents, my parents, and a bunch of relatives."

"You forgot to mention yourself," I said, "which should make it fairly obvious that I didn't write the guest list." He laughed and nodded an unspoken *touché*. "I told Barbara I didn't want a party."

"You have to have a party on your sixteenth birthday," he said. "But you could have invited some friends. I was expecting a room full of teenage girls."

I was about to tell him I didn't have any friends, but it seemed too naked a statement to make to Gray. Like leaving raw meat out for a wild dog. "So sorry to disappoint," I said, turning away from him and tugging at my necklace. I could feel the heat rising to my face, and I hated myself for it.

"You're not playing this right," he said. "The more people you invite, the more presents you get."

"But there's nothing I want."

"Nothing you want?" he said, feigning shock. "You're not a very good Lockwood girl, are you?"

Lockwood Prep, the school I attended, had a reputation for girls with trust funds and designer wardrobes who received brand-new SUVs on their sixteenth birthdays. Gray was right: I was not a very good Lockwood girl. And he would know. He'd been dating Lockwood's poster girl, Elise Fairchild, for six months. She was as Lockwoodian as they came.

"So," I said, trying to steer the conversation away from me, "this is your last year at Braeburn." Two years ago, Gray's parents had transferred him from Sheldrake, the public school in Waltham, to Braeburn Academy, an alternative school that was all about kumbaya and kindness.

"If I have to sit through one more 'harmonic huddle,'" he said, making made air quotes with his fingers, "I'm gonna impale myself with a drumstick."

"That might be a little extreme," I said, extracting a tiny smile from him. "Have you thought about where you're going to college?" I poured two inches of whiskey into my grandma's highball glass.

"I'm tired of thinking about it, actually." His eyes darted restlessly, like it was paining him to have to talk to me. My mouth went rigid, and I retracted, turtle style. I was thinking of something cutting to say when his cell phone rang. He reached into his pocket and glanced down at the display. "I have to answer this," he said and abruptly left the room.

For some reason, I felt embarrassed and enormously disappointed. What had I expected, for Gray Newman to engage in hostile banter with me for the duration of my party? I stayed in the den for a few minutes so it wouldn't seem like I was chasing after him, then went back out to the kitchen and gave Grandma her drink. Everyone was engaged in conversation, so I stepped outside to see if my dad needed help at the grill.

"Hey, kiddo," he said when he saw me. "Ever eat a tofu dog before?"

"Can't say that I have," I said, smiling.

I sidled up next to him, relishing this brief time alone with my father. For the past few years, we'd grown distant. Well, really, he'd grown distant. He'd be standing right in front of me smiling, but I'd know that his mind was somewhere else. He was a fisherman for the local fleet, handsome in a Gary Cooper way, meaning he could look rugged or elegant, depending on the context. In the middle of summer when his skin was almost bronze, he looked like a weathered lobsterman, but around Christmas when he wore a tuxedo to take Barbara to the Boston Pops, he looked like a movie star. Now, with sweat staining the back of his shirt and a damp, sunburned face, he looked like the browbeaten husband he'd become.

"Why don't you let me finish up out here?" I offered. "Go inside and cool off."

"That's okay," he said. "You're the birthday girl. Go back and talk to your guests."

How could I tell him this was the last thing I wanted to do?

Reluctantly, I went back inside. Nobody seemed to care that I'd returned, so I ended up wandering around the first floor, feeling like I was at someone else's party. In her zeal to keep the chip baskets filled, Barbara stumbled upon me in the living room and seized the opportunity to give me a lecture on feminine wiles.

"What happened to Gray?" she asked in her irritating drawl, her heavily mascaraed eyes wide with alarm.

"He got a phone call."

"Well, honey, take this opportunity to go upstairs and reapply your makeup. Your face is all splotchy and your hair is a disaster. Go now, while Gray is occupied."

I wanted to scream at her, to tell her how awful it made me feel when she looked at me like I was some kind of mutant. Why could I never be good enough for her? Why could I never please her?

It was on days like this that I missed my mother most, even if I could barely remember her. In my mind she was bright and beautiful and wild—an orange poppy or a beautifully plumed bird. Summer mornings, we used to rush down to the beach to go swimming or build castles, and summer nights we'd catch fireflies until it was too dark to see. The ocean was the place where I felt closest to her. I clutched at her necklace—a silver dragonfly with blue and green glass wings—and felt an ache for her that took my breath away.